Long Live the Cartel

BY

ASHLEY & JAQUAVIS

Copyright 2020 Ashley & JaQuavis
All Rights Reserved 2020 Ashley & JaQuavis
ISBN: 9798670717946

Edited by: Bianca Babb
@editwithb

Copyedited by: Khloe Cain
@editor_khloecain

Thank you for supporting the A&J brand.
Many of you have watched us grow up in this industry.
We thank you for believing in our work and allowing us to
share our gifts with you. Our creativity is inspired by all of you.

Our Very Best,

-The Colemans

PROLOGUE

"Everything isn't what it seems," -Unknown

The corridor was silent. The cement walls and steel bars seemed to make the place even colder than what the thermometer read. Random sounds of coughs, snoring, and echoes of the night provided an eerie ambiance in the women's federal correctional facility. Miamor Jones laid in her bunk, slowly slipping off into her slumber. A lone light shined into her cell, barely providing any source of illumination. She laid on her back and stared at the chipped paint on the ceiling as her eyes slowly closed and her breathing became heavy. She was one of the more fortunate inmates and had a cell to herself, so she only had to deal with herself and her own thoughts on a nightly basis. Just as always, her last thought was of her deceased loved ones and the love of her life.

The sound of hard bottom shoes hitting the pavement got louder and louder and Miamor paid it no mind. The guards usually did hourly walk throughs, it was all a part of the routine. As the sound got closer, it seemed to stop abruptly. A figure stood in her entrance and Miamor groggily looked over trying to see who was in front of her cell. The guard was blocking the light with their body, so Miamor couldn't make out which guard it was.

"What's the problem?" Miamor asked as she sat up, squinting.

The guard remained silent and just stood there. Miamor hadn't had any problems out of the C.O.'s, so the impromptu, middle of the night visit had her confused. She was now sitting up in her bunk, trying to make out the face of the person standing in front of her. She could only see their uniform and badge, it was too dark. She could tell it was one of the male guards because of the broad shoulders. The guard stepped forward and Miamor saw his face clearly....it was a familiar face. Her heart began to beat rapidly, and her breathing slowed as she froze in confusion. All of the blood drained from her face, it was as if she had seen a ghost.

"Carter?" Miamor whispered as she couldn't believe what she was seeing.

He was supposed to be dead and in the ground. She had attended his funeral. So, how was this happening? She looked at his face, trying to make sure she was seeing things correctly. She saw his strong jawline and broad shoulders. They stared into each other's eyes, both of them speechless. Their love was like no other. It was so unique and one of a kind. They had been through so much and had been separated for so long. Their souls cried out for one another. It was love in the purest form. Unconditional. His infamous smirk made her heart instantly flutter as she stared in awe.

Carter quickly placed his index finger on his lips, signaling her to be quiet as he glanced around. He stepped into the cell and rushed her. Miamor stood and embraced her husband, hugging him so tightly that they could feel one another's heartbeat as they stood chest to chest. They began to weep silently. Miamor broke down in his arms and for the first time, she couldn't feel his strength. A rare and lone tear fell from his eye, they both were vulnerable, trying their best to muffle themselves, in fear of someone hearing them. It had been so long since they had felt one another's embrace. Miamor's hand was wrapped around Carter's neck and she slowly slid them down onto his chest. As her palms rested on each one of his pectoral muscles, she instantly noticed he had lost some weight. It seemed as if his strength wasn't what she had remembered. Not until she heard his smooth, low baritone that she quickly remembered who the fuck her husband was; a street legend, a king amongst kings, and most of all, the love of her life. Hearing his voice made her feel his power. Carter Jones' mere presence sent her chest into anxiety and butterflies formed inside of her stomach. That man did something to her that another could never. He was her soulmate and was love in its purest form. Her eyes drifted away from his watery eyes and down to the left side of his chest. She began to feel over his left side, searching for his heartbeat.

"Everything isn't what it seems, Miamor," Carter said as he gently placed his hand over hers.

He leaned forward and gently kissed her forehead as he always did. Miamor smiled and closed her eyes, enjoying

3

the moment. The memories. What she had found in Carter Jones is what every woman dreamed about; a man that loved her unconditionally. A man that knew all of her secrets and never judged her. Oh, how she missed her man. Deep in her heart, she knew that he wasn't dead. It was nothing that Carter had to say to prove his love because Miamor felt it. Some people would never know true love, but once a woman got a taste of a real man, anything fake could never stand a chance. Carter was a real man and Miamor was grateful to have experienced him. She was grateful that somehow he was standing before her. Once again, he cheated death and Miamor wanted to ask him how he pulled it off. However, she didn't want to waste the opportunity with questions. She just stared into his brown eyes and slowly shook her head, not believing that he was there with her. Carter wiped his tear away, gently cupped Miamor's chin, and leaned in for a kiss. Miamor's closed her eyes and puckered her lips, waiting for the soft impact. The feeling of Carter's lips touching her skin sent chills down her back. It had been so long since she felt any type of intimacy and the sensation that she felt traveled through her body and seemed to stop in between her legs. She felt a pulse below. Before she knew it, Carter had slowly guided her onto the bunk and laid her down.

"Mia, I missed you so much. I'm so sorry that I had to disappear," Carter whispered, just before he smoothly grazed her earlobe with his lips. He then positioned himself over her, staring down at his love. He smiled and it instantly warmed Mia's heart. She cradled the back of his head and guided him to her neck. As he French kissed her neck, he began to unbutton her prison issued shirt. Carter left a trail of kisses. Her collar bone, then her chest, and finally down to her now erect nipples. Miamor let out a slight moan but quickly covered her mouth. Like old times, she raised her ass off the bed and Carter slid her pants and panties down. They were in perfect unison.

"I love you, Carter," she crooned as her body began to squirm in anticipation. She felt the wetness between her legs and braced herself to feel her man slide into her. She arched her back, closing her eyes as she grabbed her own breast. Carter didn't enter her, and it was driving her crazy. He was teasing her.

"Carter, stop fucking playing. Put it in," Miamor whispered as she smiled and bit her bottom lip. She was so soaked that a small puddle began to form under her cheeks. Miamor reached up to grab Carter so she could pull him closer, but she grasped at air.

"What the fuck," Miamor said as she opened her eyes, seeing that nothing was there but air. No Carter, no person, and no closure. Her watering eyes focused on the chipped piece of paint for a second and then she sat up and looked around. Her cell felt so cold; colder than it ever had been before. The disappointment sat in as she realized that her mind had once again played tricks on her. Her encounter with her late husband wasn't real. It was a dream…a wet one. She sighed in frustration, knowing that she only could see Carter in her dreams. Tears began to stream down her face as she laid back down, emotions wrecked her so

5

heavily that tears stained her pillow. She didn't wipe them away. She wanted to let them flow freely. Those tears were earned. She silently cried herself to sleep, praying to God that she could get another encounter with her husband on the sandman's watch.

CHAPTER 1

"Niggas want to beg after the fact," -Mo

We're here in the training facility of Carter Jones the second. He is a machine in the ring. Two hundred pounds of muscle and tenacity that we just haven't seen in the sport of boxing in a very long time. He is 19 and 0 with 16 knockouts. He is an executioner inside these ropes. You can hear the absolute power he has as he spars behind us, throwing jabs so powerful that they echo off the walls of this facility. He has fought his way up from the Dominican Republic and as you can see, he has the very best team with Emilio Estes in his corner. It will be an interesting fight coming May 1st. We are one month out from what critics consider is the fight of the century."

Carter didn't even hear the media circus taking place around him as his fists flew. He bit down on the mouth guard so hard that it hurt as he hit the training mitts with no mercy. He hit them so hard that they hissed with every blow.

"Psk, Psk, Psk, Psk," his trainer and longtime friend, Papi, baited him. Sic'd him. Instigating the punches. It

was a challenge and Carter's hands were like bullets. Papi was the only trainer who Carter would work with. They had come up together in the underground fighting ring in the Dominican Republic and when Carter made it big, he had brought Papi with him. Nobody pushed him like Papi. Nobody understood how far Carter had come. He had come a long way and they were experiencing the rise of his career together. Tupac blared throughout the room and Carter used the tempo of the music to keep a cadence. His gloves performed. His movements choreographed by the years of training that filled him. This was skills. The way he used his body. Never letting a counter punch touch him. He was a fucking showman in the ring, evasive, fast, and deadly. Papi's fists flew as well.

Pop. Pop. Pop. Pop. Pop. Pop. Pop.

Their sparring was always an event to watch. They had been a team too long to not anticipate the other's technique. The cameras took it all in, enjoying the show, but Carter was focused. It was like the media wasn't even in the room.

"Time."

Emilio Estes sat on the stool in the corner of the ring. Elbows met knees as Estes' old fingers pulled apart the peanut shells in his hand. He popped one in his mouth.

"You're looking slow kid," Estes stated.

Carter held his head back as the trainer squirted water into his mouth. Sweat covered him. Four hours of training per day. Effort. Discipline. Carter had it all. He couldn't slip because he was chasing the belt.

"Is that right?" Carter asked, chuckling. He spit, something he only did when exhausted and then beat his gloves together as he resumed his stance. "Got all these people in here like I'm about to do a magic trick or something. You know I ain't about all this. Private training. I requested private training."

"It's the biggest fight since Tyson and Holyfield. You can't make history and tuck your tail, kid. Deal with it," Estes said as he stood. He was slow to rise. Old bones requiring patience from Carter as he made his way over to the raven colored giant wearing the sparring gloves. "Give me the gloves," Estes said to Papi.

Carter smiled as Papi handed them over. Estes was an old man, but when he put on the leather, he radiated like father time had run the clock back a bit to the good old days. He slapped the gloves together.

"Come on champ. That's what you want right? The belt? To be the best?" Estes goaded. Carter rose on the balls of his feet. Foot work. Light work. He moved around the ring with Estes like they were waltzing to the same juke joint.

"Let's go," Estes coached. "I'm not going to break. Put some power behind that punch."

Carter threw a jab.

"C.J.!" Estes barked.

Estes knew that he had just poured gasoline on a fire. His childhood name. "C.J." was Carter's soft spot. Never wanting to be reminded that he was his father's son, his aggression exploded. Carter was a storm. Raining a series of punches that Estes blocked with the padding. Striking swiftly like lightning. Gloves thundering as they hit Estes'.

Cameras flashed around him. Every media outlet in the country was present, but Carter had left the building. He was off in his head, fighting for scraps, fighting for a piece of sanity, way back in the Dominican Republic when he was just a boy. There had been no gloves back then. No pads. No ring. Just savagery. Only heart. Carter had been taught to fight under the worst conditions and the prize back then had been his life. It was why he never lost. Other men fought for honor, for reputation, for money. Carter Jones II fought for his life. He fought to stay alive and his success hadn't changed that. Every time he slipped on a pair of gloves the instinct came back to him.

"That's my boy," Estes said. "Faster!"

Carter gritted his teeth and yelled out as he pushed his body past its max.

Estes ended the session with one final point of contact. Glove to glove and it resounded loudly.

"You keep your center and you lock in like that and you're going to bring that belt home," Estes said. He gripped the back of Carter's neck. "You're a fighter. I'm proud of you. Let's handle this press so we can get out of here."

He gave Carter a supportive pat on the back and then stood off to the side as Carter stepped to the edge of the ring, leaning down onto the ropes. His physique was like art, like God had sculpted him to precision. Not too bulky because too much muscle made him slow, but lean and defined, Carter was in the best shape of his life.

"Carter, would you say The Guerilla has an advantage in this fight because of the location of this fight? Miami is his playground." Carter looked at the ESPN reporter and rubbed his hands together as the corner of his mouth lifted in amusement.

"I have nothing to say about him. He's doing what he does. I'm going to do what I do. We'll see who does it best when the time comes," Carter said. "I don't do too much talking, I let my hands make the noise."

"Carter is it true that you steer clear of interactions with women because they are a distraction? The Guerilla is highly publicized for dating multiple women. Is there someone special in your life?" Carter's eyes found the female correspondent. *FOX NEWS*. He would have to be careful how he answered with them. He had seen them spin other athletes' words and actions to feed their narrative.

He licked his lips and then ran one hand down his wavy head.

"Women require attention. I don't have a lot to give while I'm training. There's no one special. Maybe one day," he said.

"What about your family's history in this city? The infamous Diamond Cartel was run by your..."

Fucking *TMZ*. Carter's brow dipped as he made eye contact with their fake journalist. He didn't even know how they'd gained access to his press conference. His body tensed, and Estes stepped forward.

"Interview's over," Estes stated. He motioned for security who was posted in the corners of the room. "Let's get them out of here."

11

"They ask me about The Cartel again and I'll cancel the fight," Carter muttered. He pulled down the rope and hopped out the ring. He snatched up his bag, making his way to the exit.

"Carter!" Estes called after him.

Carter turned and faced the ring where Estes stood in the center. He gave him a two-punch combo, fighting air. "You're a champion. Where you come from doesn't change that."

Carter nodded.

"Love you, kid."

Estes had been the only constant in his life. Over the years, he had become family. Their bond was unbreakable.

Carter opened his mouth to speak, but before one word came out...

BANG!

The air was snatched from his lungs as he watched the bullet tear through Estes' skull, knocking him off his feet and sending his body flipping over the ropes. Screams filled his ears as a few straggling reporters took cover. Security tried to grab him, but Carter pushed the burly bodyguard off as he dropped his gym bag and ran to the Estes' side.

"Estes!"

Carter's stomach flipped when he saw the carnage on the floor. He kneeled, allowing one knee to touch the floor and resting his elbows on the other. His chin quivered, and he reached down to close Estes' eyes. He could hear the sirens in the distance. Help was coming, but Estes had been gone before his body even hit the ground. He didn't have to wonder why this had occurred. Estes had stayed out of Miami for years to avoid this very thing. He had made enemies there and one of them had touched him. Carter's chest felt hollow. Loss was bulldozing through his body, carving out vulnerability, making him ache. It was unbearable and as he stood to his feet, he came to the realization that he was alone. Estes was all he had. Estes had taught him everything he knew. Emilio Estes had become like a father to him and he regretted ever stepping foot back in this city. No fight was worth this. No title justified what he had just witnessed. He was getting the fuck out of Miami as soon as possible before the ghosts of his family's legacy claimed his life as well.

Ashton pulled back from the scope of the gun and within seconds the long-distance sniper rifle was broken down. She put it in the backpack that rested at her feet and walked out of the abandoned apartment building. She had chosen the unit that was directly across from the training facility. The angle wasn't perfect, but her shot had been. She had put in hours at the gun range to make sure she got it right. Ashton couldn't slip. Miamor had put her to the task. Killing Emilio Estes was the first test. If she could handle that, she could handle anything. The hit was like a key that would unlock everything for Ash. Miamor had a bone to pick with Estes. He had practically enslaved her son, fighting him in the Dominican Republic like he was a prized dog…an animal.

She didn't care if her son had become one of the most noted boxers in the world. She could only imagine what he had endured getting to that spot. She knew Estes had ulterior motives. Miamor had killed his only daughter and she had never known Emilio Estes to be a forgiving man. His death had been one she had been plotting for years because even if Estes meant well, Miamor wasn't a forgiving woman.

The four years Ash had spent locked up with Miamor had been enough time to turn her into a beast. She was Miamor's eyes and ears on the outside. She was the one who would pull triggers that Miamor couldn't reach. Protecting her son was all Miamor wanted to do. Estes had to go. Miamor had ordered up his assassination like it was nothing at all. To Ash, it was like a trophy. Killing Estes, a man that had survived in a treacherous game for decades was enough to give her clout in any hood. It was a prize she couldn't claim, however.

Hurried feet carried her down the stairs and she burst out the old, rusted, back door. The alley behind the building carried her to the main street where she blended into the pedestrian crowd. She wouldn't be found. She had left nothing behind, not even regret. She had been taught by the best so the best she had become.

The Murder Mamas were a thing of the past. At twenty-two years old, Ash didn't need a crew. She didn't want one. She had no time to put her trust in others. Women weren't loyal to one another. A crew meant witnesses. Seeing eyes to curled triggers made the tally of years served go up. She was a one woman show and she had her sights on the top. Miamor had promised her a half-million dollars if she protected C.J. until her release. No way would Ash leave that bag on the table. Carter Jones II would never see her coming.

Monroe stared down at the sleeping baby girl. She was beautiful. He had never witnessed peace like that. He certainly didn't know it. The serenity on this little beauty's face as she sucked on her pacifier was admirable. He could only wish for peace like that. He leaned over her crib, his elbows resting on the bars as the scent of Baby Magic calmed him. Precious. Life was so damn priceless. He couldn't even bring himself to disturb her. He took a seat in the rocking chair beside the crib. He heard the little angel begin to stir, crying softly. If he could kill whatever was disrupting her dreams he certainly would. Instead, he welcomed her back to consciousness by picking her up. He cradled her in his arms as he took a seat again.

"Shhh," he whispered. He began to hum that only nursery rhyme he knew.

Hush little baby. No words, just the tone of his deep voice, humming, soothing. The cries stilled. The baby monitor blinked in activity as it picked up his voice. The door to the nursery busted open and a worried mother stood in front of him, silk robe open, revealing full breasts because he was sure she was still breastfeeding, and nude colored bra and panties.

"I don't know who you are but please put my baby down," the woman said.

"Come in and have a seat," Mo said.

"She's a newborn, please-"

"The first thing you need to know that will keep you and your kid alive. Don't make me ask you to do shit twice," Mo said.

The woman walked into the room. Her eyes were brimming with tears as she lowered into the chair across from him. "Give me my daughter."

"Let me explain something and you lucky you fine than mu'fucka cuz I kind of want to hit that and that's a good ass reason for me to let you make it up out of here alive. You don't call the shots. I have no problem putting a bullet through your dome and covering this little angel's face with my hand and returning her to sender. I'll send boff of y'all up out of here. Now sit ya ass down and get your bitch ass baby daddy over here. Take that tremble out your voice too cuz if you give him any indication that something is wrong, I'ma blow your head off."

The woman's chin quivered as she nodded. He could feel her fear. Her eyes never left his. He couldn't say he wasn't impressed. Grown men couldn't match his stare, but this woman, this mother was letting him know with just her eyes that if he hurt her baby, he would have to kill her too because she would do all she could to defend her child.

She dialed a number and put the phone to her ear.

"Put it on speaker," he instructed.

She did as she was told.

The baritone that answered filled the room.

16

"What up, Tash?" he answered.

"I need you to bring some diapers by. I ran out," she said. Mo was impressed because her voice didn't even shake.

"I told you I had to make a run. It can't wait?" he asked.

"She doesn't have any left. I need them now and you know I can barely even walk after the C-section. She needs them now," the woman said.

"Damn man, I'm on my way."

The woman tossed her phone. "I did what you wanted now please give me my daughter," she said.

Mo stood and carried the baby across the room. He handed her over and then wagged his pistol at them both. "You be smart cuz I can get real ignant, you understand me?"

She nodded and hugged her daughter tightly. They sat in silence as the clock ticked by. An hour and a half passed before Mo heard the front door open.

He put his gun to his lips and motioned "Shh."

"Tasha! Where you at?"

Mo shook his head informing her not to answer as he stood and pointed his gun to her head. When the man stepped into the room he froze in his tracks.

"What up, Tae?" Mo greeted. "I'ma let you choose which one you want to keep."

"Mo, man, what the fuck is this about man?"

Mo stared at Deontae Thames. Someone he had broken bread with before, someone he had put in position to get rich, but niggas always got greedy. They always came up only to bite the hand that fed them.

"Where's my money nigga? I ain't here for conversation.

17

Once I walked through these doors the time for talking was over. You been stealing from me."

"Mo, you got it wrong fam-"

Mo pulled the trigger.

The gun barely made a sound thanks to the silencer Mo had attached to the tip.

Brain matter decorated the wall behind the woman. Mo found it incredible that even in death the woman never let go over her baby.

"Nooo!" Tae shouted as he rushed to his child mother's side, scooping his infant daughter into his arms. "I'll give you your money, Mo. I swear I was just-"

"Less talking my nigga. Just run my paper," Mo stated, pushing the barrel to his head. "Where it's at?"

"In the living room," the man sniveled. Mo jammed the gun harder into the back of the man's head, leading him out of the room. "You got sixty seconds. I don't know what the fuck you were thinking stealing from me either. Slick ass nigga."

The man placed his daughter in her bassinet and lowered to his knees pulling up a loose floorboard. Money laid hidden beneath.

"Sticky fingers ass nigga," Mo muttered. He snatched the diaper bag off the living room couch and shook the contents out onto the floor before tossing it at the man's face. The man pulled out the rubber-banded stacks and placed them inside the bag.

"Please, man."

"Niggas want to beg after the fact," Mo said, scoffing.

"Run my motherfucking money." Once the bag was full Mo snatched it. Before the man could offer another plea, Mo put a bullet through his head.

Mo stepped over the body and he looked down at the baby girl. He tucked his gun in his back waistline and reached for her. He held her up in front of his face. She was evidence that heaven existed. She was beautiful. He represented all earthly things that would ruin her life. He had just taken away her parents. Her father had earned it, her mother had died by affiliation. The cost of having a baby by a fuck nigga. He sat her in her car seat and then carried her out of the apartment. He placed her in front of the neighbor's door, knocked three times before pushing through the metal door that led to the stairs. He exited the building where Joey, his right-hand man, sat curbside. Since meeting him in juvie there hadn't been a time, he couldn't remember Joey not holding him down. Fat, fly nigga, Joey had earned every stripe. Every nod of respect he received while cruising around the city was awarded out the mud. He hadn't always been the toughest. In fact, when Mo had first met Joey, he had been soft, but as they grew, the more they mobbed, the more that childhood fear faded. Joey was an unremorseful killer and Mo's most trusted man on the field. Mo skidded across the hood of the car and then hopped over the top of the convertible.

"We out," Mo said.

Joey didn't ask any questions. He hit the gas and they pulled off.

"Nigga baby mama was bad as fuck. I almost let her walk

just so I could hit that shit," Mo said as he reached in the glove box to retrieve a blunt he had rolled earlier. He fired up and leaned his head back, blowing smoke into the wind.

"Yo I would have hit that shit. That bitch been bad," Joey said, snickering as Mo passed him the weed.

They shared a laugh as Mo flipped his long, curly, hair out of his face as the wind whipped wildly. His phone rang, filling the air through the Bluetooth. Mo answered the call.

"Who this?" Mo answered.

"Monroe Diamond-"

Mo frowned and lifted the roof to the car so that he could hear the call more clearly. Niggas didn't use his government name. "Who is this?" he repeated.

"It's Einstein."

Mo's gut went missing. He hadn't heard that name in years. The attorney to every nigga that was mobbed up from East to West and North to South. He represented the most official network of gangsters the world had ever seen. He was the Diamond Family lawyer.

"I need you to meet me at my office. It's your grandfather. Estes has been murdered. It's time to bring the Diamond family back together."

"Pull over the car," Mo said.

"You good?" Joey asked.

"Pull over!" Mo shouted. Joey swerved into the right lane and pulled up on the curb recklessly. Mo hopped out the car and his body erupted, throwing up. Years' worth of discord came out of him as he balanced on his knees, gasping for air. He remembered when he was younger his father used to tell him stories about his grandfather and great grandfather. He had made them sound like legends. He had never gotten the chance to meet the infamous Carter Diamond, but he had known Estes. A long time ago, he had loved him. Years had passed since he had even mentioned his name. After discovering that Estes had rescued Carter from foster care and left him to rot over the years, the desire to see him at all had disappeared. He had wanted answers for so long but had received none. The unknown had turned to resentment, but he had always expected that one day he and Estes would cross paths, hash things out, break bread. After all, they were family. Blood-related. They were the last of a dying breed, but this phone call was the nail in the coffin. This one call had erased any chance they had of making amends. His great grandfather had died and there had been no love between them. They may as well had been enemies.

"Aye! You good my nigga?" Joey asked, leaning over the seat to scream out the passenger window.

Mo wiped his mouth with the back of his hand and spit before walking back over to the car. He snatched the door open and sat down in the seat.

"Run me by my spot so I can get rid of these clothes and clean myself up. Then I'ma need you to ride with me real quick. Estes was a living legend. If he's gone, he's leaving something behind, and all that shit now belongs to me."

CHAPTER 2

"I want the connect, that's the only legacy I need,"
-Mo Diamond

The scent of salt laced the air. The sun tanned everything under its rays and the sound of the water rushing ashore could be heard in the distance. It was a perfect Miami day. Breeze and Aurora sat in the back seat of the tinted black SUV, peering out of the open window as her driver cruised Collins Avenue. Her stomach was in knots. She couldn't breathe. It felt like the humidity had turned the air to water and she was drowning just trying to inhale. She was suffocating on dry land. *Why am I back here?* The question burned in her mind and her eyes prickled. She had so many memories on this strip. The restaurant her father had named after her had been on this very block. She scoffed when she saw they had turned it into a fast food spot. *God that was so long ago.* How she wished she could go back. The Diamond family hadn't always been cursed. They had spent some really good years together. Now her parents and all her brothers were dead. She was the last man standing. The one who had been regarded as the weakest had outlasted them all. She was left behind to carry their memories, but damn were they heavy. She almost wished she had followed them right into the grave. She had almost done it. Death had knocked so many times but somehow, she was still here, still breathing and feeling every damn thing along the way. Breeze sucked in a deep breath trying to still her frantic heart. She could feel the anxiety creeping up her spine.

"You okay, mom?"

Breeze looked over at her daughter. She put on a fake smile and feathered the cheek of the fair skinned beauty beside her. Aurora Rich. Her daughter. Her reason.

"I'm fine, Aurora," Breeze assured.

She couldn't believe fourteen years had passed since having her. Eleven long years had gone by since seeing the man who had helped make her. Every day felt like a journey, an excruciating trek through the desert and Breeze was suffering. Love had broken her. Life had torn her into pieces, but she had learned to build a wall around the parts that hurt most. Her child required a whole version of herself. A functioning woman. Breeze had grown into her mother. She was the spitting image of Taryn Diamond, inside and out.

The car rolled to a stop and Breeze waited patiently until her driver opened the door.

"Who's going to be here again?" Aurora asked. "I thought you said we didn't have any family."

Breeze glanced up at the tall building.

"You have cousins and an aunt in prison. That's all," Breeze whispered. She felt the conflict in her chest because Zyir's name rested on the tip of her tongue. She had never discussed him with Aurora. She had lied and told her daughter that her father was dead. She couldn't backtrack now. Breeze wished she could take that lie back because every girl deserved to know their father, but too many years had cemented the lie in place. It was too late to have regrets. She had to stand behind the decisions she had made when she walked away all those years ago.

"Fine. Can we hurry here so we can get to the beach? I want to tan," Aurora said as she drowned out the world, inserting ear pods. Breeze nodded and led the way inside. Every step took effort. She hadn't seen her nephews in years, and she carried guilt about that. She hadn't taken them with her, and she hoped their lives hadn't been too hard because of her abandonment. She knew Carter had found his way with Estes. She had been following his career from afar, celebrating every win because she was proud of him. She hadn't been able to bring herself to contact him, however. Everyone in Miami just reminded her of what she had lost. It reminded her of death, and she couldn't wait to get out of there. Estes' will was the only thing that lured her back in the first place.

Breeze and Aurora stepped into the elevator, letting silence fill the box until it carried them to the penthouse. She stepped inside Einstein's office and she immediately recognized the man.

"Breeze Diamond," he greeted, smiling.

"Einstein," she answered with a nod.

"It's been a long time," he said. "And your daughter! She's all grown up now!"

"Yes, she is," Breeze answered. "Am I the first to arrive?"

"We are still waiting on Mo, but Carter's here."

Breeze's spine stiffened. The sound of her brother's name put a hurting on her soul. Images of him in his casket filled her mind and she had to snap her eyes shut to stop her tears from building. She knew that Einstein was talking about her nephew, but she would always associate the name with his father. Carter Jones had been a classic man. She had loved her brother dearly from the first day he walked into her life. She hated that he was gone. She wished she could pick up the phone to call him one more time. She couldn't pick up the phone to call anyone. Breeze had no one besides her daughter. Aries called once a year to check in with her, but even then, the conversation was short and sweet because Aries didn't want to be found. Loneliness consumed Breeze.

"Mom?" Aurora called out, pulling one ear pod out of her ear and looking at Breeze in concern.

Breeze composed herself.

When you open your eyes, she can't see your hurt, Breeze thought.

Her lids lifted. "I'm fine. Let's go have a seat."

Einstein opened the conference room door and Aurora walked in first. Breeze lingered at the door; eyes locked in on the man standing at the floor to ceiling windows.

When he turned around, she couldn't stop the tears that prickled in her eyes.

"It's like somebody put me in a time machine," she gasped.

"Hey Auntie Breeze," Carter greeted.

Breeze rushed across the room and hugged him tightly. "You look just like your father, C.J.!" she cried.

Carter's strong arms engulfed her. "I don't really go by C.J. anymore, auntie. Just Carter. I don't need more pieces of that man. The junior isn't necessary."

"Junior or no junior you are your father's son," Breeze said, holding on to him tightly. "Ohh you hug like him too," she said, laughing through her tears. She pulled back, having to look up at the mountain of a man he had become. She didn't realize how much she had missed him or how happy she would be to see him until this very moment. She placed her hands on his face and shook her head in amazement. "I'm so sorry. I'm so sorry, Carter."

"No apologies," he stated. "We all made it. That's what matters."

Breeze sniffed away her emotion and turned to her daughter. "This is my daughter. Your cousin. Aurora," Breeze introduced. "Aurora this is Carter."

Aurora waved. "Cool Yeezy's," Aurora stated. "They're sold out like everywhere."

"I got a sneaker connect. I can hook you up. Whenever I get a pair, I'll just order you one too," he said.

"Yeah?" Aurora asked, smiling as she pulled both ear pods out of her ears.

"Yeah, that's no problem," Carter stated. "I get em' for free. They can throw in another one for me. What size?"

"Six," Aurora finished. "Thanks, Carter."

He nodded and turned to Einstein. "I don't have all day. Maybe we should get started."

The group took a seat around the conference table.

Einstein checked his watch. "We're still waiting on one more."

"Who's that?" Carter asked.

"Mo's coming," Breeze whispered. "Or at least he's supposed to be. Have you two kept in touch over the years?"

"I haven't seen Mo since we were kids. Damn, I know this is an L, but connecting with you. Getting in touch with Mo. It shouldn't have taken this, but..."

The sound of the elevator dinging caused Carter to pause and everyone turned toward the door as six men walked in. The smell of marijuana floated into the room with them. A walking piece of street art sauntered in last. With light skin covered in so much ink, a long wild lions' mane for hair, and a deep-set brow that covered stern, dark eyes. Denim and a white t-shirt disrespected the occasion and blinding diamonds rested around his neck. Six chains, in fact. The watch on his wrist was barely noticeable because the stones were blinding.

Breeze stopped breathing. This man was Mecca Diamond reincarnated. It was like someone had dug him up from his grave, down to the jewel that was tattooed on his neck with the phrase "Diamonds are Forever" in cursive script.

She stood to her feet.

"Mo-"

Breeze crossed the room and wrapped her arms around this grown man. The last time she had seen him, he had been a boy.

"No shit!" Mo exclaimed, taken aback by the presence

of Breeze. "Auntie B." He gave a half smile as he embraced her. It floored Breeze that she was in the arms of a full grown man.

"Last time I saw you, you were a baby," she cried.

"Yeah, shit has changed," he said, kissing the top of her head. He turned to the rest of the room. "I'm here. Let's get it over with. I got shit to do," Mo said, bypassing Breeze and sauntering to the conference table.

He sat across from Carter and leaned back in his chair, lifting his feet to the table and crossing new sneakers one on top of the other. He put his hands behind his head. His goons posted up around the room.

"This a big show cuz. You doing a lot for family," Carter stated.

"That's what this is? Family?" Mo asked. "I ain't seen you in fifteen years. I don't walk into rooms with strangers without protection, G. You know that champ. I see you out here making waves. That's what's up cutty. You done came a long way, C.J."

"Carter."

Mo lifted his brow, taken aback. "My bad, family. Carter, it is," he said as he sat up and reached across the table and extended his hand. Carter accepted the greeting as they shook like gangsters instead of gentlemen.

"It's good to see you boy," Mo said, the corner of his mouth lifting in a smirk. "Up close that is…superstar."

"Come on man," Carter answered, smirking. He would never get used to the attention that came with his career.

"And who is the pretty baby girl ignoring the fuck out of us?" Mo asked, snickering.

Breeze tapped the table with her long, elaborate, nails and Aurora looked up.

"Aurora this is your cousin, Mo," Breeze introduced.

Aurora smiled and nodded. "Hey, Mo."

"Oh, I got twin deserts ready for niggas over you, lil baby," Mo answered.

Aurora smiled and shook her head.

"Good," Breeze stated, only half-jokingly. She had been hesitant to bring her daughter back to the land of cocaine she had grown up in. With her pretty baby face, long hair, and developing body, she knew that Aurora was a dope boy's fantasy. She didn't want to introduce her daughter to that life. Breeze had been broken by that life.

"Shall we begin?" Einstein asked.

Carter leaned forward. "How about we clear the room first? There's no need for an audience," he stated.

Mo dead panned on him and Carter's gaze didn't falter. Mo, licked his lips like he was thinking on it, before nodding. "Yeah, okay." He turned to his crew. "Yo' Joey, y'all wait for me in the lobby, bruh."

"You good money?" Joey shot back.

"Yeah, I'm straight. Won't be long," Mo answered.

The men cleared the room and then everyone focused on the head of the table where Einstein sat. He opened a folder that held Estes' last will and testament.

"Emilio has left each of you a sum of ten million dollars," Einstein said. "Carter, he left you the sum of one hundred million dollars and the estate in the Dominican Republic."

"Run that back for me one time," Mo stated, leaning

forward as he stared Einstein in the eyes. "I'm the last living male heir and he leaves me a fraction of what he's worth and gives everything to C.J.?"

"I don't want it. I'm not hurting for bread. Divide it equally," Carter stated.

"Estes wanted you to have it," Breeze spoke up. "He raised you. He gave it to you for a reason."

Mo scoffed. "I don't even know why we discussing what's on paper," Mo interrupted. "You're right. Estes has a right to leave whatever to whoever, but what about what ain't on paper. I don't want that little money. Give it to baby girl," Mo said, nodding at Aurora.

"Really?" Aurora piped up, shocked as she turned eyes to her mother.

"I prefer to earn mine," Mo stated. "I want the connect."

Einstein stood. "This is where I leave you to discuss amongst yourselves." He had been in the business of representing the underworld for a long time, he didn't want to be privy to the details. What he didn't know about he could defend. He never wanted to be put in a moral disposition.

Breeze nodded, knowing that Einstein wanted no knowledge of the criminal enterprise that secretly fueled their family. Breeze turned to Aurora. "Why don't you wait for me in the hallway?"

Aurora lifted from her seat.

"Tell every single one of them niggas out there to keep they eyes down," Mo stated.

Breeze was floored at his resemblance to her brother. To both her brothers.

"Just keep to yourself Aurora," Breeze said.

The three of them waited until Aurora cleared the room.

"I want the connect. That's the only legacy I need," Mo stated arrogantly as he sat back in his chair.

"It doesn't work like that Mo. You can't just sit in Estes' seat. The people of the Dominican Republic are fickle. They operate off code, off tradition. They don't deal with outsiders," Breeze stated.

"I'm Estes blood. I'm no outsider," Mo shot back, his tone relaxed, unbothered as if Breeze was wasting her breath.

"You're an Afro-Dominican man who has never been to the island, who has never spoken a lick of Spanish in your life. You go over there, and you might not make it back. You think what your daddy and uncles did in Miami is something? The five families in the D.R. make this look like a playground. You are an American born Dominican and you're half black. Take the money and let this go," Breeze urged. "Why would you want to get in the game, Mo? You know what it did to this family. You have ten million dollars at your fingertips. Take it and live. This city is a trap."

"But it's mine, Aunt B. Miami is mine and it's clown niggas sitting on top stunting like my people ain't bleed and die on these streets. The Diamonds been gone too long. I'm taking everything I'm owed, starting with Estes' seat."

"I'll take you," Carter spoke. He had been silent, brooding, observing Monroe and all his aggression. The bravado and muscle of his cousin told a story of survival. Life had taken them down separate paths and while Carter's hadn't been easy, he could see that Mo's had been rougher. He was different. Angry. Hardened. "I know the men Estes dealt with. I know them well. I'll make the introduction and you take it from there."

"Carter," Breeze interrupted. "This family is out of the drug business. Let it die with my grandfather. Who are you going to take over with, huh, Mo? Those men you walked in here with? Back in the day, they would have never passed the test to make it to the block. Those aren't soldiers Mo, they're yes men. They're stupid, they're reckless, and they'll get you killed." Breeze had seen this time and time again. She didn't want to watch her nephew repeat the curse that plagued everyone with their last name. "Look at Estes! We still don't know who's behind that. He was murdered. This isn't a game. We've lost everything to this business. Both your fathers, Aurora's father, my father. All gone because of this city."

"That means there's nothing else to lose. Only wins from here," Mo said. He was persistent. Money wasn't driving him because he could walk away with his inheritance and be set. Breeze recognized the hunger for clout, the thirst for power, and it sent chills up her spine. Each of her brothers had been eaten alive by that same monster. Her father had lost the battle to that beast before them but if she had learned nothing else, she had learned that you couldn't stop a man from chasing the crown. Mo wanted to be king. She prayed that the road would be easier, that the men before him had paved the road smooth enough for there to be fewer bumps, but she had a feeling that Mo would drive full speed into disaster.

CHAPTER 3

"Real money is never loud.
Quiet money is usually attached to wealth, "-Estes

A crowd gathered on the landing strip as the passenger airplane sat there. Beautiful Dominican faces of men, women, and children gathered in anticipation to see their pride and joy Carter "C.J." Jones. News traveled fast that the hometown hero from their soil would be returning home. Carter sat inside the cabin, along with Mo and Papi. He looked in awe trying to figure out how did they know he was coming. He saw handwritten signs that read 'Welcome Home' and pictures of him in the ring and it brought him joy. He instantly felt the love and remembered the authentic love that the country had always provided him. He couldn't help but to smile as he looked over his shoulder and studied the crowd and sea of people. They had just landed in the D.R., to go meet Estes' former partners and attempt to establish a cocaine connection.

"Yo, this crazy as hell," Mo said as he looked at the people who anxiously waited to get a glimpse of the hometown hero. He threw his arm around Carter as he looked out of the window and he smiled ear to ear. "You a king out here."

"This is crazy," Carter said as he shook his head in disbelief. Papi rushed over to the window and smiled, feeling proud of his people. He was full-blooded Dominican and felt good to be home. He hadn't been there for years and was excited to be in his homeland.

Papi watched closely as Mo draped his arm around Carter and side-eyed him. Papi didn't like Mo too much and it showed. He had a disdain for his flamboyancy and arrogance. He still didn't understand why Carter let Mo be around them. Papi's main focus was Carter's boxing career... however, Mo had other plans. Mo wanted to reignite the family tradition. He wanted to start their own generation's cartel.

As they exited the plane and begin to descend the stairs, the roars got louder once Carter was visible.

¡Campeona!

¡Campeona!

¡Campeona!

The crowd yelled the word campeona in unison.

"What are they saying?" Mo asked as he shifted his duffle bag in front of him and he walked down the stairs.

"It means champion," Carter said as he reached the last stair and stepped onto the pavement. He instantly began signing autographs and giving high fives to the young fans as they made their way through the crowd and towards the two black sedans that were waiting for them. Two chauffeurs of Dominican descent stood by each rear door, waiting for their passengers. Mo and Carter hopped in one car, Papi got into the other.

The sun beamed down and inside the un-airconditioned car was even hotter. Mo rested his head on the headrest and took a deep breath. Mo had his hair pulled on the top of his head in a wild bun, and decided to let his hair fall as he leaned back in the seat.

"Good afternoon, gentlemen," the driver said as he adjusted his rearview mirror. He caught a glimpse of eyes in the mirror and a look of sorrow came over his face. " I'm so sorry about your loss. Estes was a great, great man," the driver said just before focusing on what was ahead of him while slowing pulling off. Carter slowly acknowledged him by nodding but said nothing.

As they slowly pulled off of the runway, the kids from the crowd began to chase the car and knock on the window anxiously, trying to get a final glimpse of their hero. They ran along the side of the vehicle reaching for Carter as Carter smiled and looked on. They were all over the car like ants and Mo was in awe as he witnessed the admiration they had for his cousin.

"They show you love out here. They love you like Pac," Mo said playfully as he tapped Carter's chest with the back of his hand.

The Dominican was everything he thought it would be. Him having Dominican bloodline made it even more alluring. He wanted that same love, but for another reason. Mo was determined to get connected. He sat back and rubbed his hands together, anticipating establishing the pipeline that would make him king in Miami, like Carter was king in the D.R.

Carter glanced over at Mo, who seemed to be deep in his own thoughts. He noticed that he had a slight smirk on his face and Carter could tell that Mo had infamy on his mind. The greed was prevalent in his eyes as he rubbed his hands together. This only made Carter more reluctant to bridge him with the Dominicans. However, he knew how much Mo wanted this and decided to do it for his cousin. Although they had been separated for years, they had a bonded past and had been through so much together. Carter felt that he owed him this one favor.

"This is the one and only time I'm getting involved in this. After I connect you, I'm never getting my hands dirty or having anything to do with this life," Carter said out loud. He was saying it to Mo, but his words were also being served as a reminder to himself that he would not get involved in the same game that consumed his mother and father.

"I got you my nigga. Just this one time," Mo confirmed as he gazed out of the window, admiring the new surroundings.

As they exited the small airport, the personality of the country came alive. Beautiful, brown faces were everywhere and the Spanish culture was colorfully vibrant. Mo had always wanted to go there as an adult, but the chance never presented itself. He felt at home. He was in the cocaine capital of the world and he felt like he was walking in his purpose. It always bothered him that he was part of the Dominican, but had no Dominican connection. It's time to take this bitch over, he thought as a small grin spread across his face. He positioned himself comfortably into the seat and reached into his pocket. He then pulled out a pre-rolled joint and began to light it. He took a deep pull and let the thick smoke set in his lungs, wanting to feel the effects of the Purple Kush.

"Yo, put that out for me," Carter said without emotion as he rolled down the window and slightly stuck his head out.

"You serious?" Mo looked confused as he frowned and looked at Carter as if he had two heads.

"Yeah, I get tested by the boxing commission randomly. I can't fuck around," Carter said assertively.

"Whatever you say, boss," Mo said sarcastically. "Just make sure you plug me and I'll play by the rules," he added arrogantly. He took one last deep pull of the joint and put out the joint in the ashtray that was in the armrest. Carter shook his head, realizing that the sooner he connected Mo with Estes people, the sooner he could focus back on boxing.

Just as the sun was going down, the air was damp and muggy. It was hot, but more bearable because the absence of the beaming sun rays. Mo, Papi, and Carter walked down the dirt road that seemed to lead to nowhere.

"Damn yo, where the fuck is this spot at? We been walking for over an hour," Mo asked as he wiped the sweat from his brow. He had taken off his shirt and draped it over his shoulders. His tattoo filled body was on full display and by him having so many markings, it looked like one big mural and his body acted as a canvas. His gold Cuban link swung back and forth as they made their way down the road.

"We are almost there. It's just up the road," Carter answered as he led the way.

They were on their way to a festival. It was a special night for the people of the D.R. Locals gathered around every Sunday night and celebrating with music, drinks, and cigars. It was a town tradition when the locals of Santo Domingo celebrated life. Carter had made arrangements to meet with a few good men and that was the destinated meeting spot.

"And why couldn't we drive to this mu'fucka?" Mo asked as he was getting noticeably irritated with the impromptu nature walk.

"We can't disrespect the culture. I didn't want to pull up in car services and luxury cars. We have to blend in," Carter said, catching Mo up on the laws of the land of Santo Domingo. Estes had taught Carter how to move correctly and to earn the respect of powerful men. He would always tell him "Real money is never loud. Quiet money is usually attached to wealth," and this was a prime example of Estes' teachings. Although Estes was the blood grandfather of Mo and had no biological connection to him, he had poured all of his knowledge and wisdom into Carter and it definitely showed.

Papi looked over at him and rolled his eyes, knowing that the Dominicans that they were about to visit would look down on Mo. He looked too ghetto and Americanized, especially to a place that was so full of culture and didn't rely on shiny things and arrogance to validate them.

"Fuck you looking at nigga? Don't get fucked up out here," Mo said boldly as he noticed the side-eyeing.

"Who the fuck are you talking to?" Papi asked with his heavy Dominican accent. He stopped and stood in front of Mo, ready for whatever. He was looking for a reason to show him how he really felt about him. Mo swiftly walked towards Papi, who was shorter than him and looked down hovering. Papi was stocky, solid, and a trained boxer, so his fist automatically balled as Mo approached.

"Don't think them boxing moves going to work against what I got for you, my nigga. All them muscles don't mean shit when we get back home. I'll put something hot in you, believe that," Mo said with a smirk on his face. The thing was, Mo meant every word he spat. Those weren't threats, but more so promises. He didn't back down a bit. Mo loved the adrenaline that confrontation often provided. The crazed look in his eyes and willingness to fight a professional boxer impressed Carter as he looked on and didn't say anything. He wanted to see what his cousin had in him. Although Mo was Monroe's son, he had the spirit of Mecca all in him. The wild hair, the fearlessness, and the craziness all were direct traits from the notorious Mecca Diamond.

"You're not even worth it," Papi said as he shook his head from side to side and stepped back. He conceded to Mo, not wanting to offend Carter. He didn't want to jeopardize their relationship over a falling out with his friend's family member. Papi stepped away, not out of fear…but respect. Carter instantly knew why Papi waved the white flag, but Mo took it as Papi being a coward.

"That's what the fuck I thought, lil man. Witcho ho' ass," Mo provoked while smiling. "Not sure who you thought I was but-"

"Leave that shit alone, cuz," Carter said as he waved off the drama and began to walk down the trail again. The men continued to walk without rehashing the drama. Mo's mind quickly refocused on the task at hand. His only goal was to get plugged, so he could do what he did best and that was get knee deep into the streets. He knew that him and Carter were not one of the same anymore. They had taken different paths and were complete opposites.

The rest of the walk was quiet as everyone got lost in their own thoughts. As they got closer to the downtown area, the faint noises of bongos and guitar strings got louder and louder. The sun had completely gone down and the wooden tikis had been set ablaze, illuminating the area where the people gathered. Carter and Papi instantly smiled, feeling the nostalgia of their childhood. Groups of people were dancing to the rhythm of the beat, swiftly twirling their hips in classic Spanish fashion. Carter led the way as they approached the ongoing festival. As they turned sideways and cut through the crowd, Mo was astonished by what he was in the midst of. He had never seen so many beautiful women in one place. It seemed like every woman he looked at was more beautiful than the last. He was in the land of milk and honey and he was beginning to like the Dominican Republic.

"Check this out, we gotta lay low. Not draw too much attention to ourselves," Carter whispered to Mo as they maneuvered through the crowd. Carter wanted to give him a crash course on mob etiquette. Carter already understood that they were being watched from the moment that they landed.

"I'm cool. I know how to handle myself," Mo said as he waved at one of the bartenders that stood to the far left of them.

"Just make sure you play it cool. This ain't the states, cuz," Carter coached.

"Just introduce me to whoever the plug is. I'll do the rest," Mo said arrogantly. Carter instantly began to regret bringing Mo to members of the five families; a group of men who controlled the drug exports out of the country. Estes was once a part of this faction, but the connection died with him.

"This way," Carter said as he noticed the familiar face sitting outside the small domino gallery. Mo veered off and headed in the direction of the bar. Carter grabbed his wrist, stopping him in his tracks. Carter pulled him close to his body and whispered.

"You gotta stay on point, man. There's no second chance with these guys," Carter said. Mo's face frowned, not used to anyone talking to him in that way. However, he quickly realized the opportunity that was in front of him. Mo pulled his arm away from Carter and nodded his head in agreement. A sound of a whistle got their attention as all of their heads turned towards the direction of the noise. A young Dominican man had two fingers in his mouth from the whistle. Once the Dominican locked eyes with Carter, he waved him over. The young man had a worn face and dark skin. He had a menacing look and didn't attempt the give them a warm welcome whatsoever. He had the eye of the tiger as he watched Carter, Mo, and Papi approach him.

"Come on," Carter said to Papi and Mo as he headed in the direction of the small hole in the wall. As they reached the entrance, the young Dominican pointed to Carter to approach him first. He wanted to frisk him before entering. Carter immediately complied and lifted his arms as the man searched him very carefully and thoroughly. The Dominican proceeded to search the other two. Once finished, he nodded in approval. He stepped to the side to give them a clear path into the spot.

The Dominican man only spoke Spanish, so Mo was having a hard time keeping up with what was being said. Papi and Carter on the other hand were familiar with the language. They walked into the empty bar and it had a very cultured and Dominican historic theme. Various tables were set up with a set of dominoes on them; each table with four chairs around it. A lone bartender was behind the bar washing off the countertop and his eyes were fixated on the crew. Mo looked closely and saw a bulge on the bartender's waist, tipping off that he was strapped. As they motioned past the bartender, they made their way towards the back and the sounds from the festival became more distant with each step. The inside was air-conditioned and cold. After a few steps, the constant humming of the air conditioner was the only thing they heard, giving it an eerie feeling. The dimly lit place was much more than it seemed. It was the hub for negotiations for some of the biggest drug deals in the world. The deeper Carter walked into the place, the more and more familiar it had become. It was the same place that Estes would come and at times and let Carter accompany him.

They followed the Dominican down a flight of stairs which led to a basement. When they reached what seemed like an underground cellar, cigar smoke filled the air. The smell of fresh tobacco was present. Papi stopped at the bottom of the stairs and positioned himself against the wall. Carter had instructed him on how to move properly the day before. He remembered when Estes used to have him do the same thing, but the day had come when he would sit at the table.

A wooden table was in the center of the room and a trio of men sat there playing dominoes. All the gentlemen were of Spanish descent and all looked to be in their sixties to early seventies. An overweight man, who had on an open silk shirt on was the first to speak. His abundance of gray chest hair was on full display as he smoked a fat cigar and was the first to acknowledge the guest.

"You're Estes boy?" the man asked with a blank face, showing no emotion. Carter humbly nodded.

"Good evening, gentlemen," Carter said as he approached the table. Mo stood next to him, remaining silent.

"Have a seat," the man instructed as he proceeded to mix the dominoes up with his fat pudgy hands. He then continued to talk to Carter, never looking directly at him. He only focused on the game. Carter looked around the table and nodded to everyone at the table, quietly greeting them all.

"I came here to talk business," Carter said with a stern look.

"Oh, you want to talk business, eh?" the fat man asked as he finally cracked a smile, easing the tension. He looked at Carter and placed his hand on his shoulder. "I'm sorry for your loss. Estes was a great man."

"Gracious," Carter said as he nodded.

"So, I'm hearing you want to open back up the pipeline?" the fat man said.

"Yes... but it's actually not for me. It's for my cousin. Who is Estes' grandson," Carter said as he threw his hand in the direction of Mo who was standing to his right.

"What up, I'm Mo," Mo interjected as he reached his hand over the table. The fat man didn't even acknowledge Mo and left him hanging. Mo slowly pulled his hand back and immediately grew a menacing look at his face, feeling disrespected. He sarcastically chuckled and let it be known that he didn't appreciate the disrespect.

"Cool," he said as he placed his hand in front of him and smoothly crossed them. Carter could sense the tension and immediately got up and leaned into Mo.

"Yo, why don't you let me handle this and wait with Papi," Carter whispered to Mo.

"Alright cool. As long as you get the plug, I ain't tripping," Mo said arrogantly.

"I got you cuz," Carter said assuring him. Mo gave a quick look at the people at the table and walked away to join Papi by the stairs. Carter watched him walk away and sat back down at the table. Carter understood the way of the land and the science of drug trafficking. It wasn't that they

46

were being rude to Mo, it was just that they didn't speak for people who weren't vouched for. There had to be an introduction in place before any type of communication was opened up. These are lessons Estes taught him as a young boy and there was no way Mo would understand this without prior knowledge.

"My apologies about my cousin, Carter said calmly as he placed his hands on the table and collapsed them inside one another.

"That's quite alright," the fat man said as they began their game of dominoes. "Do you know who I am?"

"Of course. You're Juan Miguel," Carter quickly answered.

The name sent chills up Carter's back. He was the head of one of the five families of South America. He was the head of the Sinaloa Cartel. The main source of all heroin and cocaine to the United States. They ran drugs through the Caribbean, which almost always made its way to the States. He had the power to flood an entire region in a snap of a finger. With this great responsibility came great power…which made him an extremely dangerous man. Carter understood this completely, so that's why he stepped in when he felt Mo bucking. Carter quickly realized that Mo had no idea who the man was in front of them. But Carter knew for sure and intervened before they all were killed. They were in the belly of the beast and with that knowledge, Carter was edgy.

"What can I do to help you?" Juan asked.

"My cousin needs a connect. What's in Miami isn't working for him and he wants to get the faucet turned back on," Carter said simply.

"We do not know him," Juan said as he looked at Carter and glanced over to Mo.

"I understand. However, he is the direct bloodline of Estes. I vouch for him," Carter said confidently.

"No…no, my son. It doesn't work like that. Estes is gone now. So, this falls on you. If you want the order…you put in the order. However, you are responsible for that order," Juan explained. Carter took a deep breath and sat back in his chair. He rubbed his hands together, thinking about what was just said. Something was telling him that it was a bad idea, but he felt obligated to do that for Mo.

"I understand," Carter said as he glanced back at Mo and then back to Juan.

"So, what do you want? How many can you handle?" Juan questioned, getting straight to it. Carter paused thinking about the magnitude of what was being put in front of him. He thought that this trip would be a simple introduction that he orchestrated. He had no desire to move any type of drugs, so he was conflicted. He looked back at Mo who watched eagerly, waiting for Carter to put in an order. Carter could see the hunger in his eyes, and it was as if he was nudging him to proceed without saying a word.

"Go," Mo mouthed as he slightly motioned his head. Carter clenched his jaws and dropped his head. He knew deep inside that he wasn't a drug trafficker and he was outside of his league. Although his father was one of the best to do it, it wasn't in him. He was a fighter.

"Say no more. This meeting is over. You fellas go and enjoy

the festival and have a good time while visiting here," Juan said, shutting down the possibilities of further conversation.

"Mo is knee deep and can move..." Carter began to say, but was cut off by Juan.

"Have a good day, gentlemen. Jose! See them out," he said to the Dominican man that originally brought them down. Carter was taken aback but remained silent. He stood and headed out. As he headed towards Mo, he could see the anger in his face. Mo couldn't believe that he didn't take on the weight for him.

"What the fuck?" Mo asked through his clenched teeth, as he opened his eyes the size of golf balls, as Carter approached him. He stared a hole through Carter and had never felt more disappointed in his blood. Mo bit his tongue and remained silent, but his jaw muscles flexed and it was a clear indication of his rage. Just as they began to exit, Juan added one more thing.

"If you decide to change your mind, you have thirty days to reconsider. But don't come back here. Go to Harry on Ocean Drive. That's mi familia and I will let him know that the offer stands. Thirty days padre'," he added just before he focused back on the game. Carter heard him and immediately knew that it was no chance that he would take that offer. However, on the other hand, Mo had heard all he needed to. He would make sure that The Cartel would be long lived.

CHAPTER 4

"You have to play the game smart, or you lose," – Miamor

T he sound of the gates closing behind Ashton as she stepped into the visiting room made her cringe. She hated this place. It had taken four years of her young life. Savages dwelled behind these walls and they masqueraded as guards. The inmates weren't the bad guys. Most of the women Ashton had met behind the wall were simply trying to survive. She had spent four years behind those walls without one visit. Nobody cared enough to check on her. She had been written off so long ago by her family that it didn't even hurt anymore. No commissary had come, no letters, and no names on her visitor's list. It had been a long and lonely stretch. Only one woman had made it easier. Miamor Jones.

Miamor had told Ashton not to look back once she was released but there was no way Ash would let her rot. She sat down at the table and when Miamor walked in Ash felt pride. Her long hair was pulled back and the braid was tucked inside her shirt. Her face was stern and her eyes intentional as they swept across the room.

"You're a hard-headed girl," Miamor said as she stood in front of Ashton, face unreadable. "I told you not to come back here."

Ashton shrugged and then said. "Real bitches do real shit. I'm only half free until you're out too. I just wanted to let you know I cashed that old check."

Miamor smirked, knowing exactly what her young protégé meant. She pulled Ashton in for a hug.

"I swear you remind me so much of myself," Miamor said, shaking her head. "That's not always a good thing, Ash. I didn't always make the best decisions. A lot of bad moves put me in this seat, behind these bars. You have to play the game smart, or you'll lose. Move differently than I did. I was a hothead. My emotions erased reason sometimes and it destroyed me, it ruined my family, it took me away from my son, and I lost the love of my life. Miami is not the sandbox. It's a big boy league, you have to be careful. You have to make sure my son is careful, that's he's safe. I see him living his life, boxing, making a legit life for himself and I'm so proud of him, but the enemies of his father, of me, will expect him to pay our debts. He made a mistake coming back to Miami. He has no idea what he's getting himself into. I need you at his side."

"What if he won't let me in?" Ashton asked.

"You're a pretty girl Ashton. You're smart. You're an asset to any team you choose. Choose him. Be his backbone. Be his world. Fuck him. Feed him. Praise him. Nurture him. He has mommy issues from being left alone. Raise him. They took me from him before I could, so you do it. The woman who raises him is the one he'll love forever."

"You want me to play wifey to your son?" Ashton asked.

"Not play. I want you to be wifey to my son and if anybody poses a threat, I want you to eliminate them. I taught you how. He'll provide a good life. Money, the spotlight. All you have to do is get close and play the part," Miamor said.

"What about love?" Ashton asked.

"He's his father's son. You'll love him so much he'll become all that matters."

Miamor's voice was whimsical and her eyes spaced out before closing. The history of her love for Carter Jones played behind the darkness in her mind in seconds. "Be careful how you love him. It'll take over your soul. Never let a man snatch your soul," Miamor whispered. "Because if anything ever happens to him, you'll just be an empty shell. He'll be gone and you'll just exist, waiting for the day you reunite. It's not a way for any woman to live. I wouldn't wish this shit on my worst enemy," she said. "It's a hurt that never dulls."

Ashton heard the sorrow in Miamor. She could see it. She had never noticed before, but it was all over her today. They had spent four long years together in a cell and Ashton had never seen her like this.

"Hey, keep your head. You're almost out of here. You just have a few more years to walk down. You can't let these bars get to you. You taught me that," Ashton said, noticing the somber change in Miamor.

"Whether I'm in here or out there, I'll never be free. Free is fucking Carter Jones on a Miami beach. Free is having a threesome with the love of your life in Rio. Free isn't managing without him. It's not visiting a grave to scrape up a piece of the feeling he used to give me. As long as I'm walking this earth, I'll be in prison. I won't be free until I see him again."

"But he's gone, Miamor," Ashton whispered. "He's dead. You talk about him like he's alive. You have to let go."

Miamor's flat palm slammed so swiftly against the table that Ashton jumped. "I will never let him go. Ever. Don't speak on him. That's something you can never understand."

Miamor stood, ending their visit abruptly.

"I didn't mean to offend you," Ashton said, standing too. "I just want you to be okay in here."

"I've been taking care of myself for a long time. You just worry about looking out for my son," Miamor said. "Do you got a place to live? You got a car?" Miamor asked.

"I'm figuring both out. Don't worry about me. I know how to survive," Ashton said.

Miamor tapped the table with one finger and then sat back in her chair. "You got a pen?" she asked.

Ashton shook her head. "They took everything off me when I came in," she explained.

Miamor leaned across the table. "I need you to remember this number. 810-875-0939. Let me hear you say it back to me."

"810-," Ash started.

"Come on, it's important," Miamor urged. "810-875-0939."

"810-875-0939," Ashton repeated.

"Remember it. Say it in your head a thousand times," Miamor said. "Call that number and the person on the other end of the phone will set you up. Get a place to live. A nice one. Carter's a pro-athlete, he doesn't want a gold digger. Build a lifestyle. Buy a foreign whip, not a Benz or a BMW, something an everyday bitch with a good job can't afford. A Range Rover or G-Wagon and customize the shoes. Wear designer, but not too much designer where it looks tacky and no Gucci. I need you to catch his eye for the right reasons, not because he wants to fuck you and never call you again. The person who answers that number will help you. Just use my name."

"Where did the money come from? The money I'm going to spend?" Ashton asked.

"Don't worry about that part. It's not dirty. I've got it covered. Just do what you promised."

Ashton nodded and watched Miamor walk out of the room. Miamor made it all the way to the door before she turned back. "Don't come back here Ashton," Miamor said. Ashton nodded but her heart sank. She remembered the days when she would be right beside her, headed back to their block. It was a lonely existence behind concrete and steel. The time seemed warped, moving slowly, torturing the women trapped inside. Prison politics made it impossible for anyone to serve a quiet sentence. If it wasn't other inmates starting petty beefs to establish the pecking order it was dirty C.O.'s taking advantage of the prisoners.

The years behind these walls would have destroyed her if it had not been for Miamor. Ashton had received no visitors; she hadn't gotten one letter. She had three sisters out in the world who had forgotten about her the moment she had gotten knocked. So, as she sat in time out and did her time day by day, she vowed to never step foot inside again. If things ever went bad on the outside the police would have to kill her because she would never let them put her in a box again.

Ashton walked out of the prison with a heavy heart. She hated to leave Miamor behind, but she didn't have a choice. She knew the best thing she could do to show Miamor love was to protect her son.

"I thought you said this would be a quick trip. I don't want to stay in Miami, mom," Aurora said as she stared out of the window of the rental car.

"This is home for a little while Aurora. There is old family business that I can't leave right now. I promise you; I don't want to be here any longer than I have to. As soon as we can, we will leave Miami."

Breeze's heart leaped out of her chest with every mile that passed them by. When she pulled up to the old Diamond Estate a thousand memories flooded her. Her heart filled. It was so heavy as she climbed out of the car. It still looked the same. Her father had paid for every brick to be laid. A palace. A mansion. The Diamond Estate.

"Mom, this house is huge. We can't live here," Aurora said. "Where are we going to get the money for this?"

"Don't worry about that," Breeze said. "We belong here. It's where I grew up."

"You grew up here?" Aurora said.

"With two older twin brothers and my mom and dad. My oldest brother Carter came later. I met him when I was older, but they all represent this place. They all fill these halls."

"And we're going to buy this place? With what money?" Aurora asked.

"It's already bought," Breeze answered. "And don't worry about with what money. You let me worry about that."

Estes had left the Diamond Estate to Breeze in his will. He had acquired the property after the government had seized it years ago. He had gotten many offers to buy it but somehow, he knew his granddaughter would one day return to her kingdom.

Breeze put the old code into the security gate and like magic that gates opened. She couldn't believe it hadn't been changed in all this time.

"Come on, I'm going to show you around. It's like a castle baby. You're going to love it," Breeze said growing excited as she hurried back behind the wheel. Aurora climbed in too and they drove up the long driveway to the main house. The sight of the front steps broke her heart. It was the place where Money had taken his last breaths. He had died on those steps. Her big brother. Her protection. All of them had been. Money, Mecca, Carter. Her muscle. She could hardly believe she was the last Diamond standing. She missed them terribly. Life just hadn't been the same since they had died. She had been lonely because no one understood where she came from. The thing about being the last one standing was that it was lonely as hell. No one remembered the era she came from.

Breeze remembered the blood that had stained the steps after Money's murder. The stone had been replaced but the image of those stains was permanent in her head.

"Mom?" Aurora called. Breeze shook her head, clearing her thoughts and then walked to the door. She put the key in and pushed it open, stepping into a palace.

"Oh my God! Mom!" Aurora exclaimed as she walked inside.

"This is your legacy. The Diamond Estate. Your grandfather, Carter Diamond, had it built," Breeze said.

The interior had been remodeled. It didn't look the same. It was updated, more modern. Nothing was recognizable. Different colors. Different floor. The feeling. The feeling was the same, however. It felt like home. Breeze scoffed and her eyes prickled. If she closed them, she would be a girl again. She could practically hear the bass of her father's voice bouncing off these walls. The sound of her mother's laugh. The bickering between the twins. Family had lived here once. Her family. They had existed once. She could still feel their energy.

"This is so dope!" Aurora exclaimed.

Breeze chuckled. "Come on. I'm going to show you around and then we'll head to the mall. We need to look through Neiman's home catalog. We've got to furnish this place. Make it our own."

The Bal Harbour shops were alive with energy. Aurora may not have loved the idea of living in Miami, but the mall was her favorite place to be and the way Breeze was allowing her to spend was heavenly. She knew it was her mother's way of making up for the fact that her life had been completely uprooted. She was now the new girl in a new town. She would be the new kid at school mid-year. She had no friends, no family her age. Assimilating would be hard, but the choice had been made. They were staying. The Louis Vuitton shopping bag she held in her hand was a good apology. Aurora walked through the department store in search of her mom. She found her with a personal shopper. The amount of money Breeze was spending on furniture called for champagne on ice apparently because she sipped bubbly while picking out the interior pieces of her house out of a catalog.

"Hey, mom. Can I go to Zara while you shop?" Aurora asked.

"Yeah, here," Breeze replied, reaching in her bag and pulling out ten hundred-dollar bills.

"Thanks. Call me if you need me," Aurora said as she bounced out of the store. That much money would go a long way in her favorite store. Aurora was in heaven as she ran through the racks of clothes, gathering an armful of hangers before heading to the dressing room.

"How many pieces?" the dressing room attendant asked.

"Umm, a lot," Aurora said, smiling. "I think ten."

Aurora followed the attendant to the dressing room and began to change clothes. She put on a pretty white dress and when she went out to view herself in a bigger mirror she saw a girl in the reflection behind her. With skin like brown sugar and long feed-in braids to the back, she stood barefoot and, on her tiptoes, as she turned to look at her butt in the mirror.

"My butt look big in this?" she asked. The girl looked up at Aurora. "Like does it look fat, not like popping fat, but fat fat?"

Aurora glanced at the girl in the short daisy duke shorts. "It looks good," Aurora said. "Like not sloppy and big, but not little either. If that makes sense."

The girl dropped it low, twerking in the mirror with her face turned up. "That's what I was going for. Thanks!"

The girl looked at the attendant and then went into her dressing room. As she passed Aurora she said. "That's a size too big, you should get a smaller size, show off your shape. It's bomb." She turned to the girl working the dressing room. "Hey, can you grab my friend a smaller size in this dress?"

"Sure," the girl said.

Once the dressing room was clear Aurora watched the girl go into her dressing room. She stepped into her jeans, tearing the tag off the shorts beneath.

Aurora diverted her eyes and changed back into her regular clothes. When she opened the curtain, the girl across from her was gone. The tag to the shorts was on the floor and Aurora was sure the girl had stolen them. She carried her purchases to the counter and when the cashier went to ring her up, she handed them the tag to the shorts.

A commotion by the door got her attention.

"Hey! What are you doing?" the girl screamed as the security guard at the door pulled her aside.

Aurora hurried and paid for the clothes and took the tag and the receipt, rushing toward the commotion.

"Hey! I have the receipt! She's just wearing them out the

store. They're paid for though. She's not stealing. We paid for those shorts! Here is the tag and the receipt!"

"Get off me damn! Every black person ain't a thief!" the girl shouted, snatching her arm out of the security guard's grasp.

Aurora pulled the girl from the store and they clung to one another as the girl whispered, "I owe you, bitchhh."

The two snickered as they hurried away from the store.

"Good looking out!"

"Don't worry about it," Aurora said.

"I'm Christy," the girl introduced.

"Aurora! I'm ready!" Breeze shouted.

Aurora turned to Christy.

"I've got to go. That's my mom," Aurora said.

"Mama a baddie," Christy answered. "She looks like your sister!"

"Not if you hear her fuss at me and force me to rearrange my whole life to move to Miami you'd be able to tell," Aurora laughed.

"Oh, you're new here? We got to post up! My brother throwing a kickback tonight. What's your number? I'll come scoop you if your mama says it's cool," Christy offered.

"Really?" Aurora said, surprised at how easy it was to connect with someone new. The last thing she wanted was to be stuck in the house without friends.

"Yeah, that's cool. What's your Snap?" Aurora asked. "I'll send you my number."

"EverybodyhatesChris," Christy said.

Aurora looked her up and sent the number. "Send me the deets!"

"Okay girl, thanks again!" Christy said.

Aurora walked away, rushing back to Breeze.

"Welcome to Miami!" Christy yelled across the hallway.

Ashton dialed the number she had memorized in her head. She hadn't dared write it down. Writing it down would make it real, make it useable, make it evidence, and she had a feeling that whoever would answer the other line wasn't a person that wanted breadcrumbs left behind. The phone rang in her ear and Ashton's stomach tightened as she anticipated who might answer. Miamor was connected. The most connected inmate in the prison. She was a living legend. Ashton knew that whoever was on the other end of this call was equally important. She held her breath when she heard the call connect. There was no greeting, just silence.

"Hello?" Ashton said, speaking first. Still breathing. No response. "Miamor gave me this number."

More silence. "I was her cellmate at..."

Click.

The line went dead, and Ashton wondered if she had gotten it wrong. Perhaps, she had missed a number. When her cell rang back a few moments later it revealed an unknown number. She answered.

"If you ever call me phone like dat again using dat name, I'll kill you."

Ashton was stunned, speechless in fact, she didn't know

how to respond or even who she was talking to.

"If Miamor gave you the number you should know better, girl. Meet me at de' Clevelander Hotel, on de' public beach, near lifeguard tower 10, tomorrow at 1:00 p.m. If you're even a minute late, de' window of opportunity closes. Do you understand?"

"I understand," Ashton answered.

Click.

Ashton was almost positive that she had just spoken to the last standing member of the Murder Mamas and her heart raced in anxiety. She was in way over her head. Miamor had taught her everything she knew, she had trained her and upon her release she had spent a whole year walking a straight line, biding her time at the halfway house she had been assigned to. A job at the gun range Miamor had recommended her to had been the perfect cover. From 9:00 a.m. to 5:00 p.m. every day she had learned how to shoot. Baby girl had crazy aim because of it. She walked to the bedroom and went to the closet, lowering to her knees to pull back the carpet. The loose floorboards beneath rattled as she lifted one. The cobwebs below frightened her more than the contents below. She lifted a .9mm and then the clip. Whoever she was meeting, she would be prepared. Miamor's reputation preceded her. She wouldn't ever walk into a situation unarmed. The game was murder and the stakes were high and one thing Ashton would not do is be caught slipping on these Miami streets.

Ashton walked onto the beach; her sundress blew in the salt scented wind. She looked the part, blending in with the rest of the spring breakers, only there was no liquor bottle in her beach tote, but a semi-automatic with a full clip. She looked up at the tall lifeguard towers as she traversed through the sand, wobbling a bit because walking through it in flip flops was damn near impossible. She bent down to pick them up and as she came back up a girl bumped her as she passed by. Ashton dropped her bag and shoes from the impact.

"Damn bitch," Ashton griped.

The girl didn't even apologize, she just kept walking with her drink in her hand as she stumbled down the beach.

"Drunk ass," Ashton complained. She bent to retrieve her items and found a bank card on the ground. No name was printed on the front. "Hey, you dropped your..." She looked up, figuring that the girl had dropped it unknowingly, but when she searched for her, she was gone. Ashton stood, eyes scouring the beach. Her phone rang an unknown number. Ashton answered it.

"Sorry, I got held up. I'm on the beach now...headed your way."

"No need. You have everything you need. There's a half-million attached to that account. The code is 070828. You can withdraw from any bank. De money's clean so no need to worry."

Ashton's mouth dropped in shock. She had expected a face to face meeting, not a mishap on the beach. Curiosity had made her toss and turn at night anticipating this meeting because she was almost positive she would be meeting the last standing member of the infamous female hit squad, The Murder Mamas.

"Is this Aries?" she asked.

The line went silent and Ashton held her breath. "Don't call this number again."

Ashton kneeled in front of the bed and looked at the money that was in neat thousand-dollar stacks in front of her. There were five hundred piles. $500,000. Enough to put her on, enough to keep her there for a little while, but it wouldn't last forever, so her finesse had to be impeccable. She had already spent a hundred thousand in her head. To achieve the presumption of a bad bitch she had to look the part. A car, wardrobe, and a rented beachside condo wouldn't be cheap, but they were necessary accessories to catch a big fish like Carter Jones II.

Ashton stuffed the money into her backpack and tightened the drawstring before flinging one side over her shoulder. She could finally get out of the hell hole studio apartment above the Chinese restaurant that she had been staying in since leaving the halfway house. She took the city bus to Coral Gables. She had never held onto something tighter than the bag on her back. It was every dollar she had. To execute Miamor's wishes she needed it and the cost for failure would surely be death. She couldn't afford to slip up.

The cars on the Mercedes lot sparkled under the sun and as she stepped off the bus, it was obvious she didn't belong. She stepped inside the dealership and every sales associate inside bypassed her, assuming that she would be a waste of time. Ashton looked around the building for someone to assist her. Every salesperson was busy, except a black woman who was tucked away in the last cubicle in the back. Ashton made her way to her.

"Hi, I'm trying to buy a car. Can you help me out?" Ashton asked.

"Absolutely," the woman said, perking up as Ashton stepped into her office. Ashton sat in the chair across from the woman.

"Okay tell me what kind of financing you're looking for. How's your credit?" the woman asked.

Ashton reached into her backpack and pulled out stacks of cash. "Cash. I'd like to buy a car today in cash. A G-wagon, all white, black rims, if you have it," she said.

The woman sat back, stunned as Ashton filled the desk with thousand-dollar stacks.

"Let me get my manager. I'll be right back."

She hurried out of the office and Ashton was certain that this might be a rare sale for her.

Moments later, the manager came in with a younger white gentleman. They were all smiles.

"Hi, I'm Justin the sales manager and I have one of my best associates, Stan, here to help you get your car purchased," the man said.

"Your best associate walked by me when I first walked

in here. I'm good. She can help me," Ashton said. "If the commission goes to anybody it'll be her or I can go to the BMW lot down the block."

Within an hour Ashton walked out with the finest truck on the lot. A stop at the mall and the finest luxury apartments in Coral Gables and she was set. Despite the lack of paystubs to prove where the money had come from, straight cash was power, and Ashton had pieced her life back together in the span of a day. As she stood in the empty two-bedroom apartment that overlooked the ocean she sucked in a deep breath. She had yet to furnish it and she would sleep on the bare floors tonight, but it would the safest place she had rested her head in four long years.

CHAPTER 5

"I eat off every plate at the table," -Charisma

"Yo what the door looking like?" Charisma asked.

A fly Harlem nigga in designer and jewels, he stood overlooking the pool below. He wore Cartier glasses, and braids that ran horizontally down his head. Golds in his mouth, rings on damn near every finger, it was obvious he was getting money and if the crowd was any indication of the count, his bag was full. He was stacking paper with every person who came through the door. $100 per head.

"Looking good," the manager said. "You're pushing 100k just from the door."

"And the bar?" Charisma asked.

"The bar ain't your concern. I take the bar. You take the door. That was the agreement," the manager responded.

"New agreement," Charisma said. "I want 20% of the bar. My crowd my profit. I eat off every plate on the table when I host the party. Unless that's a problem?"

Charisma didn't even look at the manager. His reputation was enough muscle to get the man to comply.

"Nah, that's fair. We all leaving out of here with a bag regardless," he said.

"Indeed," Charisma stated.

"Still the same, Ris."

He turned and Ashton stood behind him, shining like new money.

"Oh shit, I know my motherfucking eyes are playing tricks on me," Charisma said, turning to her.

"Nah, I walked that time down. Thought I'd come see the one person who didn't forget about me when I was inside," she said. "I've got something for you."

Charisma looked at the manager of the popular club. "Hold it down, I'ma grab a drink," he said.

He approached Ashton and she hugged him tight as he spun her around.

"Yo, it's good as fuck to see you," Ris said. He placed her on her feet and Ashton shoved an envelope full of money into his chest.

"That's everything I owe you, plus interest," Ashton said.

He felt the thickness of the envelope. "Come on, son, what's this? You know better. Did I say it was a loan? You know better."

"No, you didn't," Ashton said. "But you're the only person who looked out for me while I was locked up. You sent money every week for four years, Ris. My own family didn't even do that. I was down and out but you wrote me, and you made sure I wasn't down bad inside. That's every dollar you gave me plus 20% interest. I want to pay you back; I know I don't have to."

"Damn man, real shit, you realer than a lot of these niggas out here. I'm glad they gave you them freedom papers. How long you been out?" Ris asked.

"A little minute," she replied vaguely. "I had to get back on my feet."

"I see you did that," Ris said, admiring her in her Burberry bikini and denim shorts that rode up her thighs so high that the insides of her pockets peeked through the bottom. "You want to chill out for a minute. Grab a drink, some food. You can kick it in my cabana. Shit gone be live in a little bit. We got some celebrity walk thrus and shit. You gone vibe with me, make the spot look beautiful. I see you showing out and shit with your little booty all out."

Ashton laughed. "Yeah I'll stick around," she said. "Lead the way."

Ris led her to his cabana. "We at the rooftop pool with it. We got the food and shit up here, the celeb DJ, the VIP's. The main pool is for the regular niggas," Ris explained.

The vibe was completely different on the top floor. Ashton followed him to the center cabana, and he grabbed a bottle from the ice bucket, popping the top to pour her a glass of champagne before sitting.

"Ya fine ass finally home. I heard you was holding your own in there girl. Proud of you," Charisma said as he filled her flute.

"I stayed out the way, I don't know what you talking about," Ashton answered, smiling.

"Yeah, if staying out the way mean putting a razor blade to the side of a bitch face and leaving her with train tracks down the side of her shit, yeah you was out the way," Charisma added, laughing.

Ashton sipped her champagne and shrugged innocently. "I don't have nothing to say," she snickered.

More people infiltrated the party. Ris threw the most frequented and exclusive events on the East Coast and in the South. He had Miami locked down and the guest list was proof of that. Rappers and ballplayers floated in, each stopping at Ris' cabana to show love.

When she saw Carter walk in her throat went dry. The odds of him being in her space blew her mind. She had nothing but opportunity, but as she saw the entourage he had with him she knew it would be hard to get through the fanfare. His body was incredible, showing years of discipline and ink that decorated it, telling war stories that made her curious. She was judging this book by its cover and Ashton wanted to flip the pages. The attention he received was ridiculous. He could barely take two steps without giving dap or signing body parts, but somehow the smile he gave out seemed humble.

The nigga next to him was a different story. He was a show all on his own. Sand colored skin and long flowing hair would be too feminine on any other man, but it was a marvel on him. His hair was like a lion's mane around him and it was beautiful, but everything else about his presence was intimidating. He hid his eyes behind sunglasses, but somehow Ashton knew the stare behind it was cold. The most terrifying part about him was the Burmese python that draped his shoulders. Just the sight of it made her skin crawl. The pair had six men behind them, and they picked up women along the way to join them at their cabana. They ended up right beside her and she wasn't sure if it was dumb luck, bad luck, or fate. Carter Jones II had walked right into her life. Now all she had to do was weed through the vixens at the pool party who were all trying to shoot their shot.

"My man. You Ris, right?"

Charisma looked up and stood.

"Yo champ, it's good to have you. Real shit. I'ma send some bottles over. I'll put a couple waitresses on you and only you so whatever y'all need, just let them know and they'll take care of you," Ris said.

Mo looked at Ashton who sat pretty behind Ris.

"Yeah we'll take her too," Mo said.

"Don't be disrespectful because you won't like it when I take it there," Ashton said.

"I kind of think I might like it," Mo said, smirking.

"Nobody's calling you the help beautiful. We don't want no smoke," Carter interrupted. He moved to the sofa of his cabana and as if a king had sat down the bottle girls, waitresses, and peasant groupies looking for a come up flocked around him.

Ris' crew walked in next and Ashton knew they were looking for their next mark. Ris was highly successful as a party promoter, but that wasn't the real wave. The hustle was the people who attended. They partied all day and night with the elite, getting them loose, giving them a reason to pull out the bank rolls and fancy jewels, then robbed them on the way out. He had been getting rich behind the scenes for years.

Ashton remembered Miamor's words. Standing out from the crowd of groupies would be damn near impossible. This didn't seem like the time or the place to make the initial connection, so Ashton stood, deciding to leave.

As she passed Carter and Mo's table, the huge snake around Mo's neck hissed at her, rising and slithering in mid-air, blocking her path.

"Oh my God! Get this thing!" she shouted.

"Mo chill, nigga," Carter said, smiling a bit at her apprehensiveness.

"Lady ain't gone hurt nobody. She just out here trying to catch the vibes," Mo said as he lifted the thirty pounds snake from his neck, strong arms flexing as he brought it over his head and placed it over her shoulders. Ashton tensed.

"I promise if you don't get this snake off me…"

"I swear to God, I want whatever the consequence is," Mo said, smirking, taunting her.

The snake slithered close to her face, almost nuzzling her and Ashton drew in a deep breath. Her entire body was shaking.

"It's going to bite me," Ashton said. "I swear if it bites me…"

"Lady don't bite," he said, helping her hold the weight of the reptile. "She'll put the squeeze on a nigga though. Not you though. She fuck with who I fuck with."

"Boy," Ashton said, rolling her eyes. Ashton stepped directly into Mo's face. "Get this snake the fuck off me."

"Nah," Mo said as he went to sit down next to Carter,

snatching a bottle out of the ice bucket as he lowered slowly to the couch.

Carter snickered and motioned to Papi. "Get the snake man," he said.

Papi laughed as he relieved Ashton of giant and intimidating reptile, handing it off to Mo. Mo sat it on the ground in front of him. Ashton reached onto their table and knocked over every bottle that sat in front of them.

"You're an asshole," she said before storming off.

"Lil' Baby bad than mu'fucka," Mo said, snickering. "All this pussy in here and the baddest is mean as fuck."

"Yeah she nice," Carter agreed, eyes following Ashton as she headed toward the exit. He watched Charisma go after her. He knew her well; Carter could tell by the way her body language relaxed. The two went over to the bar and Carter's eyes followed. "Bad indeed," he agreed.

"My nigga drop them eyes when you looking at my future bitch," Mo joked.

"You sure about that? I don't think she knows that," Carter said, smirking. "That's too grown for you nigga. That's my type. You like the ones who be in and out the club." A random girl lowered into Mo's lap. She was perfectly proportioned. Ass everywhere, weave to her tailbone, waist unusually slim. "What I tell you?" Carter teased.

"You want to put your money where your mouth is?" Mo asked. "I got five bands I can pull that before you."

"Make it a twenty, five thousand don't move me," Carter challenged.

Mo laughed jovially slapping hands with his cousin. "Twenty it is champ," Mo laughed and pulled out dice and snapped his fingers at the waitresses waiting to serve them. "Baby, clear this shit for me, I'm about to run these niggas pockets so I can buy my new bitch a new bag." Mo was already making plans for Ashton.

A full-blown dice game was underway within minutes with thousands of dollars in the pot. Hood niggas and a champ, the groupies couldn't get enough. It was a whole movie in Carter's cabana. Miami was theirs for the taking. Young, fly niggas, with Diamond blood in their veins that had painted the town red. They were about to step into the inheritance. The Miami drug game. It was their rightful place; thrones had been vacant for too long or usurped by people who didn't belong in their seats, but with the reunion of the sons of Monroe Diamond and Carter Jones a change was coming. A change was coming soon indeed.

"Six bring eight my nigga watch that money come back," Mo bragged. Carter watched Monroe shake the dice before rolling them on the concrete. "Pay me my money, NIGGA!" Carter shook his head. Mo had been running pockets for the past hour, making their cabana the center of attention. The DJ was live, turning up the party and the mood was carefree. Money and liquor. Bad bitches and made niggas. The elite and the powerful. If you weren't a celebrity, Miami's finest, or a friend of someone on the list you weren't getting in. Carter sat back with a bikini clad beauty in his lap, but he was unamused. She was beautiful. Body right. Seductive. An easy slide, but Carter had no desire to partake.

"Listen baby, I don't know what I did to have you throwing it at a nigga like this, but I can tell you it definitely wasn't enough. I'ma need you in your own seat," Carter said. He didn't claim women publicly. He definitely didn't entertain them before a fight. The girl moved without question.

"The nigga is training, sweetheart. No pussy, no liquor, no weed. The nigga is Jesus right now," Mo said, laughing.

Carter snickered, shaking his head as he threw up a middle finger.

"Fuck you," Carter snickered.

The woman at Carter's side was more of a distraction than anything else. She had it all, packaged right. That body was on point. He was sure it was purchased but he wasn't mad at it. Fake hair down her back and no strand was out of place. She smelled good and was talking in his ear good. He was sure he could slide at that very moment. Take her to the bathroom and shake of the pretenses. Dick her down real proper right there at the pool party because he was sure she would allow it, but he was so uninterested it wasn't even funny. Once a man had partaken in one groupie, he had partaken in them all. Women like this one were for aesthetic purposes only. He was convinced they should come with a warning label and an expiration date.

The Miami heat blazed on them, and the humidity was worse. He came out of his shirt, leaving on the Burberry swim trunks he wore as shorts. Carter might as well had been a magnet, the way women flocked to their cabana to get his attention. The heat undressed the gang of men slowly as they boisterously partied with the women. Mo was popping bottles of thousand-dollar champagne like it was water as bikini clad vixens turned up around them. It was a movie. When Pop Smoke's *'Dior'* came on the entire party elevated. The energy was out of this world. A bunch of rich niggas doing rich niggas shit. Mo bit his bottom lip as a girl put her ass in front of him. He grabbed the string of her thong bikini and cranked his free hand like he was winning as she danced seductively on him.

She let it clap for a nigga.
She throw it back for a nigga.

The scene was a little too live for Carter, but he wasn't going to fuck up the vibe. He was aware of the hundreds of cell phones that were out and recording, however. He didn't need any bad press, especially before a fight, so he kept it low. Sipping water as he kicked the shit with Papi and the rest of their crew.

Carter was used to being a loner. If he wasn't training, he spent most of his time behind the scenes. He wasn't in the middle of exotic day parties, turning up in the public eye, but it had been a long time since he and Mo had been together. Years had passed them by. They had endured much trauma together, from kidnappings to…well…some things were just unspeakable, but they had battled storms in their young lives. They had once been inseparable until a cruel system had pried them apart.

Carter zoned out as those days of his childhood played in his mind. He had so many ghosts. Shit he ran from; things he worked out with his fists in the ring. His past fueled every knockout he had ever earned. He hated his father. Resented his mother. His entire family history was a stain on his soul. As he looked at Mo, slapping hands with his lieutenants and throwing up 50's and 100's like they grew on trees. He wondered if those days bothered his cousin as much. At a glance, one would never be able to tell what Mo had been through. He wore his wounds well. Carter watched him. A real trap star. A hood star. He didn't look like he had a worry in the world. He looked like he counted up pussy and money on a daily. Carter's demons were more transparent. The deep-set scowl that made him seem unapproachable was permanently etched in his forehead. Carter was a quiet storm. Despite the attention, all he wanted to do was stay low in the cut. He would rather observe than speak.

The girl in front of Mo had her hands on her knees, ass moving in a circle, her tongue was clenched between her teeth. She was in a zone, enjoying the obvious buzz she was floating on.

"You good?" Papi asked.

"Yeah, this shit just real loud," Carter said. "I'ma get a drink. I'll be back."

LONG LIVE THE CARTEL

Carter walked away from the pool area and made his way inside the hotel to the lobby bar. His Ray Ban sunglasses covered his eyes as he maneuvered through the crowd.

He saw Ashton sitting alone, sipping a mojito.

He went to the other end of the bar and took a seat. The bartender floated his way.

"What can I get you?" she asked.

"Fiji," he said.

"That's all? Just water? You can have anything, even what you don't see on this menu. All it takes is a word," she said. She was flirting. Or was she selling it? Carter knew in Miami it could go either way. The pretty bartender by day could be on a pay to play plan. So many girls sold their souls these days for clout. Either way, he wasn't fucking with it.

"Just water," he answered a smirk taking over his dark features. Carter Jones II was a spitting image of his father. Black and fine. Fine and guarded. Guarded and intelligent. He was mysterious. Hard to figure out but not hard to miss. Women loved him. Carter took the bottled water.

"You always drink water at a party?" Ashton asked, speaking across the empty bar.

Carter knew he looked lame as fuck, sitting there like he was too straight laced to let loose a little, but Carter played by a different set of rules. His lifestyle required discipline. Everything about Ashton looked like the opposite of that.

"This ain't really my scene," Carter admitted. "You always throw back shots at bars solo?"

"Mind your business, water boy," she cracked.

Carter scoffed at that and nodded his head, taking the insult on the chin and smirking in good fun.

"Too much silicone and fake hair at the pool for you? It's like dirty bathwater in that ghetto ass pool," Ashton asked.

"You got a few bundles of Brazilian up in there don't you?" Carter asked.

Ashton almost spit out her drink at the unexpected wisecrack.

"Peruvian, nigga, don't try to play me," she snickered. "There are rules to this," she replied.

"Rules, huh?" he said, amused.

"Rules, nigga," Ashton clarified.

"Care to share?" he asked. His brow lifted in intrigue. "I mean, I'm a man so I'm not privy to the way this fake shit supposed to go."

Ashton was surprised at how interesting Miamor's son truly was. He wasn't doting, overly friendly, or even mildly flirtatious. He was actually a little insulting, the exact opposite of every man at the party who had approached her so far. His conversation wasn't typical. He wasn't fishing for an afterparty nightcap, so he hit her with no lines, no obvious game...he was just being himself and Ashton was taken aback by how interesting he was. It made the job feel much less like a job. Ashton wasn't sure she would be able to fake the attraction. To her surprise he was flawless. Attractive and reserved. He had the world at his fingertips. He was a prize fighter. She was sure he was sitting on paper, but he was humble. His body, strong and defined. His skin, black and smooth. His face...her seat...Ashton wanted to sit on his whole face.

She blushed at just the thought as she spun the rim of the top of her glass.

"So, the trick is to not wear too much fake shit. Like if I have fake hair, lashes, and nails, a bitch don't need no fake titties. If I get my tits done, I don't need ass shots too. Niggas like soft shit. Don't nobody want to be laid up with a woman that looks perfect, but feels like a bag of cold wax."

"Soft shit, huh?" Carter asked.

"Am I lying?" Ashton asked. She stood and adjusted the strings of her bikini, pulling them high above her mini-jean shorts that were unbuttoned and folded over her hips.

"Ass is supposed to jiggle when you walk by a nigga, that's all I'm saying," she said, shrugging. "Have fun at this lame ass party, water boy," she said as she walked by him. "Put my drink on his tab," she said that last part to the bartender before walking away. Carter's eyes followed her.

"Soft, indeed," he smirked.

Charisma stopped Ashton halfway across the lobby and then he looked at Carter.

"Yo Champ! Penthouse Suite. We're moving the party upstairs!"

"No, I'm going home," Ashton protested.

Carter stood, peeled off a hundred-dollar bill and headed back to the cabana. As he passed between Charisma and Ashton he said, "Could use some of that real shit on the top floor."

Ashton smiled and Carter went back outside to retrieve Mo, Papi, and the rest of the mob.

Mo was already headed his way. He carried a half-naked girl over his shoulder, slapping her on the ass so hard one of her cheeks turned red. She giggled in delight, despite the sting.

Joey was right behind him with the massive snake cloaking his arms.

"Ris tell you about the gambling spot up top? You with it or you ready to break out?" Mo asked as he and Carter stopped to chop it up.

"I'm fucking with it," Carter said as they slapped hands.

The top floor suite was massive, and a card table had been set up in the middle of the room.

"Buy in is 50k," Ris said. "Gentleman don't sit at the table unless you're ready to stomp around with the big boys. Game is Texas Hold Em'."

Carter didn't do anything that could be tied to addiction. No drinking, no smoking, for damn sure no gambling. Carter never even stepped foot inside a casino. If the boxing commission got word that he was indulging in any form of wagering he would be ex-communicated. Carter had fought too hard to get where he was to allow a misstep right before the biggest fight of his career. Even this party was out of his norm.

"I'll buy in," Ashton said, entering the room.

The stakes had just got more interesting. Both Carter and Mo looked her way in surprise. There were women in the room, but none at the table. The buy in was enough to keep the novice players away.

"Shit just got real interesting in this mu'fucka," Mo said

as Ashton took a seat. "Lil' baby gone distract the fuck out of a nigga."

"You're something else, you know that," Ashton said, blushing.

Ashton took a seat. The rest of the room parlayed as the card game proceeded. There weren't many in the room: Ris, Ashton, two members from his squad, and everyone Carter and Mo were affiliated with. A few women had been chosen to accompany the group for decoration.

The energy around the room was relaxed. Food and drinks flowed while the players placed their initial bets. In the middle of the hand, the elevator opened, and a group of men walked in.

"Ris, what's good my nigga? My money ain't good enough for you? I been put the vig up for my seat. You starting without me and shit."

Charisma intercepted the interruption, placing a hand to the man's chest.

"Invite only boy. This ain't the game you bought into. Ticket is 50k. You only put up the twenty. Who the fuck let you up?"

"What you mean who let me up? Nigga, I don't ask permission to go nowhere. What up? You got a seat for me?"

"Papi, we up," Carter said. "It's real regular in this bitch."

Carter stood. "Aye cuz, I'ma call it. Get with me in the morning."

"Yup, I'll have that bet in the bag by then. Have my money ready my nigga," Mo said.

Carter smirked and he and Papi headed to the door.

"Fuck you looking at," the man by the door asked as Papi passed by.

Papi laughed. Niggas always had to be tough. Where he was from none of the bravado was necessary.

"What?" Papi asked.

"Keep it moving, Pap, not worth it bro," Carter said trying to keep his hands clean.

"Sound like it's a problem over there? I hop up and my burner gone solve em'," Mo said.

Melee erupted.

In the blink of an eye, the dude reached in his waistline and Carter reacted, leveling him with one blow. Absolute chaos erupted as women scrambled out of the way and fists flew. Would have been bullets had Charisma not enforced a no carry rule for the event. Carter didn't hesitate. He laid two more of ole boy's homies out and Papi finished off the third. Carter was a professional boxer. His fists were considered weapons. Even when he took some of the steam off his punches, they were three times harder than a normal man. Niggas in the streets couldn't fight. Not for real. Not like him. They played tough, but they didn't want real smoke. This was his profession. The fact that he was causing trauma to his exposed hands was enough to let him know it was time to leave, but when loudmouth didn't get back up from the ground his heart sank. He knew the man's jaw was broken. He had felt that much as soon as his fist connected, but he wasn't moving.

"Yo clear this shit out!" Charisma said. There weren't many

people in the room, but everyone who wasn't necessary was put out instantly.

Ashton stood, looking at the man lying lifeless on the floor. "Is he breathing?" she asked.

Charisma kneeled down and checked for a pulse.

He looked up at Carter.

"Get out of here. You were never here, bruh," Charisma said.

Mo headed for the door. "Aye, we out. Right now, bro, we got to go," Mo said.

Carter and Mo were in the elevator when Charisma said, "Yo Ash, you leave too."

She hurried to catch the door before it closed. The group rode to the lobby in silence. When they stepped out Ashton rushed ahead of them, hurrying to her car.

"This is bad," Carter said. "This is why I don't fuck with shit like this. I never should have been here."

"Cuz I'ma take care of it. I ain't never hung you out to dry. Even when we were little.

I' ma get with Ris and make sure I get that tape. You were never here. Everybody else is solid. On my team or his. You're good."

Ashton pulled onto Ocean Blvd recklessly, dodging tourists as she breathed heavily. She had never seen a man kill someone with his bare hands. One punch. It was all it had taken. How was Carter that strong? How had the quiet man at the bar with the dope conversation turn into a man that delivered death with a closed fist? Ashton didn't want to be anywhere near that hotel suite. With a body on the floor, it would have automatically sent her back to a prison cell. She would find a way to connect with Carter later. Right now, she just wanted to get out of dodge. She merged onto the expressway, heading toward her beachside condominium. She had no clue she was leading Mo right to her spot. It wasn't until she pulled into the underground parking garage did she notice his headlights shine through her rear window.

Ashton reached under her seat. She couldn't see the face of the driver. The feel of her nine milli made her feel so much better.

"Run up if you want to," she mumbled to herself. She pulled into a parking spot and hit her locks. She wasn't getting out of the car. It wasn't until she saw Mo get out from behind the tint of his car did she breathe a sigh of relief. Ashton climbed out of the car, gun drawn, pointing it at him. "What is wrong with you? Following me to my place! Are you psycho or something?"

Her voice echoed off the concrete walls of the parking garage.

"I don't know if I want to murder you or fuck you for pointing that gun at me," he said, snickering. "You're a big girl, huh?" Mo asked, stepping forward. Her gun pressed into his chest. "You gone pull the trigger?"

"What do you want?" she asked. Mo stuck his hands in the back pockets of her shorts.

"What are you looking for?" he asked as he took a handful

of ass, squeezing before removing his hands from her pockets and searching the front pockets next. Ashton stared at Mo, mugging him, as he did more than check her pockets. When his hand got to close to the prize Ashton brought her gun from his chest to the soft underbelly of his chin.

"Nigga. What. Do. You. Want?"

"I want to fuck you," Mo answered.

"You're so damn blunt and rude," Ashton said.

"I want to make it clear. You ain't see shit tonight, right?" Mo asked.

Ashton scoffed.

"You think I'm going to tell someone," she said, shaking her head in disbelief.

"Nah, I know you not gone tell nobody shit," he said as he took the handbag from her hand and opened it roughly, removing her wallet. He removed her license. "Ashton LaCroix," he read. He committed the address to memory before tossing the wallet back into her car. "You gone be a real good girl, ain't that right."

"Do you always act like you're in control when you have a gun digging into your chest?"

"Guns don't scare me. You got to be afraid to die to be afraid of a gun. Neither bother me," Mo said.

Thuggish ass. Reckless ass. Monroe Diamond II had been around his fair share of gunplay. It was in his blood. If he was going to die, it wouldn't be at the hands of a pretty little thing like Ashton. He disarmed her with ease, turning her own gun back on her for a brief second before tucking it in his back

"This little act of intimidation, following me home, making sure you have my address," Ashton said. "It's not necessary. I didn't see shit tonight and I won't say shit. Now get the fuck out my face and stay away from my house."

Ashton pushed past Mo and he leaned against her car, snickering as he watched the walk away. Ashton's walkaway was a fucking movie. Her ass was perfection. The attitude as she stormed away was even better.

"Pull up on me tomorrow to get your little bebe gun back," Mo said.

Ashton stuck up her middle finger without looking back and Mo snickered.

"Meet me at the boxing gym downtown tomorrow at three. A nigga want to take you around the city a little bit. Take you shopping, feed you, fuck you..."

Ashton turned and stormed back over to him.

"I don't know what you're used to or what type of birds you're used to dealing with, but I'm not easily impressed. You got to do a lot more than fuck and feed me to earn my respect. I will never ever go on a date with your rude ass," Ashton said.

Mo pushed his long hair out of his face. Ashton hated his arrogance. He was a gorgeous man and the hair...the hair was exquisite. Long hair on any other man would have made him look soft. It was somehow the most masculine thing Ashton had ever seen. Mo was sexy and dangerous and a fucking asshole.

"I ain't really leaving no options. When I like what I see, I take it," he said. He took out his spare phone. The one he used for pussy and handed it to her. "When I call, you answer. Simple math."

Ashton scoffed and smiled while shaking her head. "You better be very careful what you wish for Mo. I'm not your average bitch. I'll make you fall in love and then ruin you for fun. Now give me my gun," she said.

Mo shook his head. "Nah lil' baby. Tomorrow. You get the gun tomorrow and remember what I said about keeping those lips shut."

Ashton backpedaled. "One thing I've always been is solid. Need to worry about the rest of the eyes that were in the room. Matter of fact, it's the cameras that will put your boy under the jail. I should be the least of your concerns. I'll see you tomorrow Monroe Diamond."

"Yes, you will," he replied. He was completely interested, and Ashton was thrown because if Carter hadn't been the target, Mo would have been coming up to her condo right now. They were both vibes and she would have to stay laser focused to fulfill Miamor's wishes and come out of this unscathed.

CHAPTER 6

"I'ma play by your rules, you play by mine," -Guy

Aurora couldn't believe how massive the Diamond Estate was. For her entire life, she had lived with her mother in a two-bedroom condo. It was nice but modest. Always modest. Breeze Diamond had never splurged for anything a day of Aurora's life. Aurora had the best of what was important. Education, food, shelter but never abundance. Never opulence. Breeze had raised Aurora in opposition to the way Big Carter and Taryn had raised her. Never in a million years would Aurora think that her mother had been raised in this castle. She had been exploring the house for days and still hadn't discovered every room. It had been renovated from top to bottom. Breeze had shown her all the spots that she and her deceased twin brothers used to hide out in when they were children. Aurora had never seen her mother be so nostalgic. Almost every room and every story she told made Breeze's eyes water. Even now as Aurora stood outside her mother's bedroom door, she heard the cries from the other side.

Aurora knocked and then pushed open the door. Breeze Diamond was on her knees on the side of her bed, holding a picture in her hand. She hurried to her feet when Aurora entered. She sniffled and wiped her eyes quickly, clearing her throat.

"Are you okay, mom?" Aurora asked.

"I'm fine," Breeze answered. She nodded. "I'm fine."

Being home pulled out every single emotion she had hidden over the years. The picture in her hand felt like it had been taken a lifetime ago. She and Zyir Rich, sitting on South Beach. Her head in a light chokehold as he gritted his teeth behind her. They had made Aurora that night. She was sure of it. Fucking under the stars in a cabana. Life had been a thrill back then. All they knew was love, money, and power. It was before everything had fallen apart.

"Come over here, A," Breeze said.

Aurora crossed the room and sat down on the edge of the bed. Breeze sat beside her. A memory box of old photos sat on the floor.

"This is your father," Breeze whispered as she passed Aurora the picture. Aurora's breath caught and she looked at Breeze in surprise. Breeze had never been willing to divulge information about her father before. All Aurora knew was that her father was dead. Or so she thought.

"He's so handsome," Aurora whispered. Her heart fluttered. "Did you love him?"

"I did," Breeze answered. Her voice was a ghost. The ghost of Zyir Rich haunting her tongue. A sadness washed over her. "I still do. A love like what we had doesn't just go away. You look just like him."

"I kind of do, don't I?" Aurora asked in amazement.

"What was he like?" Aurora asked.

Aurora looked at her mother. Breeze snapped her eyes shut as tears clung to her lashes, none fell, but Aurora could see them building up, glistening under the chandelier.

"Mom?"

"He was perfect," Breeze finally answered. She was holding onto the sob inside her chest with all her might. "Zyir Rich was my perfect love. My only love."

"You miss him?" Aurora asked.

"Every time I take a breath," Breeze replied. "It was never supposed to be like this."

"I wonder if he would have liked me," Aurora said.

"He would have loved you," Breeze said.

Aurora stood. "I'm kind of tired."

Breeze didn't look up from the picture, but she nodded. "Get some sleep."

Aurora walked out and closed the door behind her. As soon as it closed, she heard her mother's cries start again.

Aurora would never know the ghosts that lived in Breeze's mind. Miami was a haunted universe for Breeze. The Diamond Estate, a haunted house. Aurora retreated to her room and locked her door. She peeled out of her pajamas revealing a pink mini dress beneath. She tossed the pajamas in her backpack and stuffed a pair of Breeze's high heeled sandals inside her backpack. She tossed it out of the second story window before climbing out herself, climbing down the tree next to her window until she was on the lawn. Aurora rushed across the massive estate and put in the code to exit the gates until she was curbside.

"Come on newbie!"

The sound of the girl in the car that awaited her filled the air.

"Do you want to get me caught?" Aurora said, laughing as she rushed to the passenger door.

"I can't believe you live in the Diamond mansion," Christy said.

"It's my mom's old house. Her parents built it," Aurora said as they pulled away.

"Are you fucking kidding me! You're a Diamond?" the girl asked.

"My mom is a Diamond. I don't know anything about her people. It's just been the two of us for so long," Aurora answered.

"Your family's name rings bells in Miami, girl," Christy informed.

"Can we talk about something else?" Aurora asked. "Where are we going anyway? What is there to do in Miami? I heard South Beach clubs were lit."

"Girl, that shit is for tourists. We're going to the Beans. My brother is having a kickback tonight. All his fine ass friends gonna be there," Christy bragged.

"He's going to let you party with him?" Aurora asked.

"I live there too. He can't put me out of my own house," Christy said, laughing.

The glitz of the upper class faded away as they made their way to the hood. Aurora had never been outside the safety of the middle class and excitement kindled in her chest but as soon as she saw the colorful, updated apartment complex she frowned in confusion.

"I thought this was the infamous Pork and Beans projects?" Aurora asked. "It looks pretty regular to me."

"You been listening to too many rap songs, sis," Christy said, laughing. "This is the Beans. Brownsville all day, but they tore the PJ's down. Came through and fixed up the hood. The shit looks better but it ain't better. Change the paint but you can't change the wall. Underneath all this shit is still the same ole' motherfuckas that make the Beans the Beans."

Aurora followed Christy up the stairs. There were so many people hanging out around the apartment building. The music was loud, pumping out of the apartment. The smell of weed seduced the air. Aurora worried about the potent scent sticking to her hair and her clothes. It would be a sure giveaway that she had snuck out. They weaved through the crowd of guys that surrounded the front door, squeezing by.

"What I tell you about bringing your little friends here, Chris?"

Christy paused, turning to the handsome man who leaned against the railing across from the apartment door.

"You gonna walk into my house and not speak?" he asked.

"Looks like that's what she was going to do to me," one of the men said.

Aurora smiled bashfully.

"I don't know you. I was just minding my business," she said, her sweet voice filling the air.

"Come mind my bi'ness," the man said. "Come over here beautiful."

Aurora walked toward him stopping in front of him.

"Closer," he said as he hit the blunt.

Aurora felt a lump in her throat. He was so damn fine. Just rough. Brown skin that seemed to be marred with battle scars. She noticed a line on the side of his face, an old cut perhaps that had bubbled a little. He had tattooed the word Brownsville over top of it. His lips were dark, undoubtedly from the weed he smoked. Apparently, it was habitual. It seemed like she was looking up to a giant he was so tall or maybe his presence was just that grand that it shrank her.

"I can't come any closer," Aurora answered.

The man grabbed her waist and pulled her into his body. Aurora's body screamed in adulation.

"When a nigga say come closer, come closer. All on his dick. That's where I want to feel you," he said.

Aurora was speechless but the feeling felt amazing. Sinful.

"Leave my friend alone, Guy," Christy said.

"Nah, this my friend, Chris. My new best friend," he said as he leaned down into Aurora's neck, whispering in her ear. "Ain't that right?"

Aurora smiled, giggling.

"Say that's right," he said. "You know I'm right."

"That's right," Aurora replied.

"You smoke?" he asked.

She nodded. She had before. That's all she and her friends in Arizona used to do. There was nothing else to do in the desert but get high and wonder what it would be like to live in places like this...Miami, Florida. Where hood niggas with big dicks and charisma whispered in your ear at midnight.

He handed her his blunt and released Aurora. "You in rotation. You with me. All night. Stay right next to me. I'll keep you safe," he said with a wink.

"What? You like somebody! You actually being nice to one of my friends?" Christy asked.

Guy snickered, waving his little sister off. "Get out of here with all that," he said.

Aurora puffed and passed to Christy.

"What's your name?" he asked.

"Aurora," she introduced.

"Niggas call me Guy," he replied. "You a baby out here. It's past your bedtime. What you doing out?" he asked.

"I do what I want," she answered.

"Oh yeah?" he asked, smirking because he was highly entertained. "What you want to do? Out here in the Beans tonight lil' mama?"

Aurora shrugged. "Just looking for a little fun," she answered as she hit the weed one more time before passing it back.

Guy scoffed and he pushed off the railing.

Aurora lingered with Christy outside.

"Bring a new little light skin around and niggas act like they ain't got no sense," Christy teased.

"Come on girl, let's grab a drink," Christy said.

Aurora followed Christy inside, and even more people partied there. The small two-bedroom apartment was live wall to wall. There was barely room to walk through. It was nice for what it was. New furniture. Big screen TV. Nice big sectional. By hood standards, they were living good. Compared to where Aurora now laid her head it was a hell hole.

Christy led the way to the kitchen and grabbed a bottle.

"Light or dark?" she asked.

"I've never drank. I don't know," Aurora said.

Guy walked into the kitchen, overhearing her answer.

"Hold that," he said, handing Aurora his blunt. She took it and puffed it. Guy lifted her onto the countertop.

"What are you doing?" she asked.

"Don't trip. They're my counters," Guy said, smirking. "How old are you Ms. Aurora?" he asked.

"18."

The lie came off her lips so fast. Without even thinking. He was clearly older. She didn't want to seem like a baby, but Aurora was a baby. Fourteen. Almost fifteen.

"How old are you?" she asked.

"Not 18," he answered as he poured himself a drink. Henny. VSOP. He took a sip then held it up to her. "Dark. Always choose dark."

She hesitantly took the red cup and took a sip. Trying to swallow it was like trying to swallow fire. She grimaced as it went down.

"It doesn't taste good!" she said.

"It ain't supposed to taste good. It makes you feel good," Christy said as she took a shot.

"I'ma take a ride, you want to roll with me?" he asked.

"I guess," Aurora said, nervously.

He grabbed his keys and turned around, heading for the door.

Aurora hesitated.

"Is he cool?" Aurora asked.

Christy nodded. "Yeah, my brother ain't gone let nothing happen to you out here. You straight with him."

Aurora hopped down from the counter and followed behind him. They were silent until they got to the parking lot. The shiny red Mercedes told her he was important. Just like a girl to measure the importance of a man by something as unimportant as a car.

"You want to drive?" he asked.

"I don't know how," she said.

He paused, leaning into her, backing her against the passenger's door.

"You're not eighteen, are you?" he asked.

Aurora didn't respond. She was so nervous. He smelled amazing. It was like his cologne fogged her mind because she could barely form a sentence with him standing this close.

"How about you keep your age to yourself and I'll keep mine to myself?" he asked.

His 25 years was old enough to know she was way younger than she said.

"I'm good with that," she said.

He can't be too old. He doesn't look that old.

She climbed in the car and he walked around to the driver's side.

"I'm young," she said, fidgeting, her leg bouncing as he turned over the ignition.

"Too young?" he asked.

"It depends on what we're doing," she said.

Guy leaned over the armrest and kissed her cheek.

"What if I'm doing that?" he asked.

Smooth. The nigga was real smooth with it. He moved her hair out of the way and kissed her neck. "You too young for that?" he asked.

"No," she whispered as her head fell to the side.

"You ever had your pussy ate, Aurora?"

Her entire body tensed.

"No," she whispered. His tongue was all over her neck, by her ear and then he turned her face to his and it was in her mouth. She had kissed boys before, but this was the best kiss she had ever received. It made her ache everywhere.

"I want to suck on that pussy, baby. You gone be my lil' mama?" he asked.

Aurora moaned. It was all happening so fast, but it felt too good to stop. Her body hummed and it felt like the back of her neck was tingling. The liquor and weed were doing their jobs.

His hand was up her dress and slipping inside her panties.

"That feels so good," she moaned.

"You sure you not too young for that?" Guy asked. "I'll take real good care of this pussy if you let me. Can I do something with it?"

He never stopped kissing her as he spoke, and his fingers never stopped working her middle. She was practically in the backseat; he was making her feel so good.

He reached across her body and leaned her seat all the

way back and then continued to explore her wetness.

"This little pussy wet for me," he said. Guy leaned his seat all the way back and rubbed his dick.

"Come here," he said. "Climb over this shit."

Aurora was too hot to slow it down, but her heartbeat out of her chest.

"I'm a virgin," she said.

Guy paused. "You young like that?"

"Fourteen," she answered. "I mean this feels good and I want to, but…"

"Get out my car man," he said.

"I want to, it's just…"

"Go back to the party. Chris is 18. What you even around for?" Guy said, irritated. "Get out."

Aurora was mortified. She popped open the door and rushed back to the building.

"I thought you were going to the store," Christy said as she came back inside.

"He went," she answered.

"Turn up then," Christy said, handing her a shot glass full of clear liquor. Aurora needed it to take the edge off. The tequila was the perfect recovery from the embarrassment she had just endured.

Her eyes watched the door anxiously as she laughed and drank with Christy and a few of the neighborhood girls. When Guy walked back inside, she felt sick. She felt like apologizing. She felt like talking to him. Before he had found out her age it was like he had seen her. Now he walked by her like she was invisible.

It made her feel sick. She just wanted to explain herself. He couldn't be that old. How old was old? He looked young, maybe 20 at most. Aurora couldn't get her mind off the way she felt when he touched her, but when she saw him take interest in another girl at the party her heart sank. She retreated to the bathroom just to gather herself. Suddenly she just wanted to go home. When she emerged, the party was even more crowded. She pushed open one of the closed doors and stepped inside.

"Get out."

She jumped, not expecting anyone to be inside, but she recognized his voice. She turned on the light and closed the door. He laid across the bed, eyes to the ceiling, smoking a blunt.

"Can I talk to you?"

"What you got to say?" he asked.

She walked over to the bed and sat beside him, twiddling her fingers nervously.

"I lied because I like you and if you knew I was fourteen…"

"Go back to the party, man. Teasing and shit. Playing them lil' girl games," he said.

"I'm not a tease," she said.

"A nigga like me gone bust that lil' pussy wide open. If you ain't trying to do that you a tease," he said.

"Maybe I'm trying to do that. I mean. If you take it slow."

"You trying to get me locked up. I'm 25, baby. I'm trying to do grown man shit," he answered as he blew smoke into the air. He sat up and held the blunt to her lips. Aurora puffed, coughing slightly before blowing it out. "You fuck with me and I'm daddy. You mine after that. I kill for mine. Ain't none of these little niggas out here coming after me, but you got to hold it down. You got to be good at keeping secrets cuz you jailbait."

"I wouldn't tell anybody," Aurora whispered. "I just don't want you to be mad at me."

He snuffed out the blunt and came to his knees in front of her, opening her thighs.

"Let me show you what kind of secrets you got to keep," he said.

Aurora's eyes rolled to the back of her head when he went down on her. She had never felt anything quite like this. She whimpered, a merciless victim to his tongue as he ate her for half an hour. He let her orgasm four times back to back and when he came up, she saw how hard he was.

Aurora held her breath as he laid her down on the bed, parting her legs and coming out of his jeans. He was gentle when he entered her, but he still tore Aurora in half.

She bit her bottom lip to stop herself from crying out.

"Condom," she whispered. "You should wear a condom. I don't want to get pregnant."

"This my pussy now. I do what I want with it, baby girl, and I don't want nothing in the way," Guy said, kissing her slowly.

It felt like he was hypnotizing her. Aurora felt victorious for getting his interest. He was clearly the big man in the room, the man all the women flocked to, the man all the men respected. This felt like it gave her clout in Miami. Like she had won a trophy. She had no idea she was the trophy. Better yet, she was the race, but she was at a vulnerable age and Guy had years on her.

The pain gave way to an unbelievable amount of pleasure. That pleasure blinded her. It blocked out everything she knew to be right, flooding her with emotion as she experienced her first orgasm.

Head gone. Aurora heaved as he hovered over her.

Niggas loved new pussy and there was nothing better than a virgin. It would be a while before he grew bored of her. Men like Guy liked them young because they were easier to manipulate. Aurora would put up no protest. No smart mouth. No bite back when he asked her to do something. Young girls were easy. Both mentally and physically.

"This is between me and you. It's for us. I don't even mess with young girls but it's something about you. People ain't gone understand what this is. All they gone see is age, but it's more than that. I want to fuck with you for real for real the long way but if we going to do this, you got to hold me down. Hold me down like I'ma hold you down. You got to keep it between us. Can't go running back to your parents or your little friends telling them about what we do. All they need to know is you and Chris are friends and I'm her brother. You can do that?"

Aurora nodded. "Yeah I can do that," she replied.

"Good girl," he said.

"I have to get home before my mom wakes up," Aurora said.

"I'ma play by your rules you play by mine," he said, kissing her lips. "I'ma get you home, baby girl. Keep you on mommy's time so you can stay on daddy's time, you hear me?"

She nodded in adulation and agreement. Always agreement. She would never protest.

Aurora couldn't believe that she was laid up under a man, her man, like this. Moving to Miami had felt like it would ruin her life, but her young naïve heart was all in now. She only prayed her mother never found out.

Carter stood on the dock to the waterfront mansion he was renting while in town. Miami wasn't supposed to be a permanent stop for him. It was supposed to be temporary, but with the death of Emilio Estes, the closest thing he had to a father, the entire world had stood still. Still, he was expected to fight. Estes wasn't even in the ground yet and no one seemed to care. It felt like he had lost a part of him. The man who had taught him to use his fists to work out all his emotional turmoil was gone. He couldn't lie and say the shit didn't hurt. All his teachings. All the discipline had gone right out of the window.

Carter had killed a man with his bare hands. It was hard for him to gauge his own strength at times. The gloves helped take some of the deadliness away when he was in the ring, but when his fists connected with the skull of a man without a barrier between the two, it would always be fatal. He was a monster in the ring and outside of it he had just become a murderer. He had felt the man's soul lift out of his body on contact. He was just waiting for the police to knock at his door. He had hardly slept the night before from the anticipation that they would come. No news outlet had reported the incident yet and he knew once any evidence of that fight surfaced his life as he knew it would be over. He had dealt with the system once before as a child. It hadn't been kind to him. He was ill prepared to face a judge again.

The ocean glistened under the moon and the soft sound of the waves echoed through the air. It was so quiet he heard the footsteps approaching from behind.

"He's dead?" Carter asked. He didn't need a response. He already knew. He was hoping for a different response. Praying that what he had felt behind his knuckles had been a lie, but his fists never lied. *Nigga's up out of here,* he thought grimly.

"He's dead," Mo informed.

"That's a big problem," Papi said. "We were all over that suite. The cameras. There's no way this won't lead back here."

"I'ma handle it," Mo said.

"How?" Papi asked.

"Don't question me, bro, I said I'ma handle it. I ain't gone leave my family out to dry. I got it."

"We ain't leaving nothing undone. Questions are necessary," Carter said. His back was still turned to them as he spoke.

"I'll handle it. Just stay out the way. Give me a day. You my family. I ain't gone half step," Mo said. Carter stood and walked between Papi and Mo.

"Get out," he said as he retreated to the inside. He had half a mind to go back to the Dominican Republic on a private jet tonight, but there was nothing to go back to but crime. He had fought his way out of those foreign slums. He was chasing a legitimate title. This one misstep could ruin his entire future. He had encountered nothing but bad luck since he had returned to Miami. He had a feeling this city might be the beginning of a long end.

Mo walked into the empty nightclub. He had been before, but it was drastically different in the sunlight. The city was silent. He could hear the echo of hard bottom shoes in the distance as he stood in the middle of the empty dance floor.

"Another step and niggas gone start shooting, fam." Ris' voice announced his presence and then he appeared in the rafters above.

"I ain't know you could fit a gun in that tight ass suit," Mo said.

"You don't carry steel with Tom Ford my nigga. My niggas carrying heavy though." Ris leaned over the rail and nursing a glass tumbler filled with brown liquid in his hands.

The sound of guns cocking erupted, suddenly Mo saw hidden figures in the room. Shooters. Ris had a room full of chameleons, waiting for someone to run down with a problem. If anyone had problems, Ris and his wolves had answers.

"You strapped?" Ris asked.

"I'm always strapped but it ain't for you," Mo answered.

Ris scoffed and then nodded. "Let him up."

Mo walked up the stairs and Ris led him to a table.

"Have a seat, man. You want a drink?" Ris asked.

"This your spot?" Mo asked.

"Every Sunday it is," Ris said. "I'm a promoter. I don't need a building; I control the crowd."

"Let the city tell it, you way more than a promoter," Mo said.

"I don't know what this fake ass city say, man," Ris said. He pulled out a chair and sat down. Mo looked around. Six guns against his one if this went bad. He sat down too.

"I got twenty-five bands for the tape from the hotel last night. You got the leverage. We both know it. You see an athlete that can cash out way more than that for the tape, but my twenty-five and my friendship is worth way more than a one-time bag," Mo stated.

"I don't do friends," Ris stated.

"You want to do friends down here homie. This ain't Harlem. Friends are off limits. Everything outside of friends owes a city tax my nigga," Mo said.

"City tax?" Ris said, scoffing in amusement. "You got no room to put no threats down on the table."

"No threats, just facts. It's just how I'm running shit down here. I know your hustle. You throw a party, invite the city out, and collect a nice little bag at the end of the day or night. Most niggas think you making it off the door, maybe a percentage of the bar, but I know you and your niggas taking hella risks robbing whales at the end of the night. The real money is in the lick."

"Whales and licks, huh?" Ris asked as he sipped.

"The big fish. Athletes, sometimes rappers, never the drug dealers though. They don't rap about the shit. Us Florida niggas live that street shit. It ain't an easy lick round this way," Mo said.

"This how you plan on getting that tape?" Ris asked.

"You gone give me the tape because I'ma make you rich, bruh. I got the pill game on lock. Niggas walk through these doors to party. Whatever you need, I can supply. Right now, I'm serving Premo and his parties go off because the people know they gone have access to my product. He clearing paper that could be yours. I'ma need that tape though."

Ris nodded. "You was always getting the tape, Monroe Diamond. I took care of that problem. Cleaned it right on up. The champ ain't got to worry bout that coming back. It's been handled properly. That partnership you talking about though. A nigga with all that. I know the pedigree. I respect it. Let's chop up the details." Ris motioned a waitress over to them. "Bring us a bottle and some food out here."

"Anything else?" the girl asked, lingering as she looked Mo up and down.

"Nah, lil' baby I'm good," Mo said.

"You busting that down, my nigga?" Mo asked.

"I ain't sticking nothing that bleed once a month," Ris said.

Mo's brows rose in recognition. The rumors about Ris' sexuality was true. Nothing about him screamed that he preferred men. In fact, Ris had more bitches than Mo who were waiting for him to change his mind and swing their way just one time, but his preference was his preference. Ris was a fly ass, flashy ass, designer label wearing ass nigga who got money by the boatload, but he shared his bed with men.

"That's your business, my nigga," Mo stated. "But look I'ma leave you to it." He pulled out his phone. "Lock me in so you can hit me about that first package."

"You good on the meal? My chef can whip up something real proper. Celebrate this new partnership cuz these bands about to go up," Ris stated.

"Way up," Mo said, slapping hands with Ris. "But nah. Just the tape."

Mo wasn't fucking with it. If Charisma had never told him, he would have never known, but now that he knew breaking bread over drinks and five-star cuisine sounded like a date.

"You ain't my type, nigga," Ris snickered, standing.

Mo laughed. "I'ma get with you. Be looking for my text."

Mo swaggered out of the club, checking the time on his phone. He was supposed to be meeting Ashton, but with this new partnership with Ris, Mo had to link with Joey and get Ris' first package prepared. If Mo could secure the Dominican plug, they could all get rich. Ris' guest list was the perfect clientele. They came looking for a good time and Mo could supply them without problem. This was bigger than moving pills through the trap. This would prove lucrative and the more product they moved, the more valuable they became to the connect. Mo lived to win a wager but Ms. Ashton would have to wait. Business always came first.

CHAPTER 7

"Sacrifices," – Mo

Mo pulled up to the training facility, where Carter instructed him to meet. The small gym was just north of Dade county and away from the flashy Miami that the rest of the world knew. It was just a small spot, tucked away, but that was by design. There was little distraction, no fast food joints, and two-lane highways leading to it. It was the stomping ground for Carter and his training team. On that day, Mo was officially a part of Carter's boxing team and as explained to him; the entire focus was getting Carter ready for the next fight. Carter thought bringing Mo in would quench his thirst to establish a Dominican coke connect; however, it did the complete opposite. It gave Mo entryway into Carter's inner circle, so he could wreak havoc. Mo was a street nigga and it was running ramped through his veins. There was no amount of legitimate money or boxing championships that could keep him away from what he was destined to be and that was a motherfucking gangster. Mo wasn't trying to hear that shit. This is why he was in the parking lot an hour before anyone was expected.

It was just before 9 a.m., and Mo was dead tired. He hadn't gotten up that early for years and wasn't what you would call an early riser. He had been partying the night before, so he was functioning off of three hours of sleep. However, he had to make sure he was there to meet Joey. He had sent him on a mission to retrieve something for him and it was a must that he met him there before Carter and his entourage made it. He looked down at his diamond encrusted watch and checked the time. Just like clockwork, he saw his friend's car pulling next to him in a tinted out old school Chevy. Mo smiled as he saw Joey roll down his window, exposing his face.

"Top of the top, my nigga," Joey said as he pulled on the joint that was between his fingertips, slowly blowing a thick cloud of smoke, then swiftly sucking it back into his lungs making it disappear within a millisecond. Mo heard the light thumping of Nipsey Hustle's song *Ocean Views* resonate through the bass filled subwoofers.

"Top of the top," Mo replied as he threw his head up, acknowledging his righthand man.

"Nigga, I ain't never seen you up this early," Joey said in a raspy tone as the smoke was still in his lungs.

"Gotta handle that business. Sacrifices," Mo said calmly as he released a smirk.

"Sacrifices," Joey repeated as he smiled, blew the smoke out, and nodded his head in agreement. He raised the joint, held it out the window, and gestured as if he would share it with Mo.

"Nah, I don't want to smell like trees when these square ass niggas pull up," Mo said, sounding almost disappointed that he couldn't partake in the smoking festivities. He shook his head and then focused on the task at hand. He continued, "you got that for me?" he asked.

"Yessir," Joey said as reached over to his glove compartment and grabbed a wrinkled, brown paper bag. He tossed it out of his window and into Mo's car. Mo alertly caught it and then proceeded to open it. He saw a few baggies filled with white powder inside of it and smiled. He reached in and grabbed one, held it up, and examined it.

"This it, huh?" Mo asked as he looked at the unfamiliar powdery substance.

"Yep, my guy said that shit gives a mu'fucka wings, you hear me? He say a nigga can punch a hole through a brick wall on that shit there," Joey bragged.

Earlier that week, he sought a black-market dealer that dealt steroids, all at the request of Mo. The drug purchased was called Stanozolol. It was an anabolic steroid that can help an athlete get stronger, build muscle mass, boost acceleration, and recover faster from workouts. Basically, the drug turned any man into the incredible hulk. It was also the most easily detected steroid through a blood test and urine samples. Mo had strategically done his research to narrow it down to this particular drug. He was plotting on Carter. Not to deceive his cousin, but only push him into what he truly was; a fucking Diamond.

"Bet. You didn't mention my name did you?" Mo double checked.

"Come on, family. You know I'm smarter than that. Told

him I was trying to get my weight up," Joey said as he made a strong arm, causing them both to laugh.

"Cool," Mo said as he slid the substance in his pocket.

"A'ight, I'm about to slide. I'ma let you go in that joint and play with those sweaty mu'fuckas. Me…I'm about to get some sleep."

"Shit, I ain't fucking with this boxing shit. You know what I'm here for," Mo jokingly confirmed.

"I already know. Get this nigga to jump off the porch so we can flood this bitch," Joey said, fantasizing about the possibilities.

"That's the plan. How we do last night?" Mo asked, checking on their trap spot.

"We sold out. We was out of product by six o'clock. Everybody started flocking over there to Pork and Beans when we tapped out. We lost out on so much paper," Joey said as he shook his head in frustration. The news only justified what Mo was planning to do. He was losing money by the day because he couldn't keep up with the demand for drugs. He could not find a plug that could keep a steady flow in, so in return, he gave other crews room to get the money that he felt was his. This infuriated Mo and he clenched his jaws, so tight that his jaw muscles began to show through.

"Them niggas got weight over there?" Mo asked, trying to get more intel of the projects that was nicknamed Pork and Beans, a moniker that stuck with the apartment complex for decades.

"Yeah, they switched up the game recently. Ma'Dear got them boys selling everything," Joey answered.

He mentioned the name Ma'Dear and Mo instantly knew who she was. She was an older woman that had a lot of respect in the city because of who her past lovers were. She only dated kingpins and somehow made the biggest, most feared men fall in love with her. It was like an art form that only she mastered. Her age and years of street life had caught up with her and her looks weren't what they used to be. However, she was said to be one of the most beautiful women that stepped foot in Miami hands down. Old pictures showed that she looked like Claire Huxtable and had a mean walk that could rival any runway model. Nevertheless, now she was just an old lady with many stories to tell. She also was like the project's street mother and basically raised the entire projects. This was how she garnered the name *Ma'Dear*; a southern term that black people would call their mother as a sign of respect and gratitude. She was known for her great cooking and selling dinners out of her apartment. However, over the recent years, that hustle of hers became much more. She was supplying much more than fried chicken and dressing. She was giving young hustlers a way to eat literally and figuratively.

"I heard she supplying the whole projects. Who's her plug? We need to go see her," Mo confirmed.

"I already pulled up on her. She looked at me like I had three heads when I asked her about some weight. She keep her shit low. She damn near cussed me out and asked me was I hungry afterward," Joey said shaking his head.

"That old bitch think she slick. I ain't tripping off that anyway. She probably ain't got a real plug. Probably still eating off of one of her old niggas connect," Mo said, guessing.

"Probably so. Whatever it is…it's got them niggas around her loyal. They treat her like some type of queen round that bitch. They protect her like they on a chessboard.

"Oh yeah?" Mo asked, learning something new.

"Yessir. We can take that whole area if we get that D.R. plug," Joey simply said. "A'ight, I'm out family. Hit me later tonight."

"Bet," Mo said as he threw his head in an upward motion and rolled up his window.

Ding!

He watched as Joey pulled off and then looked down at his phone that had just chimed. He received a text. It was Ash. The text read: *I'm about to pull up. You there yet?*

Mo smiled, remembering the beautiful girl he met at the pool party. He had just remembered that he had invited her to the gym and flaked on her. He instantly thought about how he stood her up and his arrogance led him to believe that she was trying again. But the reality was she wanted to see his cousin again. *She want a nigga*, he thought as he replied to her text. He shot her the location and smiled, thinking about the bet he and Carter had. He loved competition and brought her there purposely so Carter could witness him finesse her out of her panties. It was all a game to Mo and that just made the day more interesting.

"That's it, champ," Papi yelled as he stood behind the punching bag and held it in place firmly.

"*Hmph! Hmph!*" Carter grunted with each power punch as he alternated left and right hooks.

With each punch he slightly swayed the bag, moving it and his trainer a little each time. Carter has a brick house and swung with such ferocity that the spectators could literally feel each punch. He was shirtless and his chiseled physique was on full display. Muscles bulged from his body and his calve muscle tensed up with each swing. Sweat dripped off him, creating a puddle beneath him. His tight Nike boxer shorts were soaked, and he breathed heavily as he put in work. The sound of his gloves crashing against the plastic bag resonated throughout the gym. Each punch seemed like a force of nature as the hums of his arms cutting the air, sounding like whizzing bullets. All eyes were on him. He looked like an African God.

Mo watched carefully as he stayed to the side. He quietly plotted. He was waiting for the right time to act out his plan. He had conveniently called the boxing commissions anonymous hotline and gave them a tip about Carter, which would strategically set his plan in motion. Carter and his next opponent agreed to Olympics style testing which enabled them to be tested randomly and at any time. This played right into Mo's deceitful plans. He knew that a representative would be showing up at the end of practice, so he had to get the drugs inside of Carter before then.

Mo eyed the Gatorade bottle and was studying the level of fluid in it for the past hour. He anticipated its completion. It seemed like it took forever for Carter to finish off the bottle. He filled it with the steroids before Carter and his crew came in and made sure that he shook it well so no remnants would show.

"Time!" Papi yelled. It was followed by a round of clapping. Carter stopped movement and placed his hands on his hips as he began to catch his breath. Papi grabbed the laced Gatorade bottle and tossed it over to Carter, which he caught. Carter downed the drink and Mo couldn't help but smirk.

"Let's go, champ!" Mo yelled as he clapped. Carter nodded his head at his cousin, thinking he was commending him for a good round of working out. However, Mo was celebrating the death of Carter the boxer and the birth of Carter the hustler. As Mo was clapping, the sound of the door being opened, and everyone's attention went to it. There was Ash, who walked in looking beautiful. She dressed down but still managed to be stunning. She wore black leggings with a snug black shirt. A distressed jean jacket was hugging her upper half tightly and her shape was on full display. Her hair was casually and neatly pulled back as her baby hairs rested on the edges of her scalp. She wore oversized shades that covered half of her face. It was easy to see that she was drop dead gorgeous. Mo quickly walked over, smiling, walking with a gangster bop that only a Dade nigga possessed.

"What's good lil' baby? Thanks for coming," Mo said as he approached her. Ash smiled and slowly took off her shades as she scanned the entire gym. Her eyes landed back on Mo and responded.

"What's up," she said, smiling ear to ear, showing her beautiful rows of teeth. Mo instantly loved her swagger and confidence.

"Thanks for coming," he said as he stood before her and ran his tongue across his top row of teeth.

"Thanks for having me," she responded. She looked over Mo's shoulder and saw Carter. He nonchalantly threw his head up, acknowledging her. Ash stood on her tip toes and waved at him.

"Come kick it with me," Mo said as he threw his head in the direction of the bench that was just outside of the boxing ring. He headed over and Ash followed and took a seat right next to him. Carter was entering the ring to spar and they had front row seats. Mo was trying to talk to Ash, but her attention was on Carter. She loved the way his sweaty body looked and was surprised at how she was intrigued. She tried to small talk with Mo, but as Carter skillfully floated around the ring, while punishing his sparring partner, it garnished her full attention.

"Ma!" Mo said as he nudged her, making her snap out of her stare down of Carter.

"Yea, what's up," Ash said as she turned to look at Mo.

"Man, fuck you," Mo said playfully as he shook his head. He already knew that he had lost the competition.

"What?" she said after she giggled. Mo had a funny and hilarious vibe. She couldn't help but to laugh.

"At least hook me up with one of yo fine ass friends. I know you got some," Mo said conceding defeat.

"What you mean? Ash said while smiling, almost blushing.

"You can't even hide the shit. You might as well, jump in the ring and give him the pussy," Mo said playfully.

"We are well acquainted. You late," Ash informed him. Mo was salty, but tried his best to save face.

"You gave him the pussy already? God damn. I need to start boxing if it gets you the pussy that quick," Mo said jokingly.

"You're crazy," Ash responded while shaking her head.

"No, I'm smart actually. A blind man can see you feeling him. I ain't tripping. I know the game. Just hook me up with all yo friends so I can fuck on em'," Mo said jokingly, but dead serious. He reached out his pinky as if he was making an agreement with her. Ash smiled and reached out her pinky, respecting his honesty. She liked Mo. Not romantically, but she fucked with his realness. She respected people like him and knew they would get along fine.

"I'll see what I can do," she laughed while shaking her head.

Real always recognized real. Just as they were unlocking their fingers, a group of white men came through the door with clipboards. They stuck out like sore thumbs, which confused everyone. However, Mo glanced at them and smiled. He knew exactly who they were. That's because he was responsible for their presence. It was members of the boxing commission. They were there to test Carter.

"Let's go," he whispered to himself and watched them approach the ring. They were beelining directly to Carter.

"Huh?" Ash asked, thinking she was talking to her.

"Nothing. Nothing at all my nigga," Mo said as he watched his plan unfold perfectly.

CHAPTER 8

"We got one life to live…why play with it?" -Mo

Mo sat inside his all black, smoked out, tinted car. He was smoking some of Miami's finest Kush. Mo puffed on the blunt that was placed in between his fingertips. He inhaled the thick smoke deeply, leaned his head back, and blew out the cloud of ganja. A small smoke cloud formed on the roof and began to dance in the air as Mo watched closely. The air conditioner blew against his torso and face with force, so he didn't feel the hot and humid air that was waiting outside. It was mid-day and nearing one hundred degrees on a hot summer day. He was on Ocean Drive and parked right outside a small Tex-Mex restaurant. Mo had parked in that same spot for three days straight, contemplating about going in or not. He was hesitant to go in because he would be going under false pretenses. Carter made it clear that he wanted no parts of the drug game, but with Mo's recent stunt, he was trying to force his hand. He still didn't budge, so Mo was running out of options.

Mo looked over to his right and saw his lieutenant, Joey. Mo passed him the blunt and began to weigh his options before he went into the spot. Mo's hand was itching, and he was ready to make some moves, but Carter's reluctancy was throwing a wrench in his program.

"Did homie ever get back with you?" Mo asked as he watched Joey hit the weed. "What he say about hitting us with them joints?" Mo asked, referring to the bricks of cocaine he wanted in on.

"Nigga won't pick up the phone. I been hitting him all week. Nothing," Joey confirmed. Mo shook his head in disappointment.

"What about Bless in Michigan?" Mo asked, trying to jog his mental rolodex, thinking of anybody that could supply him with a steady pipeline.

"He changed his number," Joey answered.

"Fuck..." Mo whispered as he shook his head in disbelief. He hadn't had a steady plug since he had been in the drug game. Mo's name carried weight; however, it didn't equal wealth. Sometimes he felt having the last name Diamond was a gift and a curse.

Joey wanted to ask Mo what was stopping people from dealing with him, but he knew how hot head Mo could be at times. He didn't want to be on the receiving end on one of Mo's tirades. Mo looked at Joey and immediately knew that something was on his mind.

"Say it, my nigga. What up?" Mo quizzed as he reached back for the blunt.

"It's just..." Joey hesitantly started. "How can your family be infamous Miami's Cartel...and you not plugged. We grew up hearing stories about how they ran shit for years.

Now niggas act like you a rat or something. Nobody will touch you," Joey said in honesty.

"That's because niggas scared. After my aunt got locked up and the feds came in, it put a target on the back of anybody waving that Cartel flag. If I get a plug, it's not going to be from the states. I need a plug out the country. Niggas is pussy."

"Makes sense," Joey agreed.

"And that's why we're here," Mo said as he threw his head in the direction of the Tex -Mex restaurant. It was the hub of a Dominican connection. A connection that he had no right to visit. He took a mental note while in the D.R. and remembered when Juan Miguel mentioned Harry on Ocean drive, so Mo did his homework which landed him there. Mo had contemplated going in all week, but couldn't bring himself to do it because his approach would be foul. He had to go behind Carter's back to get the pipeline and Mo was conflicted.

"What's in there?" Joey asked.

"My legacy, my nigga," Mo replied as he took a deep pull and put the blunt out. "Hold it down. I'll be right back," Mo said as he stepped out of the car and headed into the spot.

Mo entered the empty restaurant and the place was just as hot as it was outside. It lacked any air conditioning and smelled like mop water. However, it was by design. The Dominicans didn't want the restaurant to be known as a comfortable place, nor to have good food. A satisfied customer was the last thing on their priority list. It was just a front and a central hub for the distribution of heroin and cocaine, directly from the D.R. As Mo walked in, he noticed a few guys scattered throughout the room. When he walked in, the chatter had stopped and an older Dominican man with olive color skin approached him. He had a soiled apron on a gapped tooth smile as he put on a happy face. The man dug into the front pocket and pulled out a small notebook as if he was preparing to take Mo's order.

"How may I help you?" the man asked in broken English.

"I'm here to see Harry," Mo said as he looked around and noticed that everyone was looking at him.

"Oh, you here to see Harry, eh?" the man asked as he slid the notebook back into his pocket.

"Who sent you?" the man asked as his friendly smile now turned into a much sterner expression. It was as if he was a completely different person than what he was just moments prior.

"Juan Miguel in the D.R.," Mo said, feeling his morality leave just as the words left his mouth. He was playing with fire while in the belly of the beast. But he didn't care. He wanted to get in the game, and he knew this was his only option. The Dominican man turned to one of the men and began to speak Spanish. Seconds later, the man that he was speaking to, got up and headed behind the bar. He reached down and grabbed a large black phone that had a long antenna on it. Mo had never seen a phone like it before. It looked like something that came from the eighties. While the man began to dial a number, the greeter focused on Mo.

"So, you met Juan?" he asked again, trying to make sure.

"Well yea, me and my cousin Carter."

"Carter? Carter? Estes boy?" he asked.

"Yeah. He sent me to place an order. So here I am," Mo lied confidently.

The man yelled something over to the other guy on the phone, the only thing Mo could make out is that he mentioned the name Carter. After a few seconds, the man on the phone nodded and the greeter turned and looked Mo in the eyes. He extended his hand.

"I'm Harry. They gave the go ahead back home for Carter. How much do you need?" he said simply.

"How many can I get?" Mo asked, feeling like a little kid on the inside. He didn't show his excitement, but his adrenaline pumped, and he couldn't believe what he was hearing. Every hustler's dream was to have an overseas connect and he had just achieved that.

"As many as you can stand," Harry said without blinking.

"I need a hunnid," Mo said, not fucking around. He didn't know if this would be the first or the last time that he got hit with some much-needed work, so he decided to shoot for the stars.

"Done. Come back tonight after the sun goes down. Pull around back and we will take care of you," Harry said as he walked over to the table to continue talking with his friends.

"Twelve a piece," he added nonchalantly. Mo couldn't help but smile. Bricks were going for damn near thirty in the streets. He began to do the math in his head.

That's like a mil and a half profit, he thought as he rubbed his hands together, thinking about how he was about to flood the streets of Dade county. It was the day he had been waiting for, for a very long time. Mo stepped out of the spot and into the blazing sun. He had a different bop in his step and Joey watched from the car. Joey began to smile from ear to ear as he took another pull of the smoke.

"Let's go," Mo said under his breath harshly as he slid into the car.

"We on?" Joey asked just to confirm.

"We on," Mo replied as he slowly nodded his head and stared out of the window, looking at nothing particular. He couldn't see anything but the money that was in front of him.

"How many?" Joey asked, wanting to begin to strategize. Mo smiled and looked over at Joey.

"A hunnid," Mo said surely.

"Get the fuck out of here," Joey said as doubt instantly spread over his face.

"Swear to God. Let's take this bitch over," Mo said as he put the car in drive and slowly pulled onto Ocean Drive. He was on his way to put his team into position to flood the streets. But first, he had to break the news to Carter. Mo didn't give a fuck at that point. He knew that to gain power, some things had to be done that weren't always pretty and this was one of them. He was headed to tell Carter they were partners in crime if he liked it or not.

"This is crazy. It's obviously some type of mistake. I don't fucking juice! I don't need to!" Carter screamed into the phone as he paced his living room. He was furious and pleading his case to the boxing commission. He had been on the phone all day, trying to get retested to prove that there was a mistake. However, it would be for nothing. He had been banned for an entire year and the decision was final. Out of pure rage, he threw his cell phone against the wall, causing it to break into multiple pieces, while also leaving a hole in his drywall.

"Fuck!" Carter yelled as he plopped down on his couch and tried to understand what happened? Why would Papi try to ruin him? All of those crazy thoughts ran through his head and he couldn't make sense of it all. Papi had cost him his biggest payday ever and what he had been working his entire career to get to. He was projected to make a five-million-dollar purse with his next fight and now it was gone. Carter was in shock and for the first time, he felt the void that Estes had left.

At times like this, Estes would always know how to navigate through the madness. He looked over to his right where a picture of him and Estes sat. Carter smiled thinking about the good times they shared and all of the talks they had that molded him. Right next to that picture, was a picture of his mom and his father. Miamor and Young Carter. They were in the back of a Rolls Royce. His mother was relaxed in his father's arms and they both had their middle fingers up, smiling from ear to ear. Just from the picture, you could tell that they were in love. Carter automatically frowned, remembering how the streets stole his parents away from him. They were everything to the streets but damn near strangers to him. His parents were street royalty but by his account, they

LONG LIVE THE CARTEL

were shitty parents. He focused on his father's face and couldn't help but notice the resemblance. It was as if he was looking at a picture of himself. They shared the same skin complexion, facial bone structure, and piercing eyes. He was the spitting image of his father and this made him think of the small amount of time that they had spent with one another. He barely knew his father and learned more about him through old stories and rap songs honoring his historic hustle. He never wanted to be like his father; however, it was inevitable.

"Yo!" he heard a voice coming from the front of the spacious home and sound of the door being closed. He immediately stood up and looked towards the entrance. It was Mo, who was accompanied by his friend Joey.

"You don't know how to knock, nigga?" Carter asked slightly annoyed with Mo's brashness.

"Why would I knock and the mu'fuckin door was unlocked? You gotta think," Mo said playfully as he tapped his temple, making his friend chuckle at his joke. Carter returned to his couch and plopped down, not really ecstatic that Mo had popped up without an invitation. He hadn't seen him since the steroid incident and wasn't really in the mood to talk about it.

"What up? I know you didn't come over to shoot the shit. What you got up yo sleeve?" Carter asked suspiciously. Mo slowly walked around the living room and admired the rows of trophies and boxing awards. He also studied the pictures of Carter with various legendary boxers and flicks with him in the ring. Mo paused and looked back

ASHLEY & JAQUAVIS

at Carter and a wave of disappointment spread over his face.

"Damn, cousin. I'm offended. I can't come check on you? We family, right?" Mo asked as he picked up a trophy and examined it. He looked back at Carter with a half-smile.

"Yeah, we family," Carter answered reluctantly.

"Exactly we family," Mo said as he walked closer to Carter and began moving his hands as he talked, emphasizing his words. He continued. "This is why we have to continue our family's legacy, by doing what the fuck we supposed to do."

"Doing what we supposed to do? What you mean by that?" Carter asked, already know what he was getting at.

"Taking this bitch over. That's what the fuck I mean. We got one life to live, why play with it? We only young for a short time. You supposed to chase the fucking bag. Live life to the fullest. The way our grandfather did. The way our pops did! A short run could set up us for life. It's fucking millions to be made and you scared to jump off the fuckin porch!"

"Yo, that's not me. That's not what I'm on. That was our fathers' legacy….not ours. I box…" Carter started to say but was cut off before he could finish his sentence.

"Nigga, boxing is out the window. You're not a boxer! Not anymore. Nigga you banned. I know you ain't got paper like that."

"You talking real slick. I'll lay you the fuck out," Carter yelled as he swiftly stood up and jumped into Mo's face. Mo didn't flinch at all. He looked directly into Carter's eyes as they stood toe to toe. It was a tense moment of silence, but Mo quickly lightened the mood by winking and stepping back, creating a little distance between them. Not because he was fearful, but because he knew that he needed Carter to accomplish his goals.

"I'ma be honest with you my nigga. I'm not about to box with you. But if you touch me, I'ma shoot you until you catch fire," Mo said with a smirk on his face as he playfully held his hands up.

"Yeah, that tune changed real quick," Carter said in a low tone as he was noticeably bothered by Mo's harsh words.

"Relax. I'm just trying to motivate you to step into who you really are," Mo added as he returned to the wall and once again viewed the pictures and continued. "What you gon' do huh? Estes ain't here to take care of you no more. You got to pull up your bootstraps and get the fuck outside. The streets waiting on us. Think about it….Us in the streets like our pops used to be? The streets would go fuckin crazy!" Mo smiled, thinking about the possibilities.

"I am not my father. Why can't you get that through your head? Do you even remember the shit that we had to go through back in the day?"

"Yeah, I remember," Mo answered calmly, dropping his head.

"That shit wasn't normal. Look around. There is nobody left. All of the men in our family are dead. This game gave my father an early grave. He died of a heart attack in his thirties. Think about that. What was on his heart, that it quit on him that early? The streets drain you. Don't you see that?" Carter explained.

"You just don't get it," Mo said as he shook his head from side to side in disappointment.

"What our family did will live on forever. They made all that money and set the blueprint for us to know what to do and what not to do. Their problem was they didn't get out of the game. They didn't have an escape plan. I do!" Mo exclaimed.

"I'm not fucking with it," Carter said as he shook his head. Mo just stared at Carter, knowing that he wasn't budging on his position.

No matter how hard he pushed him, he just couldn't get Carter to jump into the game with him. He knew convincing him to pick up the bricks from Harry later that night was out of the question. He was tired of begging Carter, so he knew at that point he would have to force his hand one way or another. Mo was determined to do exactly what he wanted to do, and that was to continue the tradition of his family's cartel.

"This nigga scared," Mo said as he looked at Joey, pointed at Carter, and half grinned. "Let's go," Mo said as he began to head towards the door. Joey shook his head in disappointment as well and followed Mo's lead out. Just as Mo reached the door to exit, he yelled back.

"Oh yeah. Aunt Breeze wants all of us to come over tomorrow night."

"A'ight," Carter said as he watched Mo exit his home. He focused his attention on the television screen where ESPN played. He saw his picture and the words 'Boxing Phenom Caught Cheating' on the screen. He grabbed the remote and quickly clicked it off. He stood in the middle of the floor with his hands on his hips, wondering what his next move would be. Something had to shake.

Mo and Joey pulled into a driveway and drove all the way to the back of the modest home. It was a lowkey two-bedroom house just outside of the city limits, that served as their stash spot. They kept their street money and drugs there for the past two summers, they were the only two who knew about the house. The entire car ride there was quiet. They didn't say one word. They had never had a car ride where they didn't speak, but this time was different. As Joey put the SUV in park, he took a deep breath. He looked to his left where Mo was sitting on the passenger's side. Mo seemed to be staring into space and not focusing on anything in particular. It was as if he was in a daze like state. That was maybe because he was. He had been waiting on that day for years and it had finally arrived.

"How you feeling?" Joey asked, breaking up the silent monotony.

"I feel heavy," Mo said as he smirked and sunk down into his chair more comfortably. He leaned the chair back and took in a deep breath.

"Heavy?" Joey asked not understanding what Mo was trying to say exactly.

"Yea nigga, about a hundred kilos heavier," Mo said.

"Let's go!" Joey said as he playfully hit Mo as if he was

boxing him. They had just picked up one hundred bricks of pure cocaine from Harry on Ocean Drive. Mo felt an adrenaline rush like had never felt before. He felt like he had finally arrived.

"Let's unload this shit and get to it," Mo said as he beamed and rubbed his hands together, anticipating the money and power was about to gain from his new acquisition.

They stepped out of the car and began to unload the truck. They entered the home and began to place the bricks on the table. By the time they were done, it looked like a real-life Tetris board. Mo's eyes were glued to the plastic wrapped bricks and the sight of the fish scale. The shiny crystals and the sheen look that it gave off, earned its nickname. This usually meant uncut, pure cocaine, and was a drug dealer's dream because it meant that it could be doubled or sometimes tripled because of its potency.

"This is beautiful," Mo said as he picked up a brick off the table and admired it. The sparkly specs were like eye candy to him and he knew that the takeover had just begun.

"You already know," Joey said, agreeing with his partner as he pulled off his hoody and prepped the cutting process. He reached under the table and pulled out the compressor. Mo placed the brick back on the table and walked over to his snake tank where his Boa constrictor was slithering around. He tapped on the tank, causing his snake to look at him.

"We gotta stamp these joints," Joey said, knowing that when you put a new product on the street, stamping it gives it brand recognition. It's like having a secret commercial for your coke. Mo picked up the snake and wrapped it around his neck. He felt comfortable as the snake rolled its big body around his upper torso.

"We going to put a snake on that mu'fucka," Mo answered, with a smile on his face.

"Say no more," Joey said as he smirked and prepped the table, so they could begin busting the bricks open and cutting them to make even more profit.

"I see them scales from all the way over here. It's only right to put a snake on that bitch. That's the purest coke Miami has seen since my family used to be out here running shit."

"It's crazy you mention that. One of my OG's just posted an old video on Instagram of your uncle."

"Yeah?" Mo asked as he frowned slightly and turned his head. He didn't see too many videos and pictures of his family because of their unwillingness to take pictures and get in front of cameras. Their lifestyle didn't allow them to be at the forefront. Their stories lived on through old stories and urban legend.

"Yeah, check it out," Joey said as he pulled out his camera and began to scroll through it until he found the post he was referring to. He turned his phone towards Mo so he could get a better view of the video clip an OG had posted for nostalgia. Mo walked over and his heart instantly felt full seeing his uncle and his father at a barbecue. It seemed as if everyone was enjoying themselves as the music played loudly in the background. You could barely hear the voices over the music, but you could if you listened carefully. Mo's attention went on his Uncle Mecca who was right square in front of the camera. Mo smiled, noticing how they resembled so closely.

Both he and Mecca had long wild hair and their voice cadence were even the same. Full of confidence and cockiness, Mecca looked dead square into the camera and smiled, showing his bottom row of the gold grill that he sometimes wore. Mecca's tattooed body was on full display and the letters DC were bold and big on his chest. Mo instantly knew that those letters were for *Diamond Cartel*; a street moniker that stuck with their family, which made them famous.

Yo, we run these streets. Niggas ain't getting money like this and making it look this good. The Cartel make sure everybody eat. That's why the streets will forever love us. Our name gone ring bells for 100 years. Believe that!

Mo watched closely and studied his uncle's mannerisms. He grabbed the phone so he could study it even closer.

I'm about to hang this shit up though. I gotta little boy on the way, so I'm going to retire on top and become a family man or some shit like that. Mecca laughed and then chugged a bottle of Cristal. His silk Versace shirt was open and a gold Cuban chain rested on his chest, swinging left to right as he talked into the home-video camera.

Mecca threw his arm around his twin brother who had a low neat hair cut with no jewels on. Although the two brothers resembled each other, their styles and demeanor were complete opposites. Mo watched as his father, Monroe 'Money' Diamond, shied away from the cameras and avoided eye contact as his twin brother talked his shit. That small video clip was a great depiction of their two contrasting personalities. Mo smiled seeing his young father on camera; however, it was his uncle that he was getting the most entertainment from. He was so charismatic…so free. Mecca Diamond was everything he wanted to be and that video served as a subtle confirmation that he made the right decision to use Carter's name to get the bricks from Harry. In Mo's mind, the plug was rightfully his so he didn't feel like he did anything wrong.

Mo handed the phone back to Joey and the words of his uncle replayed in his head. He didn't know about Mecca having any children, so he wondered what child he was referring to. He also got motivated by the brashness of Mecca. He then looked at the bricks on the table as he played with the snake around his neck. He smiled from ear to ear and couldn't wait to put his new product on the streets. He only had one step left, and that was to break the news to Carter that he had used his name. He reached in his pocket and pulled out his cell phone to make the call. He hoped that Carter would see the bricks on the table and click on…so they could get money like their fathers did; together.

CHAPTER 9

"I didn't come back to Miami to bury more Diamonds," -Breeze

The slap of the body bag erupted throughout the training facility as Carter threw aggressive jabs. The impending appeal he had filed with the boxing commission had him on edge. Carter was an athlete. He had always played the game fair in his profession. No steroids, no enhancers, just pure skill and demons of his past fueling his fists as he fought his way to the top of the boxing industry. He had never put anything synthetic into his body a day of his life. Proving his innocence was important to him. He had worked hard to build a legitimate name, outside of the tarnished legacy his father had left him with, and now with one test it had all been destroyed.

Sweat covered his body and he grit his teeth, grunting with every blow that connected to the bag. His body was like a machine. Trained to do much more than win a fight, but his discipline kept him from crossing the lines that the boxing commission established as fair. Estes had been the nucleus of his team. He would have known exactly what to do to mitigate this storm. Without him, Carter felt like he was fighting an uphill battle. On top of that, he was now on the hook with the Dominicans. Mo had used his name to establish a connect.

Carter had steered clear of the drug game for years, despite being raised by Emilio Estes. He had been around. He had soaked up the knowledge from Estes' criminal enterprise. Only the upper echelon of drug dealing had taken place and he had been witness to it all. He knew price, he knew cut, he knew how to break down bricks of cocaine, how to stretch heroine, how to package pills. He knew how to steal, how to kill, how to flip, but he never partook in any of it. Estes had only made him one time after a losing fight. His only loss as a young boy. As long as he was winning Estes rewarded him with legitimacy. He never put Carter in the field with Papi or the other losing fighters, but he had to win. It was contingent on being the best and so he was.

Now he was knee deep in a relationship with a faction of gangsters so deadly they weren't even known. They operated in the shadows of the D.R. getting rich, taking lives, and moving pawns around on the chessboard. He was the pawn. One of many and Carter hated it, but he knew his aunt was right, once inducted there was only one way out.

The sound of the metal doors opening didn't distract him as he kept sparring with himself. He was his biggest component. The man in the mirror had always been the greatest competitor and he envisioned his face on the bag as he delivered bone shattering uppercuts. The sound of heels clicked against the concrete floor and he shot a quick glance to find Ashton approaching. Still, he didn't stop.

"This is private property," he said, hissing through clenched teeth as he felt his fatigue fighting back. He had been sparring for an hour straight.

Ashton stood, staring up at him, admiring how focused he was, how deadly each blow seemed to be.

"I was invited," she said.

"Not by me," he shot back. He delivered one final punch and then staggered away from the bag, gasping for air. He bit down on the mouth guard and leaned onto the ropes.

"I'm meeting Mo here," she said. "But I'm half an hour late and he's not even here, so I'm feeling like he's not coming at all."

Carter scoffed. "Who knows. Being prompt ain't really his thing," Carter said, chuckling.

"I see," she said, looking around.

"You're welcome to wait," he said.

"I'm really sorry about the fight," she said. "For the record, I believe you about the steroid allegations."

Carter inspected her from head to toe.

"You're a boxing fan?" he asked, surprised that she knew about his circumstances.

"Not really, but you're kind of a big deal now aren't you?" she shot back. "Which is why you should have never been in Ris' suite last night."

Carter's eyes went cold and he didn't respond.

"I don't know what you talking about," he answered.

Ashton smiled. He was smart. He didn't do too much talking.

"Good answer," she replied. "Which is why I know you're not stupid enough to take steroids."

"Yeah, well you might be the only person who believes me," Carter said. He lowered one of the ropes. "Climb in the ring."

"What?" she asked, confused.

"You want to wait here you got to help me train, ain't no bystanders," he said. "Put your Birkin down and come help a nigga out."

Ashton smiled and shook her head in disbelief. "I have on four-inch heels."

"Take em' off," he said.

Ashton stepped out of her designer shoes and climbed into the ring. Carter removed his gloves to help put hers on. He rolled the tape around her small hands as she watched him.

"You ever been in a fight?" he asked.

"Not really," she lied.

He slid the gloves onto her hands and then put his back on, holding them up. He took a light jab at her.

"You're wide open. Protect that face," he said. "Hands up, like this." He held a defensive stance and Ashton modeled after him.

She was pretty as hell. Her body was on point, face hard to forget, but out of all the things he took in, it was her smile that quickly became his preference.

Ashton threw a jab at his face and Carter smirked as he dodged it with ease.

He checked her chin lightly when she left her face unprotected.

She was so stunned that she came out of her stance and Carter followed up with a left hook. The softest blow tap landed on the side of her head.

"Okay, you not about to just beat my ass, boy," she said, taking off the gloves and throwing them at his head.

"Love taps, that's all. I ain't doing too much."

"You're a prize fighter. Even the love taps hurt!" she argued, laughing.

Ashton had a small temper problem and every time he tapped her it was a bruise to her ego. If Carter wanted, he would be getting the best of her and it irritated the hell out of Ashton. She was swinging with all her might, but Carter was playing with her. He was so light on his feet she couldn't even touch him. He floated; he was so quick. She understood why they called him the best.

"My bad," he said, licking his lips.

Carter sat on the edge of the ring. She sat beside him, leaving a little space between them. "You lucky I ain't feel like fucking you up," she said.

He laughed aloud at that, baritone echoing through the facility. "Yeah? You get like that?"

"When provoked," she admitted.

"Remind me not to ever provoke you," he replied, amused. He hopped down to the floor. "You gon' wait around for Mo or you want to quit bullshitting and let me take you to lunch?"

Ashton smiled. "Is that what you do? Steal girls from your cousin?"

"Nah. You ain't his girl and I ain't looking to do too much. It's just food."

"I guess you do kind of owe me since you beat me up and all," she answered.

"The least I can do," he said, chuckling.

Ashton smiled. She was showing a lot of teeth around this nigga. It was easy. He was comfortable. "Sure. Lunch sounds great."

"You mind waiting around while I shower?" Carter asked.

"I'll be here," she answered.

Ashton browsed the facility, looking at all the trophies Carter had won over the years. There were pictures of him in frames from boyhood to manhood. Pictures of him sparring with other fighters, and dozens of pictures of him and Estes. One after the other. When Ashton got to the picture of him and Miamor she froze. Miamor hadn't aged. She stood with Carter who couldn't have been a day older than three years old and the smile on both their faces revealed nothing short of love.

"You ready?"

Ashton turned to Carter to find him fully clothed. Black jeans, white fitted t-shirt, J's, and jewelry, not too much, but enough to blind her. Just enough to be noticeable but not to attract unwanted attention. Carter was an athlete so each time she had seen him, he had been dressed like one. At the pool he had, and now dressed down in street clothes, he was an entire vibe.

Fine ass, she thought.

"Yeah," she answered.

Her phone rang, well the phone Mo had given her rang and Ashton looked at the screen.

"You need to get that?" he asked.

Ashton sent the call to voicemail.

"No," she replied. "I'm good right here."

He took her to a little hole in the wall, across town, where they sold Cuban sandwiches.

"This is your idea of a date?" she asked.

"This is my idea of being polite. We not dating. If we were dating, I'd have you in my bed by now and we'd be ordering in," Carter said.

She froze because he didn't say it on the sly like he was trying to be cute. He said it like it was a fact. Ashton blushed so hard she felt herself get jittery. Miamor was right. Her son was his father all over again. There was nothing like confidence and certainty in a man. Carter Jones ll had both.

"You sound so sure of yourself," she laughed as she reached for the Styrofoam cup and took a sip.

"Nah not really. I'm sure of you. Sure of how you'll react when the vibe is right and a nigga earn his keep," Carter stated. "The energy that comes after that is inevitable."

"The energy?" she said, turning in her seat so that her back leaned against the door and she faced him.

"Real shit," he said. "So this ain't a date, but it's a vibe. It's chill. It feels good. I'm enjoying you, you enjoying me, but it's not pressure, we just cooling," he said as he leaned over the armrest. He pinched her chin and pulled her face to his. "So when a nigga kiss the first set of lips ain't no protest…"

Yeah, this nigga was his whole daddy because just that quickly Ashton forgot she was planted in his life. All of this chemistry couldn't be real because his mother had sent her into his life. An arranged circumstance. He pecked her lips and Ashton reached for his face, kissing him back as her lashes fluttered.

"The first set?" she asked as she stared at him through lowered lids. He kissed her again.

"Yeah I plan to show appreciation elsewhere," he said. Another soft kiss and then he pulled back. "If we get to that. That requires a little trust first unless you trying to go back to waiting on Mo."

Mannish. Carter Jones II was mannish. Who would have fucking thought? She liked that shit. Her heart fluttered and she hated it because that feeling often made emotion chase logic right out of the window.

"I don't wait on anybody. You show up on time for school or you miss the lesson," Aston replied.

Carter smirked. "Real shit, I feel that," he said as he put his car in drive. She rolled her pretty eyes out of the window as she faced forward in the seat.

"Drive fast," she said. "I prefer to do everything fast. Drive, fall in love, it's all better that way…"

Carter applied pressure to the gas pedal of his Lamborghini and Ashton shouted in excitement as they flew by the other cars on the Miami street. He felt a bit of guilt about wagering on her. When he'd first seen her, he had been intrigued. She had been the only girl in an atmosphere full of rich men who didn't seem impressed. She was beautiful, not the baddest in the room, but definitely the most memorable with her mean girl vibes that left her unapproachable. It was hard on the regular girls these days. Day parties brought out the most elite women in the city. Looks wise they were winning. Build-a-bitches with manufactured waists, fat asses that no amount of cornbread could produce, fake hairlines, fake lashes, and fake eyebrows. Bitches were perfection these days and amongst all that had attended sat Ashton, an imperfect girl. She was regular and her body was natural.

As Carter watched Mo shoot his shot, he couldn't help but be a little relieved when she shot him down. The bet was the male ego, a little fun wagering to make an uninteresting party more interesting. With her sitting beside him, with the scent of her perfume floating in the air as they rode top down through the city, he felt a bit bad. He liked her. He was intrigued enough to want to know more and for a man, as disciplined as Carter, that was a big deal. He never wanted to know more. He had never been seen with a woman, never dated openly. Sex with no conversations to avoid complications was how he moved, until today. Today, he took a girl to lunch and it felt good. He decided then and there to let Mo know all bets were off with this one. Carter wasn't interested in playing games. He wanted to see where this could lead.

"Look where this mu'fucka at man, I ain't got all day. The nigga must not want to do no business if he late. Money show up on time," Mo said as he sat on the porch of the Opalocka trap house.

Joey passed Mo a blunt and waltzed down the short staircase. "This nigga move a lot of product. He working out of Pork and Beans for Ma'Dear. They getting a lotttt of money round that way. We can make a lot of money over there if they fuck with us to get the work," Joey said.

"Ma'Dear? Like a grandma, nigga?" Mo asked, face balled in confusion.

"Just like that," Joey said. "Lil' ol' bird in Liberty Square who run all that shit. Niggas respect her, bruh. Ain't nothing moving out that way without her say so."

"We getting enough money over here. I don't really need no partners," Mo said as he pulled on the blunt and then blew smoke into the air. His wild hair fell like a cloud around his face. Humidity was tearing his man apart, expanding it by the minute. Mo was a beautiful man. In another world, he would be a model. In this one, he was a thug and his temper was flaring the longer he waited. "I'ma peel this nigga top for making me fucking wait. Real shit."

A red S-Class pulled up on the block with limousine tint and custom shoes on the wheel.

"Flashy ass nigga, man. Who the fuck you got me doing business with Joey?" Mo asked as he stood to his feet.

"He's good money, bruh, you know I ain't gone have no clowns pulling up. Just hear him out," Joey said.

Mo's goons stopped the man as he approached.

"The nigga got sense man. He don't want no smoke," Mo said as he waved off his men and allowed the man to approach.

Joey greeted the man with a nod.

"What's good, baby? I been waiting on this conversation all day. This the money talk," the man said.

"You walking up to this bitch late. You don't want to make no money," Mo said.

"Aww, man. I don't mean no disrespect. I'm coming with nothing but respect. I got this little bitch in the whip. I lost track of time. Bad lil' bitch too. I was stretching that out a little bit," he said, chuckling while bragging and glancing back at the car. "My fault. I lost track of time. I'm here now though. It's all love. I'm just tryna make some paper with you. I heard of you. Your name ring bells in Miami. It's respect," the man said.

"Pussy don't stop my timeline, nigga. You gone have to tighten up if you fuck with me. I left a bad bitch on hold just to take this meeting. You don't think I'd rather be getting my dick wet right now, nigga? Money is first. Always," Mo said. "What's your name?"

"Guy," the man introduced. "You right. That's my bad. Won't happen again."

Mo glanced at the car, nodding. "And don't bring no bitch I don't know nowhere around me when we talking business. Get that bitch out the car so I can see who ya' ass done used my name in front of."

"You joking, right? Aye Joey, fam, I thought..."

"Joey don't speak for me. Do it look like I'm a comedian?" Mo asked, deadpanning on Guy. "Get the bitch out the car."

Guy walked back over to the curb and knocked on the passenger's window. Whoever was inside refused to roll it down. Guy walked around to the driver's side and got in, igniting Mo's suspicion.

"This nigga move funny, man," Mo said, hiking up his pants as he eyed the car suspiciously.

He swaggered across the lawn and around the front of Guy's car. He could hear the couple arguing inside.

"No, please, I don't want to get out, Guy. I don't have anything to do with your business."

Mo might not have recognized the voice immediately, but all it took was one glimpse of her face as the window rolled down to light a fire in his chest. Aurora sat in the passenger seat, trying to shield her face from Mo's view.

"My bad man, she a little shy..."

Mo reached through the driver's side window and snatched Guy out, yanking him as he gritted his teeth.

"Nigga get yo' ass out the fucking car! She's 14!" Mo shouted as he snatched a screaming Guy out of the hundred-thousand-dollar car.

"Mo! Stop it!" Aurora screamed, hopping out of the car as Mo snatched the man's gun from his waist.

"Fuck you doing with this nigga?" Mo screamed. "Go in the house!"

Mo beat Guy mercilessly. "Nigga if you ever put your hands on her again, I'll kill you!" Mo said, sneering in Guy's face as he lay sprawled over the concrete.

"Mo please stop it!" Aurora cried as she pulled at her big cousin's arm, trying to pry him off.

Mo staggered away from Guy and extended his arm, hand gripping his pistol, finger wrapped on the trigger.

BANG!

Guy screamed as he writhed in pain at the bullet that tore through his foot.

"Mo, no!" Aurora screamed in horror.

"Get your ass up out of here before I put the next one between your eyes," Mo warned.

He was so livid he grabbed Aurora up by her arm.

"Let me go, Mo!" Aurora fussed as she snatched away from him. He grabbed her up again.

"Get in the car so I can take ya' bad ass home, out here fucking with these lame ass niggas. Grown ass nigga fucking on little girls. You lucky I ain't kill that nigga!"

He never thought he would be the one to discipline anyone, but the sight of Aurora with a grown ass man made him sick to his stomach. Guy was 25 years old. He had no business with a fourteen-year-old girl. Mo wasn't a saint, but when it came to his bloodline, he would blow a nigga's head off for the disrespect alone. If Guy hadn't known Aurora was affiliated before, he knew now…the entire hood knew too, and it was a lesson they wouldn't soon forget.

"What were you thinking?" Breeze shouted.

"Mom! I just wanted to have some fun!" Aurora defended.

"Fun with a grown ass man! Miami isn't fun! Miami is dangerous! Men like that are deadly!" Breeze yelled so loud that Aurora had tears in her eyes. "He'll have your little ass tied up somewhere Aurora! It is not a game out here!"

Mo was silent as he stood behind Breeze. He almost felt bad for telling Breeze what had gone down.

Breeze was so irate that her voice was trembling. Breeze had underestimated how cold the streets of Miami could be once upon a time. There had been a consequence to pay for that. Ma'tee had done unspeakable things to her, kidnapping her and trapping her so far away from her family that she wished she had died.

"I wasn't unsafe! He treats me good, mom! If you would just give him a chance!"

Aurora's defense pissed Breeze off more. She hadn't been in Miami for a full month and already she was headed in the wrong direction.

"You don't even know him! That's a grown man! I WILL HAVE HIM SENT TO HIS MOTHER IN A BOX!"

There it was. The spirit of her bloodline coursing through her. She had always been the docile one. Soft spoken and gentle. It wasn't because it wasn't in her, however. The thought of her daughter being taken advantage of by a grown man brought out a different type of ruthlessness in her.

"Mom!"

"You're not to leave this house with anyone that is not blood related to you and you will turn on your locations every time you are out of my eyesight."

"What? Mom, that's unreasonable!"

"I don't need to be reasonable. I need to keep you alive down here. Go to your room," Breeze said.

Aurora rushed out of the kitchen and Breeze blew out a breath of frustration. She stalked over to the refrigerator and snatched it open, retrieving a bottle of wine.

"Thank you for bringing her home, Mo," Breeze said. "I remember the days when your Uncle Mecca was snatching me off the street." She poured a glass of wine and lifted the liquid relief to her lips. "It's ruthless out here. I won't let Miami corrupt my daughter."

"Never thought I'd see the day I'd be snitching like a mu'fucka," Mo said. "I lost it over her out there today. I saw her in that nigga's car, and I went stupid."

"She can't handle the streets, Mo. There is an allure down here. These Miami niggas will pull my baby in and I can't let that happen. I haven't been around for a long time. I need you to keep an eye on her," Breeze said. "She doesn't belong to the streets, Mo. She's my baby. She's all the proof I have that..."

Breeze paused and took another sip of wine.

"Proof?"

"Proof that her father existed." Breeze hurt tremendously over the thought of Zyir Rich. She had so many regrets. "I could have loved him for the rest of my life."

Mo didn't know what to say. It was like Breeze wasn't even talking to him.

"I'ma leave you to it, Aunt B," he said, knocking on the counter to bring her back to the present because her mind was somewhere in the past.

"Thanks, Mo," Breeze said. She walked him to the door and before he exited, she said, "There might be blowback over what you did today. Wars have been sparked for less, Mo. Be careful out there. I didn't come back to Miami to bury more Diamonds."

CHAPTER 10

"Baby, you know better than to talk to Ma'Dear like that…"-
Ma'Dear

The air was full of moisture as the morning dew sat on top of the grass blades. Birds were chirping and the dawn's fog was present. The dangerous housing projects known as Pork and Beans was the setting, however, one wouldn't imagine how deadly it really was when the night fell. In the middle of this warzone was a well-kept garden. It was leafy and vibrantly green with specs of bright colors from the various fruits and vegetables. The garden was about twenty feet long and twenty feet wide. It was outlined by beautiful flower beds and was a bright spot in this dark place where many called home. No matter what chaos ensued or what went inside the projects, the garden stayed unbothered and intact. It was a local treasure, and some would call it a sacred patch. It had been there for nearly twenty years and became legendary in some circles. Not for the fruits and vegetables, but for the green thumb that managed it. None other than Renetta Pollard, better known as "Ma'Dear." Right in the middle of it was a middle-aged woman on her hands and knees tending to what she called "her babies."

Her brown skin seemed to be kissed by the sun and her pretty hazel eyes were dreamy. Her hair was healthy, bouncy, and silver as steel. She was simply beautiful and carefully aged. Crow's feet had formed just outside of her eyes, hinting at her age, but her beauty still shined through. A few early morning hustlers sat on a stoop across the way and a couple of zombie like fiends wandered around, looking for someone to open up shop for them to get their fix. However, Ma'Dear sat in the middle of the concrete jungle just a' humming away.

Ma'Dear got her name because of how she mothered the young boys, who eventually became men, who then eventually became her army. She had the respect of every gangster, hot girl, woman, and child of those projects. She was the unofficial mayor and that was undisputed. She wore a big straw sunhat as she kneeled with her knees in the dirt. She was cutting collard greens that were ready for picking.

Ma'Dear hummed Patti Labelle's *Somebody Loves You* as she picked the greens and placed them in her small wicker basket that sat right beside her. Like she did every morning, she sang to her plants, fruits, and vegetables. She smiled as she genuinely found peace in her safe place right in the middle of hell's kitchen. She was so focused on her garden, she didn't realize the man approaching from her rear. A tall, stocky thug with the skin completion that was dark as tar stood there.

"Top of the morning," he said with a heavy southern drawl. Ma'Dear stopped humming and slowly turned around to see the man. It was Tar. He got the name because of the obvious reasons and he had been a resident of the projects for a few years. He also was a pill man. He pushed all the Oxycodone, Percocet, and Xanax pills to name a few. All from which he got from Ma'Dear wholesale. Ma'Dear had many hats when it came to the black market. Whatever you needed, she had it or knew how to get it. She was the plug for anything you couldn't get at Walmart.

"Good morning, baby," Ma'Dear said as she smiled and went back to picking her greens.

"I was trying to get right," Tar said, cutting straight to the point and letting her know he wanted to re-up on the pills.

"Oh is that right?" Ma'Dear asked nonchalantly, without even looking at Tar.

"Yeah, I need a hunnid pack of the Perc 30," he said

"About that...I been wanting to bump into you. A little birdie told me that one of those got into the hands of a fourteen-year-old in building six."

"Shit, I don't know. I sell all around this bitch," Tar said, seemingly becoming irritated by the small talk. He was becoming antsy because he had a few sells on deck that he was missing because of being sold out.

"See...that's the thing," she said as she slowly stood up and dusted off her knees and then pulled off her gardening gloves. She placed her hands on her hips and slowly walked towards Tar.

"Now...that baby ended up in the hospital last week. He had a seizure and had a lot of people worried about him," she said. She was now standing directly in front of Tar who was at least a foot taller than her. He loomed over her as she sternly looked at him, searching for an explanation.

"What that got to do with me?" Tar asked as he slightly frowned, wondering what Ma'Dear was hinting at.

"The problem with that is that boy is fourteen years old. You know my rules no kids or pregnant women. Ms. Jenkins was looking out of that window just above the alley and said she saw you sell to him," she said with a smile on her face. She was cool, calm, and collected while talking to him.

"I didn't know he was that young, Ma'Dear. And to be totally honest, I'm not trying to hold mu'fuckas hands while they trying to be grown."

"Yeah, I hear you, baby. But we have to work together. It takes a village...." Ma'Dear said, but was cut off by an agitated Tar.

"Fuck all that. Do you have the pills or what? It's too early to be talking about all that bullshit that doesn't make me money. I mind the business that pays me," Tar said arrogantly as he pulled out a black and mild cigar and lit it. Ma'Dear eyes got low as she took in what Tar had just said to her. She looked down and let out a small, quick chuckle. She looked left and right, scanning the projects. She then took a deep breath and looked back up at Tar. She still had that famous warm smile spread across her face.

"Baby, you know better than to talk to Ma'Dear like that," she said as she slowly pulled off her straw hat and shook her hair out, so it could lay neatly just above her shoulders.

When she took off her hat, a few guys from across the parking lot who sat on the stoop, began to make their way over to where she was. Also, a young man emerged from a parked car that was just to their left. He had a menacing look

ASHLEY & JAQUAVIS

on his face and was staring a hole through Tar. It was a signal that she secretly orchestrated with her boys and even when she seemed to be alone, she never was. Tar instantly began to regret his words as he noticed the group of guys coming their way from different angles. He instantly began to change his tune and tone.

"I'm just saying. I couldn't tell that it was a kid. You know these lil mu'fuckas be looking grown as hell nowadays," Tar said as he was now circled by Ma'Dear's goons.

"We have to protect the kids, baby. You have to be smarter," she said as she gently placed her hand on Tar's cheek and tapped it. A love tap.

The most intimidating part about it was that Ma'Dear acted as if they were alone. She kept a smile on her face and her voice was warm. It was crystal clear that she was playing a mind game with him and he then understood why she was queen. He didn't see her viciousness through her facial expressions, but he felt that negative energy surrounding him. Although she herself was smiling, all of her goons were looking as if they had a deep-rooted hatred for Tar. Tar looked around and saw that everyone had their hands under their shirts or in their pockets. He already knew what time it was and understood that he was standing in the belly of the beast, so he wanted to choose his words wisely.

"I get it," Tar said carefully. He had his gun on him, but he knew he didn't stand a chance if he reached for it. He decided to play it cool to live to fight another day.

"Good. Come on by and get you a plate later. I'll make sure you get what you need then," she said as her smile

157

spread wider and winked. She then put back on her straw hat, turned towards her garden, and placed her hands on her hips as she observed her masterpiece. Tar took that as a signal and left towards the back of the projects, leaving Ma'Dear and her protectors there alone. Ma'Dear looked at the man who emerged from the car and nodded her head.

"Guy, baby...come help me pick up this basket. Carry it to the house for me," she ordered. Guy made his way over and had a noticeable limp. Almost like he had stepped on glass.

"I got you," Guy said as he gingerly headed over to her basket and picked up the collard greens. He headed towards Ma'Dear's apartment.

"Hold up. I'ma walk with ya," she said as she walked beside him. The others went back to their post as they strolled towards the buildings. "So, what's this I hear about someone putting hands on you? They say you got a little flesh wound?" she asked as she reached into her breast, pulled out a cigarette, and lit it.

"You heard about that?" Guy said, almost embarrassed that she knew the news.

"Now you know that I know about everything that happens. Plus you're walking like you're missing a toe. The streets be talking, baby. And I always have my ear to the streets to see what's going on. So tell me...what happened?"

"Some bitch-ass nigga hating that's all. I'ma catch him slipping though," Guy said. He was infuriated from the embarrassment. He clenched his jaws so tightly that muscles flexed and formed in his jaw.

"You have to keep a cool head. I need you out here moving work, not getting into petty fights." Ma'Dear said, knowing that Guy meant what he said about getting the guy back.

"He shot me in the foot. I can't let that ride," Guy said with hatred in his tone.

She had known Guy since he was a young boy and he was one of her lead earners. She also knew that he was a live wire. The last thing she wanted was any unwanted attention brought to her section and this had police attention written all over it.

"Who was it?" Ma'Dear asked as she quickly inhaled a cloud of smoke, making it disappear into her lungs.

"This nigga named Mo," Guy answered.

"Mo? Where he from?" she asked.

"I don't really know. He's a Diamond though. I do know that," Guy answered. Ma'Dear stopped walking and placed her hand on Guy's chest so he would as well. She wanted to get the information straight.

"You say he a Diamond? He a Cartel boy?"

"Yep," Guy answered. Ma'Dear rolled her eyes and continued to walk.

"Let that alone, Guy," Ma'Dear said as she shook her head from side to side.

"Nah…I gotta get…" Guy started, but Ma'Dear cut him off by placing her hand on his chest once again. The cheerful look on her face quickly dissolved and a frown appeared.

"Listen to me. Leave it alone," she said as she pointed at his face.

"Yes, ma'am," Guy said, not wanting to upset her any further.

"Good. Gon' and take the greens in there and place them in the sink," she instructed as she threw her head in the direction of her building. She stayed and watched as Guy headed into her apartment. She took a deep pull of her cigarette and thought about what she had just learned. She hadn't heard anything about The Cartel in years. However, she knew enough to know that that was a path she didn't want to go down. She decided right then that she would take an impromptu trip into the city and put out a small fire before it became a raging blaze.

Breeze and Aurora sat in a small coffee shop, just around the corner from the Diamond Estate. Breeze was having a latte while Aurora enjoyed a milkshake. Breeze had taken her on a small girl's day out. They had just gotten their nails done and did a little shopping. They were having small talk and it was a good vibe for them on that day. They sat in a small booth and weren't paying attention to their surroundings too much. A small framed woman with silver hair approached with a smile, interrupting their casual conversation. It was Ma'Dear.

"Excuse me. You're Carter and Taryn's baby girl, right?" Ma'Dear asked with warm eyes. Breeze and Aurora paused their conversation and an awkward moment of silence occurred. Breeze had never seen the lady in front of her a day in her life, so she was hesitant on revealing her own identity. She was gamed up to know that a lot of people idolized The

Cartel and her family name, but she also understood there was a few that hated them. Breeze was unclear if the woman was friend or foe. Breeze looked the woman up and down and saw the expensive belt, shoes, and the diamond rings on multiple fingers. Big, oversized Cartier glasses covered Ma'Dear's face and diamonds were in the bridge of the nose. She was sparkling and looked like a million bucks. She obviously kept up with the Joneses, so her guard went down.

"Yes, I am. I'm sorry…but have we met before," Breeze asked as she turned her head to the side and gave Ma'Dear a half grin.

"Oh, how rude of me," Ma'Dear pulled her shades off and placed them inside of her Chanel purse. She then reached out her hand and extended it to Breeze. "I'm Renetta, but everyone calls me Ma'Dear. Nice to meet you." She greeted. Breeze reached out and shook her hand, still trying to figure out the woman's angle. Ma'Dear continued.

"I knew your mom and dad. We used to run the streets together back in the day. A long…long time ago." Ma'Dear said as she looked over at Aurora. She placed her hand over her mouth and smiled. "And you must be Aurora? You look just like your grandma when she was your age. You're just cute as a button," Ma'Dear smiled and brushed her hair away from her face.

"Thank you," Aurora said, letting out a small chuckle and blushed.

Breeze began to ease up and become a tad bit more comfortable because of Ma'Dear knowing her mother. Aurora did in fact closely resemble Taryn, so Breeze believed that she had known her mother at some point. Ma'Dear focused back on Breeze.

"Sorry to bother you, baby. But I was wondering if we could talk for a bit," Ma'Dear asked.

"Sure," Breeze answered.

"Alone," Ma'Dear added as she glanced over at Aurora who was in her phone, not paying too much attention to what was being said.

"Ok. Aurora, why don't you let us talk for a second," Breeze instructed as she placed her hand on Aurora's wrist.

"Sure," Aurora said, without giving it a second thought. She slid out of the booth, headed over to the bar area, and placed her headphones in her ear. Ma'Dear and Breeze watched as she walked away and once she was settled at the bar, that's when Ma'Dear slid into the booth. The two women were now sitting directly across from one another and Breeze was interested in what Ma'Dear wanted to talk about.

"You don't know who I am. However, I know who you are and I'm aware of who your family is. This is why I'm here. I have extreme respect for the Diamonds. So, I wanted to do this the right way," Ma'Dear said.

"I'm not understanding what you're trying to say," Breeze answered with confusion on her face.

"It seems that a little incident happened the other day involving one of my boys and your nephew."

"My nephew who? Mo or Carter?" Breeze asked.

"Mo," Ma'Dear replied.

"Ok, I'm listening," said Breeze.

"Well, your nephew out here playing with that pistol like

it's a toy. He shot my boy in the foot. Thank God he was playing. However, it could have been a lot worst if something would have happened to him."

"Worst like what?" Breeze asked as she felt hostility coming from the woman who sat across from her.

"See, I can tell you're getting a little riled up, baby. I'm a grown ass woman. I leave the childish games to the children. I'm just trying to come and see if we can call a truce before somebody really gets hurt," Ma'Dear spat.

"I'm not sure what's your aim here. But I don't get into the business of my nephews. I'm not sure if you didn't notice, but I'm a grown...ass...woman as well. So games aren't a thing I'm into playing. This, what you're talking about, is none of my business ma'am," Breeze said with a heavy attitude.

"Oh, but that's where you're wrong, baby girl. This is called street politics and you are in in if you like it or not. As long as you have that last name, you are a part of it. Now by you being the elder, seeing as you are the oldest Diamond living....I would expect you to help me resolve petty things like this. I've seen wars started for less," Ma'Dear explained.

"Good day, ma'am," Breeze said as she rolled her eyes and took a sip of her drink. She was done talking to the stranger and didn't want to participate any longer. That wasn't why she returned home. She wanted nothing to do with anything street.

"You enjoy your afternoon, baby," Ma'Dear said as she grabbed her glasses from her purse and smiled. She stood up and walked away with her head high. Before walking out she tapped Aurora on the shoulder. Aurora pulled her earphones out and looked back at Ma'Dear.

"See you later, pretty girl," Ma'Dear said with a big smile.

"Bye. Was nice meeting you," Aurora said, smiling from ear to ear as well. As Ma'Dear headed out, Aurora returned to the booth, rejoining her mom who seemed to be in deep thought.

"She was nice," Aurora said just before she put back in her earphones and focused on her phone.

"Yeah, baby. She was," Breeze dryly answered. Breeze then picked up her phone to call Mo. She had to see what was really going on and who this mystery woman was who popped up on her.

Mo drove wildly through the streets, gripping the steering wheel tightly. He had just left the Diamond Estate from talking with his Aunt Breeze. She explained to him everything that happened at the coffee shop. He took it as a threat rather than a plea for a truce. He felt disrespected and the fact that Ma'Dear had the audacity to confront his aunt had his blood boiling.

"Who this old bitch think she is? Pulling down on my family like that? Like I'm a game or something." Mo talked to himself as he maneuvered through the pothole infested streets on his way to Pork and Beans projects, the stomping ground of Ma'Dear. He looked in his rearview mirror to make sure that his team was keeping up with him. Joey and a few others were trailing him on their way to address the issue.

Finally, Mo pulled into the projects while his team laid back as instructed. He didn't want to draw any attention coming in. He knew that the P & B boys didn't play games, so he wanted to move smart. Just as he thought, Ma'Dear was in the middle of the garden on her knees, tending to her fruits and vegetables. He could spot her from afar because of her signature straw hat. He had gotten all of the inside information on her from a girl that he was dealing with who happened to be from these projects, so he knew just what to expect. Although he was aware that she was always being watched by her goons, he still had to address the issue head on.

As he parked, he began to take deep breaths to calm himself. He understood that he had a hot temper and he wanted to try his best to remain calm while letting her know that he was ready and willing to go to war over disrespect to anyone in his family. He looked down and saw the gun sitting on his lap. He slid it into his waist and pulled down his t-shirt, trying to conceal it as much as possible. He then casually stepped out of the car and made his way over to the garden. Kids were horse playing in the parking lot and a group of young girls where double-dutching while singing a song in unison. Mo's hair was wild and it blew in the wind as he walked towards Ma'Dear, passing the children in the process. He was an unfamiliar face, so he caught the attention of a lot of people and all eyes were on him. He made it to the garden and he stopped where the garden began. Ma'Dear's back was turned to him, so she didn't see him approaching.

"You Ma'Dear?" he asked, letting his presence be known. Ma'Dear paused her humming and answered without turning around.

"Who wants to know?" she asked.

"Mo Diamond," Mo answered, not hiding who he was.

"Aw...so you the one that like to shoot feet, right? she asked as she sat straight up and began to dust her hands off, shaking the access dirt from it. She took a deep breath and finally turned around to look at Mo. She stood up and slowly began to walk towards Mo, taking her gloves off in the process.

"Actually, I don't shoot feet at all. I shot him in his foot, but I was aiming for his dick. Since he has a problem with sticking it in the wrong places," Mo said, referring to Guy's nasty ways.

"How may I help you, young man?" Ma'Dear asked, not wanting to get into the small talk.

"Got word that my auntie got a surprise visit from you. Wanted to come and see what that was all about," Mo asked as he crossed his hands in front of him and slowly rocked back and forth, not taking the older woman for granted. He knew how deadly she was and he wasn't going to let the sweet face of hers fool him for one second.

"Just a little girl talk. Wanted to send a message to you, to see if we could kill the situation before it went any further," Ma'Dear said as she placed her hands on her hips and looked in Mo's eyes, trying to read him.

"Nah, it ain't too much to talk about on that situation. That's between me and homie. But, what me and you can talk about is doing some business," he said, using that opportunity to place some of his work in the Pork and Beans Projects. Just as quick as the words came out of Mo's mouth, Ma'Dear had begun to chuckle.

"Baby. We're doing just fine with what we have. You know what they say about having snakes in the garden. They will eventually bite you if you keep them around long enough," Ma'Dear said.

"You sure about that?" Mo asked, knowing that she was subliminally telling him something.

"Baby, I'm positive," she answered with certainty, leaving no guessing in her decision.

"Alright cool. Well check this out. I don't like uninvited guest and I'm pretty sure my auntie feels the same way. Let's not make that a habit. You never know what might happen if you do silly things like that," Mo said with a sinister smile on his face.

Ma'Dear paused and returned the smile. She was trying to decide whether to take off her hat or not. She knew that if she did, Mo would be surrounded within thirty seconds. But she was smarter than that. She knew what cloth Mo was cut from, so she decided to dig deeper.

"You came here alone?" Ma'Dear asked as she looked back at where Mo's car was parked.

"Now, you know better than that. You know them hittas close," Mo responded arrogantly.

"That's what I figured," Ma'Dear said as she turned back to

Mo and nodded her head slowly.

"I'll tell you what. I will leave that situation alone and not turn up the heat on your boys. In return, I just want you to shop with me. We can split it 50/50 and I'll sit them on you with no money up front. We can be like partners," Mo proposed again.

"Baby, I told you I'm good. You can find your way out. Make sure you walk around the garden," Ma'Dear said as she began to put on her gloves and turned her back to Mo.

She got on her knees and began humming as if Mo wasn't even there. Not until she heard water being poured did she turned around. She looked back and saw a slightly erect penis hanging from Mo's hand and he urinated on her dirt, smiling from ear to ear. He was so subtle with it, others didn't even notice, but she did. Ma'Dear was irate and clenched her jaws tightly at the blatant disrespect. She shook her head in disappointment, knowing that she would have to eventually kill Mo for his bad choice.

"You shouldn't have done that," Ma'Dear said in a low tone as she watched him smoothly put his dick back in his pants.

"Little water won't hurt," he said, entertaining himself. He walked around the garden and back to his car as Ma'Dear watched. She saw some of the boys on the stoop staring at her waiting for her to give a signal to light him up, however, kids were around playing, and she couldn't greenlight it. That was the beginning of something very bad to come, both Mo and Ma'Dear knew it.

CHAPTER 11

"I like monsters..." -Ashton

That thing taken care of?" Carter asked as he sat in the barber's chair, receiving an edge up as Mo, Joey, and Papi sat in chairs beside him.

"Ain't no thing," Mo replied. "I don't even know nothing worth discussing. That's how taken care of it is. I got a way to move them bibles."

Carter lifted his hand, signaling for the barber to stop cutting.

"Jimmy, can you give us a minute?" he asked.

"Yes sir, boss man, you the only client I came in for today. I'm on your time," he said. "I'll be in the back."

They waited for the old man to clear the room before they resumed the conversation.

"What's the move?" Carter asked.

"The nigga Ris turned over the tape in exchange for a partnership. We supply his parties."

"Where is the tape?" Papi asked.

"I said I took care of it," Mo said.

"Took care of it how?" Papi asked.

"We ain't into answering questions around here. We don't

report to you mu'fucka," Joey said, growing irritated. "You ain't the boss."

"Answer the question. This ain't a game. Ain't nobody walking down that 20 years if this goes bad but me, so my nigga, when a question is asked, I'ma need information. My name and my life is the one on the line," Carter said.

"It ain't on the line but it can be on the line my nigga. Any day just say the word," Joey said.

Carter scoffed. "Where you find this guy?" he asked. He was so unenthused. Unbothered. Unintimidated. Joey was a tough guy who felt the need to prove it every opportunity he got. Carter wasn't tough at all. At least not intentionally. He had no desire to hide his humanity behind bullshit creeds for the sake of appearances. He was human as fuck which meant people received different versions of him depending on his mood. Today he felt like rocking Joey's top. Disrespect had never been a trait he could vibe with.

"Chill, Joey. We all on the same team," Mo said.

The bell above the door rang, pulling their attention as Ashton walked inside.

The conversation ended as Mo stood, hiking up his pants as he bit his lip.

"You stalking a nigga?" Mo asked.

"Not here for you, actually," she said, smirking. "But you can return my property anytime."

Ashton walked right past him and stood in front of Carter.

"So this fresh cut is a good look on you," Ashton said. "Cleans you up a little. I like it."

"Glad it pleases you," he said. "You want to tell me how

you just pulling up on me out the blue? You following me? I'd like to know in advance if you're crazy."

Ashton laughed. "Mo posted your location on IG," she said, pulling out her phone and holding up the screen to show the picture of them smoking cigars in the closed shop. "I was in the area."

"Yeah you stalking me for sure," Carter said, winking at her. He was only half playing. It was pushy as fuck for her to pull up uninvited. He couldn't lie and say he didn't like it though.

"I just wanted to stop by and thank you for lunch," she said. "You haven't called so I didn't get a chance to."

"You haven't called me either," Carter said.

"Oh, is that how this works? We're both playing hard to get?" she asked.

"I ain't into games much. I see it. I like it. I get it," Carter answered.

"Come get it then cuz we both know you like it," she replied. Carter smiled. Her straight forwardness was refreshing, but also put him off. He didn't know how to dissect her confidence. It could be a defense mechanism or arrogance. Only time would tell. He stood and placed a hand to the small of her back, leading her out of the shop.

"Not gone lie I don't love the pull up," Carter said. Ashton was interrupting an important conversation. As he looked at her, he couldn't deny she was a sight for sore eyes. She was a beautiful fucking distraction. He had to give her that much.

"I can leave. I've never stayed where I wasn't wanted," she said.

"There's just a time and place," he said. "Neither of those things are here at the moment," he replied. "I'm not trying to be an asshole or nothing…"

"Just because you aren't trying to be an ass, doesn't mean you aren't, but it's cool," she said. Ashton turned on her stiletto heels. Carter felt like a bit bad, but he let her walk away. He had never entertained a woman before, not like this, not enough to allow her to show up in his life unannounced. It was a little extreme for her to show up without invitation thinking that would be acceptable. He hated that he was flattered. He scratched the top of his head and rubbed it in distress as he watched her climb in her car and drive away.

He walked back into the shop and Mo had resumed his cut.

"Yo that bitch pulled up on you cuz. That's red flags like a mu'fucka. No lie, I would fuck baby girl before cutting her loose," Mo said.

"You crazy as hell for sending her on her way," Joey agreed, snickering. The friendly banter had begun.

"That bet?" Carter said as he sat back in his barber's chair.

"The bet I'ma win?" Mo asked.

"It's off," Carter said.

"It's like that?" Mo said.

"Could be," Carter answered.

He might have sent her home, but she was still very much on his mind. Running through his thoughts because the vibe had been easy. He had thought of her a lot in the moments after she had left him actually. She didn't need to know that, however. Her stalking tendencies told him she had done the same.

"I'ma respect it," Mo said. "You might want to find out why somebody like her is carrying though. I pulled up on her after the pool party to let her know how to move with the information she knew, and baby pulled the heater on me. Surprised the shit out of me. I should have closed out that deal that night," he said, chuckling.

"She pulled a burner on you, bro?" Joey asked.

"Hell yeah. I took her pistol. I'll let you deal with returning it since you on another level with it, but my question is what's a girl like that carrying for in the first place?"

"Maybe it's for protection," Papi speculated. "A single woman, living in Miami. Wouldn't surprise me. It's actually quite smart."

"If it was for protection the serial numbers wouldn't be scratched off the side. She was strapped and the way she held that mu'fucka let me know she was prepared to use it if she had to. Be careful with that shit."

"Always," Carter replied.

Ashton looked in the mirror, gripping the sink as she waited for the phone to ring. She needed a better plan. Carter had seemed interested at first, but after the shade, he had given her at the shop she wasn't sure if she had done enough to pull him in. If she was unable to protect him from the inside, she would have to do it from afar.

She couldn't force Carter to like her. Perhaps they just weren't compatible. Her phone rang and Ashton answered quickly because Miamor wouldn't have much time to talk. The guards on Miamor's cell block would walk by every half hour so they had to chop it up quickly so that Miamor wouldn't be caught with contraband. Just having a cell phone on the inside could get her more time added on her dwindling sentence.

"Miamor," she answered.

"How is everything going?" Miamor asked, jumping right into business. "How's my son?"

"He's everything you said he would be. I've sent you pictures. I snuck and took pictures of him. Had me sitting at a bar by myself looking pathetic, but I stuck around long enough to get those."

Ashton thought of telling Miamor about the fight Carter had been in, but there was nothing Miamor could do from inside, and Ashton didn't want to add to her distress. There was nothing worse than overthinking about something you couldn't change. Miamor couldn't do shit about it so Ashton wasn't going to say shit about it.

"I saw. It's like I'm staring at a ghost," Miamor stated.

"I don't know if I can be in his life the way you want me to. He ain't feeling me like that," Ashton admitted. "I can protect him without being up on him."

"You can't. His father died when I wasn't up on him. Whenever I was there, he was safe. I should have been there. If I had just been there..." Miamor took a deep breath. "You protect your man from the inside and without acknowledgment. The woman behind the man. Just because Estes is no longer a threat doesn't mean my son is safe. He'll never be safe in Miami. Tell me about the steroids."

"He didn't take those. I don't know how the tests came back dirty but that's not him. He loves boxing too much to risk his entire career. It's not in his character," Ashton said.

"That's a lot of defending for someone who says they're not getting anywhere," Miamor said.

A knock on the door interrupted Ashton's response and when she pulled open the door her mouth fell open in surprise.

"You ain't the only one who know how to pop up," Carter said.

"What are you doing here?" Ashton asked.

"Fixing a mistake. My bad about earlier. I was harsh with you. It's been a long couple of days," he said.

"Is that my son?" Miamor asked.

"Yeah," Ashton whispered. "I've got to go."

"He likes you. I can hear it. I grew his heart inside me. I know him."

Click

Miamor hung up and Ashton looked at Carter.

"You gone invite me in?" he asked.

"No. I'm not welcoming to people who aren't welcoming to me," Ashton said. "Get off my doorstep, Carter."

Ashton attempted to close the door, but Carter's sneaker stopped it.

She huffed as he pushed it back open.

"We can skip the fighting. I don't wanna do that," he said. "It's a little dramatic for my taste."

"Your taste is not my concern," she replied. "I was feeling you a little bit. Now I'm not. I don't really let a nigga play me twice. When I pulled up your energy was different. You were around your homeboys and I guess you were playing it cool, acting uninterested or something. Well, now I'm really not. I don't play bullshit games like that."

"What you expect from me? We hang out one time and all of a sudden you pulling up like you're my girl. Tracking me down on I.G. Shit screams fucking fatal attraction," he said. "I'm a high-profile athlete. I have to move a certain way."

"Got it," she said. "Well make sure you float like a butterfly and sting like a bee your ass off my store step," she stated.

She prayed she wasn't going to hard. Carter was a man who didn't like a girl who tried too hard. She hadn't realized that before, but she did now.

He likes to work for it. Easy bores him. It's why he didn't smash one of the chicks from the pool party.

Carter dead panned on her and then removed her gun, the one Mo had confiscated and handed it to her. He then turned without saying another word and left as she had requested. She was certain he had never been turned down a day in his fine ass life. She was indeed the first to ever deny him and she knew it would only put the ball in her court.

Meet me at the club. 911.

Ashton awoke to the text from Ris and she frowned as she crawled out of bed. She knew better than to text anything further. 911 meant face to face. She showered and dressed quickly, effortlessly throwing her hair into a top knot and opting for short jean shorts and an *Off White* sleeveless sweatshirt that showed off her entire side. She wore a bikini top and bottom beneath because if she was going to South Beach to meet Ris, she was going to enjoy the ocean afterward. She had been free too long without feeling truly free. She wanted to feel the water wash up on her toes.

She slid into Hermes slides and grabbed her keys. Traffic made the drive longer than usual and parking was horrendous. By the time she arrived, she was more than frustrated. She huffed as she gave the valet her keys and a hundred-dollar tip.

"Keep me out front. I hate waiting when its time to leave," she said.

Ashton didn't wait for a response. Her heels clicked against the concrete as she made her way inside.

"What up Ash?" one of Ris' goons greeted. "When you gone let a nigga get on?"

"You do too much, Juice. You'd have me out here slitting tires and bleaching your good clothes," she said as she stopped to give him a quick hug.

"A nigga wouldn't even get mad at you, either. Swear to God," Juice said. His Suge stature engulfed her but he only kept her for a minute. "Smell good than a motherfucka."

177

"Gone Juice before I climb that tree," she said, laughing as she hit his shoulder and wiggled out of his grasp as she continued up the stairs.

"Always knocking niggas off they square. Juice you even check her?" Ris asked, shaking his head.

"Felt up all the good parts," Juice said. "She good."

"Come on up," Ris said.

Ashton took the stairs to the top and when she saw Carter and Mo sitting at a table, she halted.

"We just need to talk. Make sure everybody's on the same page," Ris said.

Ashton's gut tightened. "What is this?"

"Sit down Ash. You know I got you," Ris said.

"I got me too so somebody better start talking or I'm walking up out of here."

"We just need to know that you're in line. What you saw is a liability to everybody."

"What I saw? The whole fucking room saw it. There were at least fifteen people in that penthouse," she hissed.

"And you're the only one still breathing," Mo said.

"We're trying to keep it that way. Sit down," Carter added.

How stupid she had been finessed into a set up.

"Trust me," Ris said. "I ain't never pulled no snake shit on you."

Ashton blew out a breath of frustration and then stormed over to the table.

"Have a seat," Carter said.

Ashton pulled out her chair and sat down.

"You were on the phone with somebody yesterday when I

pulled up. I heard my name on the other end of the phone. Was it a cop?"

"A what?" she asked, brow dipping in confusion. "I don't fuck with the police. It was my fucking sister. I was telling her about the rude ass nigga who had just curved me. When you knocked on my door uninvited, might I add, she asked 'is that him?' That's what you heard. Ris this is nuts you know me. When have you ever known me to be anything less than honorable?"

"Never, I told them that. I vouch for her on any given day of the week. I met Ash years ago in Houston when I was promoting heavy out that way."

Ashton grimaced because Ris was unknowingly doing too much. Giving out information that she didn't normally share. People only got her in the present. Details of her past were never a part of the package. Just the here, the now, the why. It kept her safe, kept her anonymous.

"We want to make sure it stays that way," Mo said as he leaned down and reached under his chair, pulling out an MCM duffel bag. He removed two large plastic wrapped piles of money and placed them on top of the table. "For being solid."

Ashton looked at the money and then lifted eyes to Carter. "Keep your money, just refund me my time because you were a waste of it," she said. Ashton was beginning to think that Carter had only taken her to lunch to feel her out and it was a blow to her ego like none other.

Ashton stood. "Are we done?" she asked.

"Yeah Ash, you all good," Ris said.

She made her exit and was absolutely mortified when both men let her. Neither Carter nor Mo stopped her. She had just known that she would have leverage with one of them. She floated out of the door with Miamor on her mind. Perhaps there was no job present to be done. No protection needed. Miamor had been locked up for a long time. The streets of Miami had changed a lot since the days of the Murder Mamas. The Diamonds were legendary, but old school, no one was checking for them these days. Although Mo was getting money there was no present threat. Maybe Miamor's streets sense was off. Maybe it was for nothing. She had half a mind to leave Miami altogether.

Ashton pushed out of the nightclub and when she got to valet, she handed the man her ticket. She couldn't wait to get out of there. She hated that Carter's cologne lingered in her nose. He smelled amazing and looked even better. Ashton just wanted to run her tongue across the tattoos on his neck. There was so much mystery about him. Mo was easy to figure out. Hood nigga with a hood creed and probably good, hood dick to match. A paradox that seemed impossible to figure out. Moody and honest. He seemed like he was from the bottom, but he wasn't super hood, not from the ghetto like her, but he had seen some things, he knew struggle. Forward and frank. Most of all observant. Carter was a different type of man.

"I'm sorry your car isn't available at the moment," the valet said.

"What the hell does that mean? I asked you to keep it upfront," she said, frowning in confusion.

"He asked me to retain the keys, ma'am," he said.

Ashton turned to see Carter exit the club.

"Nigga, if you don't get my car," she threatened.

"Thanks man," Carter said, tipping the valet even more.

"Where is my car? What are you doing?" Ashton asked.

"Make a little time for me?" he asked without looking at her.

Ashton was floored. Carter was so up and down. Hot and cold. She couldn't figure out if he was interested or turned off. He opened the passenger door for her, and Ashton glared at him before sliding inside. He shut the door and then rolled down the window. "Just tell me now. Are you bipolar or something because I swear you be switching up," she said.

He bit his bottom lip. The fucking sexiest lip bite she had ever seen. Ashton twisted her lips and shook her head.

"You can get out if I make you uncomfortable," he said. "But you ride out with me and I promise you won't regret it."

Ashton turned in her seat and rolled up the window, crossing her arms stubbornly across her chest.

"Off and on ass nigga," she mumbled as he joined her, sliding behind the wheel.

"Where are we going?" she asked.

"You ask a lot of questions," he answered.

"You evade a lot of questions."

He pulled out into traffic and they rode in silence until they arrived in the most unexpected of place.

"A vegetable farm?" she asked.

"I only eat fresh produce," he said. "It all affects how my body works. How I fight depends on it."

181

"You plan on fighting today?" she asked.

"Affects how I fuck too," he replied.

Ashton's face burned red and she couldn't even help the smile that spread across her face.

"And you plan on doing that today?" she asked, laughter in her tone.

"Come on, man, come help me out," he said, smirking as he climbed out of the car.

Ashton got out and Carter led her through the fields. They were the only ones there besides an aging white man in overalls who was headed their way.

"Champ," the man greeted as he held out his hand for a shake.

"Knaus. Good to see you again," Carter greeted.

"You normally come alone. Who is this pretty young lady?" the old man asked.

"Ashton," she greeted, extending her hand, which he captured and then kissed.

"Nice to meet you. I'm Mr. Knaus," he said. "You know the lay of the place. Since you have company, I'll set up with some nice refreshments when you're done."

"Appreciate you, Knaus," Carter said. He led Ashton through the vegetable garden.

"You've got to fill it up. The reddest ones are ripe. Look out for mold though. The leaves should be real green too," Carter instructed.

Ashton picked up a strawberry. "Is this one good?" she asked.

He shook his head. "Nah that one ain't ripe enough. It's still got some white on it."

He bent down to pick one for himself. He fetched a hose that was lying in the dirt nearby and sprayed it. He held it up to her mouth.

Ashton looked at him hesitantly and then opened and bit the strawberry. She was surprised at how sweet it was. She took a second nibble and then a third, then she bit his thumb gently as he stared down at her. She could practically hear her heartbeat. This was what she was talking about. His moods. The constant switch of them. She was exhausted and exhilarated from being in his presence all at the same time.

"It's better than anything I've ever tasted," she said. "I'll never want a store bought one again if I eat too many of these."

He chuckled. "Yeah, you couldn't pay me to eat no store-bought shit. My bad about the bullshit. It ain't how I want you to view me. Like a monster."

"I like monsters," she replied.

She saw the amusement in his eyes. He was pleased with her. Intrigued even.

"You're dangerous. Like a sharp cliff around a curve," he said. His mind went to the cliffs that filled the mountains in the D.R.

"I'm dangerous? I'm not the one with hands strong enough to take a man's life with one blow," she said.

"Does that scare you?" Carter asked.

"For some reason, nothing about you scares me. Except rejection."

"I reject everybody. Ain't too good at keeping people close. Estes was it. My boxing coach, but he was like a grandfather to me. My own mama and daddy left me behind so since then it's been fuck everything," Carter explained.

"That's a hard sentiment to get around," Ashton admitted. "I'm not looking for a damaged ass man. Like if it's going to be fuck me too, we can stop before we start."

"I feel that, but since the day we met, I can't get my mind off fucking you. That's all I want to do is fuck you," Carter stated.

Ashton's body protested. A full-on riot started fires in her heart as her pussy clenched.

"That's bold, like you're bold as fuck right now," she said, blushing and laughing as he wrapped a hand around her waist, snatching her closer to him and burying his face in the crook of her neck.

"Real shit. I want to do that. I want to know you like that," he whispered. He spoke different because he was different. Raised on the island amongst the citizens of the Dominican Republic he had learned to be very forward. Mannish even. Carter had much restraint but when he decided he wanted something he went after it aggressively.

The air from his words aroused her ear and her nipples hardened as she giggled.

"Oh, do you?" she asked.

"Blood racing for it," he answered. "Your vibe asking for it. I don't know how long I'ma be able to act like a gentleman with you either."

"Being a gentleman is overrated," Ashton said, grabbing his hand. She guided it down the front of her shorts, bypassing that bikini bottom as she stared in his eyes.

"You're trouble," he smirked.

"The best type," she gasped as her eyes closed slowly and he took her clit for a spin. It was swollen and meaty. Wet as fuck as he played in her pond as she bit her lip. Her forehead pinched.

"Hey! You two fill those baskets, yet?" Knaus' voice caused Ashton to pull in a sharp breath as Carter removed his hand.

"Yeah, we got some pretty good ones!" Carter shouted. He grabbed her hand and Ashton blushed as they walked side by side back toward the front.

When they entered the building, Ashton smiled. "This is really cute!" she exclaimed.

Knaus had set up a small picnic by the window. Strawberry pie and homemade strawberry lemonade sat on the table as well a bottle of wine with fresh cut strawberries, meats, and cheese.

"We treat the pretty ladies nice at Knaus Farms," he said.

"You sure do!" Ashton laughed. "You could teach this one a thing or two."

"No, you're in good hands. Best man I know here. A gentle giant. Don't let the guy in the ring fool you," Mr. Knaus said, playfully sparring with Carter.

"You can set your things there," Mr. Knaus instructed.

"We aren't sitting here?" Ashton asked.

"No, no, no," Mr. Knaus said.

"We get to take the pie home, but not without making one to replace it first," Carter explained.

"Really? Oh, I'm a terrible baker," Ashton said, waving her

hands, opposing. "Trust me. You don't want me to make any type of pie."

"I'll help you, no worries," Mr. Knaus said.

Ashton reluctantly followed Mr. Knaus into the kitchen with Carter following behind.

All of their supplies were already set up.

Ashton felt giddy.

"Did you plan this?" she asked.

Carter shook his head. "Nah," he said. "This is all Knaus."

Ashton and Carter washed their hands and then put on the aprons that awaited them. Carter did his first before lifting Ashton's over her lead.

"Is this considered our first date?" she asked. "Or would it be a second date?"

"When I take you on a date, you won't have to ask if you're on one," he said.

She smiled and turned around so he could tie her apron. He stood behind her and wrapped his arms around her and reached for the flour that was on the countertop.

"Flour, water, salt, butter," he said.

"You've made this before?" she asked.

"Many times," he answered. "Knaus taught me the first time Estes brought me to Miami when I was a kid."

"Long time ago," Knaus said. "It's a shame what happened to him. God rest my good friend's soul. A good man he was." Knaus grew visibly quiet. The sound of the bell announced the entrance of another patron. "I'll leave you to it. You're in good hands. He knows the recipe better than me."

When they were alone Carter stepped closer to her, looking over her shoulder. "Mix them together to make the crust."

He kissed the back of her neck as Ashton began to combine the ingredients.

"Mix the butter in slow, in small chunks and then add a little water," he said.

"You really know what you're doing," she said, completely shocked.

He kissed her neck again. Ashton felt that kiss resonate throughout her body and she turned to him.

He lifted her onto the countertop and occupied the space between her thighs as he stole her tongue. Long and deep he kissed her. Her hands around his neck, his hands planted on the sides of her hips, eyes closed. It felt incredible. When he pulled back, he rested his forehead to hers.

"Your kisses feel like sex," she panted, slightly dizzy.

"Sex is a bit better," he said with laughter in his tone. "If that's all the thrill a nigga been giving you, you've been fucking with the wrong niggas."

Ashton laughed. "Clearly," she agreed "You gonna finish showing me how to make this pie?" she asked.

He nodded and stepped back, opting to move around the island.

"Why are you all the way over there?" she asked.

"You don't want me on that side with you," he said, face pulling up as he fought a leer.

"You and Ris are close. He vouches for you. How long y'all been rocking?" Carter asked.

187

"A while. He's just my homeboy. Met him on the scene years back," she said keeping it vague.

"You came through his spot dolo?" he observed.

"There's something wrong with that?" she asked.

"Nah, I just noticed."

"I don't have many friends. I got a big family, so I never needed a lot of friends. My sisters were enough." She regretted it as soon as she said it. She had given him too many details.

"How many sisters?" he asked.

"Three," she answered. "They don't live here. We haven't talked for a while." Her voice grew sad at that. "We fell out a few years ago and I just don't know how to put it back together. I miss them though. I'm the baby. I need my big sisters sometimes." The vulnerability in a girl who had been nothing but tough as nails called to him. He knew about need. There had been a time when he had needed people. His mother at a point in time. His father for as long as he could remember. His aunt Breeze. Mo right after they had been separated. He had trained himself to erase the need for them all. "I don't really want to talk about family," she said as she blended the dough.

"Okay now what?" she asked.

Carter took the bowl and walked it to the refrigerator and retrieved a dough package that had been previously chilled.

"Now we leave that one for the next person and take one of these," he explained.

Carter took her through the steps to the homemade recipe until they had crafted a perfect pie.

"Let me guess. We leave this one to cool and you're going to pull one out of the fridge?" Ashton asked.

Carter shook his head. "Nah, we get to take this one home," Carter said.

"Which home? Mine or yours?" she asked.

"Whichever one we gone wake up in tomorrow," Carter stated.

"Oh, you get real fresh. You're too much." The consent was in her tone and the red hue that dusted her cheeks as she blushed.

"I'm not trying to assume so if that's not where this is headed just say so. I can drop you back to your car and keep it light, but if it's up to me..."

He paused.

Ashton waited with bated breath. It was up to him because she was with it. Wherever he wanted to take this was where it would go.

"It's up to you."

The kitchen door swung open. "Oh, I'm so sorry. We got busy, busy, busy, but how's my favorite couple?"

"We're all done," Ashton said, smiling.

"Oh good. I hope you will join us again soon, Ms. Ashton," Mr. Knaus said.

"If I'm invited, I'll be here," she said.

Mr. Knaus bagged them up and sent them on their way. The conversation was easier, simpler, on the way home as Ashton took a fork to the whole pie. To her surprise, Carter didn't take one bite.

"Natural sugar only during training," he said.

"What if they don't let you back in, Carter? Have you thought about what your life looks like after boxing?"

"I don't want to have to think about it. If I do my part, stay healthy, stay active, when the truth comes out it'll be like no time has passed. I just have to be ready. I'm already making an exception to my lifestyle with you. I'm not normally this undisciplined."

"So, you don't date?" Ashton asked.

"We aren't dating," Carter said.

"You don't fuck?" she corrected.

"We ain't doing that either," Carter replied.

"You pull over this car and we can change that," Ashton answered as a mischievous smile brightened her face.

The ball was in his court. To her surprise, he didn't pull over. He simply leaned back in his seat and gripped the steering wheel with one hand as he finessed his chin between two pinched fingers.

"You always been like that? A do what you want, say what you want, no matter what anybody thinks type?" he asked.

"I care what you think," Ashton said, not looking at him but the road as it passed them by at 80 mph. "Not many people though, but for some reason, I'd love to be a fly on the wall of your mind when it comes to me."

"You shouldn't," he shot back. "I'm nobody's judge."

"Your place is amazing," Ashton said as she entered Carter's oceanside villa. "Are you on the water?"

Carter walked through his home turning on lights.

"Yeah, it's a dock on the back for the yacht," he said.

"You have a yacht?" she asked.

"Estes had a yacht," Carter corrected. "Somehow, I inherited all this."

"It's beautiful," Ashton complimented.

"It's a lot for one person. I don't stay here often. I usually post up at the Mandarin," he explained.

"So why here tonight?" she asked.

"Seemed like your speed."

She smiled and he turned to walk through the rest of the house, headed toward the back. She followed without invitation.

He led the way to the backyard. The pool sparkled as the blue aqua lights lit up the bottom. The moon spied over them and made the ripples in the ocean water ahead seem mystical.

"This is definitely my speed," she said. "It's incredible out here. Who chooses a hotel over this?"

Carter chuckled and took a seat in one of the oversized clamshell chairs.

"The hotel has security, a full gym, and chefs. Here it's just me. It's easier to train from the hotel. This house gets too quiet sometimes. The silence is loud. Estes is dead. I had to get rid of my man, Papi. It's just too big."

Ashton sat beside him.

"Well why don't we make a little bit of noise?" she asked.

Ashton leaned into Carter slowly and he captured her neck with one hand and squeezed as he pulled her in. As soon as her lips touched his she felt what she had heard Miamor describe for years. Chemistry. Undeniable spark. Carter was a chip off his father's block. He kissed her lips and her body responded. Ashton stood, reluctantly breaking their kiss. She unbuttoned her shorts and came out of her top revealing the bikini beneath. She pulled at the strings of that too. She tossed the pieces at him and Carter tried his hardest not to blush. She was beautiful. Somehow slim and thick, all at the same time. Her curves were unexpected. The sea air drifted in off the ocean and kissed her nipples, pulling them to attention.

"What you doing, man?" he asked with laughter.

"Being really loud," Ashton said. She ran toward the pool and screamed as she jumped in, butt ass naked.

She came up moments later, treading water and screaming at the top of her lungs.

"Wooo!"

He stood on the edge.

He came out of his clothes and Ashton lifted her hands, clapping in appreciation.

"Boy you working with something," she teased as she gave her stamp of approval. He slid into the pool, but kept his distance as he threw his arms over the edge of the pool. Ashton went to him and he pulled her in with one hand around her waist.

"You feel real different," he said as he stared down at her. "I don't know if that's good or bad."

Ashton didn't want to answer that. Instead, she kissed him again only this time he pulled her thighs around his waist and walked her over to the stairs of the pool. He carried her out effortlessly and into the freezing cold house. He had no time to take it upstairs. The dining table would have to do. He turned her around, bending her over as he placed one of her legs on the table, while the other balanced on the floor. She could feel how much he wanted her. That thang pressed against her ass. Hot. Ready. The only warm thing in the entire house because the air was on freeze.

"I don't have condoms here, Ashton," he said.

The moment almost mirrored one that his father had with his mother. These two young souls had a choice. To press STOP or GO. Ashton turned around faced him.

"So do we press pause? Maybe we should," she panted. "Maybe we should call it a night."

He nodded and Ashton went to retrieve their clothes. They dressed in silence and as she listened to the sounds of the night bounce off all these walls; she completely understood what he meant about the silence being loud.

"I have to go back to get my car," she said.

"I'll have it brought to you tomorrow morning. It's too late for you to be all over the city tonight," he said.

"I'm a big girl," Ashton protested. "Don't go getting all extra on me."

"No extras, just making sure you make it to the crib," Carter said.

She loved it. His concern. She hadn't felt like someone cared enough to worry about her in a long time.

They walked to his car and to her surprise they laughed and talked the entire way to her place. When they arrived, he pulled into the parking garage at her building. He put the car in park and Ashton turned to him. Leaning over the armrest, she put one hand to his cheek and kissed him. Carter tasted like an orgasm. Ashton climbed over into his lap, straddling him awkwardly as he placed a hand to the small of her back.

"I have condoms," she whispered.

They paused, panting as she pressed her face to his. They were considering things. Did they want this to go to the next level? Their bodies said yes, but did their hearts comply? Was it a good idea? He gripped the back of her neck and the way he massaged there in that one place at the base of her neck, like he was trying to rub anything bad that had happened to her away, made Ashton close her eyes.

"I like this," she whispered.

"I don't," he said. And he didn't. He didn't like the pit in his stomach when she was close to him. Didn't like that he hadn't thought about training all day. He didn't like that she made him want to cut into a slice of pie and defy the years' worth of clean eating he followed to make sure his body was a well-oiled machine. Most of all he hated that when he remembered that he didn't have protection, he wanted to fuck her anyway. Even now in this car, he couldn't even wait to get upstairs. His dick pressed into her body, the only thing that separated them was clothes.

"You will," she said, kissing him again. "I'ma make sure you love it. After tonight you won't want to live without it." Ashton reached down, feeling his hardness and then she popped open the door.

The elevator was private enough. As soon as the doors closed, she was unbuttoning his jeans, freeing what she knew was amazing. She didn't know how, she just knew. Thick and long. Shorty had a head on that thing, and she couldn't help but to go to her knees to make introductions. She went down as the elevator went up and Carter groaned, resting his head against the wall as his hand guided her pace.

The ding announcing her floor brought her to her feet and she led the way to her penthouse, rummaging for keys as he French kissed the back of her neck and slid his hands in the front of her shorts. She almost wanted to stay locked out it felt so good, but instead she pushed forward into the dark condo. As she walked forward the string to her top was captured between his hands, it unraveled, falling to the floor. She shimmied out of her shorts and kept walking toward her bedroom without ever glancing back.

Carter stood in the middle of her living room. He second guessed only for a moment before following behind her.

By the time he made it to the bedroom, Ashton was sitting on the edge of the bed, legs open, the skin of her fresh wax looked like a delicacy, and her back arched as she used her middle finger to rotate her clit.

She was motherfucking perfection. There was nothing like a woman comfortable in her own skin. Ashton and all her flaws. A real body in a land of plastic was enticing as fuck and when she stuck that same middle finger up at him, flicking him off before curling it.

Nigga fuck all that shit you thinking and come here.

He knew what it meant. His dick jumped. She was a

firecracker. She knew what she wanted, and he wasn't leaving before giving it to her. She reached in her nightstand and held up a condom and Carter peeled out of his clothes.

Ashton's stomach tensed as she watched him bite open the foil and roll it on himself. It wasn't the size of his dick that called to her most. Although it was impressive. Pretty as hell. A lighter color than his brown skin with a fat head that she knew would knock on every wall. It was his lip bite as he looked down at his dick. It was the way he used both hands to roll it up his girth. It was the way it hung heavily in midair, bouncing, lunging for her. He knew he was about to tear that pussy up and so did she.

He came down onto the bed, hovering over her and robbing Ashton of all her kisses. She put her common sense right in the bag with them. Her thighs butterflied and he put a hand around her waist, pulling her into his body.

Years. It had been years since Ashton had gotten some dick and even then, it had been childish dick. She had been super young, and it had been bad. She hadn't even orgasmed.

Carter put a blessing in her soul as he knocked down her door, knocking that bitch off the hinges, in fact, as he explored her deep end. Either she was shallow, or he was extra-long because he was tearing her up. Him on both knees, her legs over his shoulders, his hands on her waist pulling her in... pounding her, stretching her out.

"Oh my God," she moaned as she lifted her hands above her head. He used one hand to play with it, thumbing her kitty with quick strokes. It was so tender that she screamed his name.

196

"Damn," he groaned as he slowed and deepened his rhythm. His full lips devoured hers and suddenly he pulled out, going south, until he kissed her pussy, sucking her clit into his mouth so hard that Ashton gripped his head.

"CARTER!"

He sat up, smacked her ass and Ashton turned over. Titties to the sheets, hands behind her like he was about to arrest her ass. He might as well had called her a shrink now because when he slid in Ashton went crazy. She felt dick in her stomach he was hitting it so good. There was no way Carter was as disciplined as he claimed. Men who served dick like this had hoes. He took it out every few strokes and beat up her clit with his tip. It felt so good. Euphoria. Like everything any nigga before him had ever done to her body had been a joke.

"This pussy good baby," he whispered. He spent forty-five minutes putting in work, taking her right to the edge so many times she lost count but he never let her go all the way. It was torture. Sweet torture, waiting for her pussy to explode.

"Fuckkkk," he groaned. Carter flooded her. He didn't feel shit but bliss. Not a condom, not a care in the world that it had broken, just the warmth of her as she contracted around him and the sting as she drug long nails through his back as she came too.

He rested on his elbows, covering her, still inside her as his manhood retreated and their hearts steadied.

"I think the condom broke," he whispered.

"Honestly, right now, I don't even care."

197

He laughed and Ashton found herself falling into a comfortable titter as she covered her face with her hands.

"That was amazing. I'd be your baby mama if that's what it comes with," she said, blushing.

He scoffed and climbed out of bed. "You mind if I shower before I break out?" he asked.

"You're leaving?" she was stunned.

"Discipline," he said. "A part of that is knowing when enough is enough."

He grabbed up his clothes and Ashton pointed to the hallway. "Bathroom's on the left."

Before he walked out, she called him. "Carter?"

He turned to look at her.

"It's enough," she said. "So be as disciplined as you want but know that I have absolutely none."

He stood there, staring at her as if he were weighing his options. He walked back over to the bed where Ashton sat, Indian style. He pulled her chin up as he leaned over to kiss her.

"This is a mistake," he said.

"Then why did you walk back over here?" she asked.

"Because it ain't enough for me either," he said. He sat on the edge of her bed and leaned over onto his knees, rubbing the top of his head like he was carrying the heaviest burden. Maybe this was a burden. Maybe love would be. Maybe trust should be. Whatever it was it was too late to undo it. Ashton might have been planted there, but unexpectedly, she liked it. He felt like he had never been loved before. He kissed her like he had never kissed before. Touched her like it was forbidden. She climbed across the bed and sat next to him, leaning her head on his shoulder.

"There's no pressure from me to get it wrong. Even if it goes wrong it'll be worth the moment," she said. "I just want what's in front of us. Today, right now. Each moment for whatever we make of it."

"That's good. I'm not trying to sell no dreams. With my career, ain't no telling where I'ma be in six months. Ain't no telling what I'ma be doing in two weeks. I've never been good with attachments. Today. Right now. That's all I can guarantee," he said. Another kiss. "That don't mean I'm on no bullshit though, just prefer to keep shit light. As long as we both understand that, nobody gets hurt."

"Agreed."

CHAPTER 12

"It's like the graveyard throwing a party for all the real niggas…" -Mo

Breeze sat on her plush, comfortable couch, as the fireplace provided the scarce lighting for the room. She had mixed feelings about her family's house. On one hand, she had great memories, growing up in the mansion, but on the other, every nook and corner reminded her of a deceased family member. She sipped a glass of sweet red wine as she closed her eyes and grooved to the sounds of chilled R&B. She was in her feelings that night because it was the eve of her father's birthday and she had almost forgotten. Slight guilt made her sad, however, the thought of him spoiling her as a young girl made her smile. He would always treat her like a princess, giving her all the love, attention, and anything material that she desired. She smiled as a tear ran down her face, thinking about how both of her parents were gone and leaving her as the last of the originals standing. She lost her brothers to the game as well and her life was that of trials and tribulations. She swayed back and forth as she felt the words of the song, feeling that it was speaking directly to her soul. Beyonce's *Just like my Daddy* was pumping out of her home speaker and Breeze was vibing thinking about the one and only Carter Diamond.

I want
My unborn son
To be like my daddy
I want my husband to be like my daddy
There is no one else like my daddy
And I thank you (thank you)

As Breeze was vibing, she saw Aurora coming down the porcelain stairs and she quickly smeared away her tears. She didn't want her daughter to see her crying. She sniffed, wiped her face, and ran her hand through her hair quickly. She gathered herself and smiled as the very moment Aurora reached the bottom stair.

"Hey beautiful, girl," Breeze said, putting on a forced smile, attempting to mask her sorrow.

"Hey, ma," Aurora gleefully answered. She wore comfortable sweats and a simple jean jacket. She had a book bag draped over her shoulders and big gold bamboo earrings on. Aurora smiled and walked over to the couch and fireplace where her mom was sitting.

"Hey, can I go over Christy's? We were going to chill and watch some movies," Aurora asked.

"Christy?" Breeze answered, not being too familiar with the name.

"Yeah, the girl from the mall? She's pretty cool. We've

been talking on Snapchat and Facebook ever since then. She doesn't live far at all."

Breeze needed to be by herself. Aurora's request was right on time. Breeze knew that she needed to cry, so her baby being away for a few hours was just what the doctor ordered.

"I'm glad you're meeting new friends. Do you need me to take you over there?" Breeze replied.

"No, it's okay. Her mom let her use the car to pick me up. She should be pulling up any second now," Aurora replied as she looked down at her phone.

"Okay, well make sure you don't stay out too late. Tomorrow morning we are going to visit the cemetery to tell your grandfather happy birthday," Breeze said just before she took another sip of wine.

"I won't, ma. I'll be back before curfew," Aurora assured. Her phone buzzed and she looked down and smiled. She then rushed over to Breeze on the couch and gave her hug and a quick peck on the cheek.

"Okay, ma. She's here. Love you!" said Aurora.

"Love you too, baby," Breeze whispered as she hugged her daughter tightly. Breeze felt grateful to have her because everyone else was dead or gone. She watched as Aurora hurried out and noticed she had the book bag on her back.

"What's the bag for?" she quizzed.

"Oh. We're going to do each other's makeup and post some TikToks," Aurora answered, referring to a popular social media platform. "Bye!" Aurora yelled as she quickly headed out, leaving Breeze home alone to grieve. Breeze returned to her vibing session and grabbed the remote, turning her speaker volume up all the way. She raised her glass and smiled, feeling tipsy.

"Diamonds are forever," she said, repeating a line that her father would always say. She pulled out her phone and started a group text, contacting Mo and Carter. She wanted them to meet her at the cemetery so they could pay homage to the man who started it all.

Just outside of the house, a car sat waiting. Aurora hopped in and quickly began to take her clothes off.

"Hey Christy," she said as she continued to get undressed.

"Hey girl," Christy responded as she watched her friend strip down to her panties and begin to rummage through her book bag that sat at her feet. As Christy slowly pulled out the driveway, Aurora began to give her instructions for the night.

"Thanks for coming," Aurora said. Christy was a convenient excuse to see Guy again. The last thing she wanted to do was for her mom to find out that she was seeing someone older.

"I got you covered. Don't worry girl," Christy affirmed. Aurora slipped on a tube black dress that hugged her body so tightly, it looked like it was spray painted on. She popped the rubber band, causing her hair to fall down her back. She ran her fingers through it and pulled down the visor mirror to give herself a glance over. She reached into her bag and pulled out some red lipstick. She began to apply it, running it smoothly across her lips, and puckering them. She wanted to make sure it was applied evenly. She smooched and smiled as she looked at herself in the mirror. She was on her way to Guy's house so they could watch a movie and chill. He promised her that he would be a complete gentleman. After days of sweet talking and late-night text, he got her to agree to come over to his place. Aurora's nose was wide open, and Guy was making love to her mind, slowly grooming her to open all the way up for him.

Carter drove down the highway in his drop top Porsche doing nearly eighty miles per hour. The cocaine white vehicle was one of the only things he had to show his hard work instead of the ring. His mind was racing, thinking about finding out that he was banned. He keep thinking about how drugs got into his system. He had never touched a drug and was very conscious of what he put inside of his body. He just couldn't wrap his mind around it.

"This shit don't make sense," he said as he gripped the steering wheel tightly as he gradually applied pressure to the gas pedal. He glanced down at the speedometer and he was creeping north of 100 miles per hour as he switched lanes on the four-lane highway. He was en route to an address Mo had texted him. Mo had hit him randomly, promising him he had an answer to the steroid debacle. Carter was desperate at that point to get to some type of resolution. Just at the snap of a finger, his whole life was swept from underneath him. One day boxing was his entire life and in the blink of an eye…he didn't know what was next. Thoughts of how it happened began to run through his mind. He questioned Papi for days, asking him to recount his steps that morning when prepping his daily vitamins. Over a dozen times, Papi explained that he did everything as he had been doing for years. He swore to the heavens that he didn't make a mistake by giving him steroids. Papi went to the same natural vitamin store monthly for Carter's supplements and administered it to him before every workout.

"What the fuck is going on? Gotta be some shit in the game somewhere," Carter said to himself as he followed the GPS directions and pulled onto the exit on the highway. Carter began to think about potential invisible enemies. This was something that Estes had always warned him about and expressed that those kinds were the worst. He compared it to fighting in the ring with a blindfold, which made perfect sense. Carter's mind began to think about possible enemies within the boxing commission. Little did he know, that the problem was much closer than he could imagine.

A few minutes later, Carter was at the back door of the trap house that Joey and Mo were in. They had been there for hours prepping the dope for distribution. Inside the small house, Mo and Joey sat at the kitchen table. Bricks of cocaine were stacked in multiple rows; all of them were saran wrapped and had a snake stamps square in the middle. Mo smiled as his dreams were unfolding in front of his eyes. He sat at the table as his snake maneuvered around his back, neck, and shoulders. Mo was in awe and he was ready to step into what his destiny called for.

"How is this nigga going to turn down all of this? This is the key to everything a nigga would ever want in life. It's right here, Joey," Mo said as he leaned back and stretched his legs out. He raised his hands over his head and yawned.

Glancing over at the clock on the wall, he saw that it was approaching dusk.

"With him or without him, we about to flood this mu'fucka. Everything moving in Miami will be coming off of this. The quality is too good. Shit crazy," Joey responded as he shook his head in disbelief while smirking.

"Where this nigga at? I texted him an hour ago," Mo whispered under his breath. Just as the words left his mouth, the flash of headlights peered through the blinds and the sounds of a roaring engine resonated. Joey stood up the slightly pulled down on the horizontal blinds to peer outside.

"It's him," Joey confirmed.

"It's time. Cuz gotta step into the family business."

"You think the nigga in his feelings about you using his name to secure the plug?" Joey questioned.

"I don't give a fuck about no feelings, my nigga. I'm standing on what I did. That's supposed to be my plug. He betta get with the program, feel me?" Mo said as he stood up and lifted the snake off of his neck and gently sat it in its cage.

Aurora's heartbeat rapidly as her nerves were getting the best of her. She stood at the door of the condo, waiting for the door to open. She ran her hand through her hair and straightened out her dress, pulling it down right below her butt cheeks. She had just been dropped off by Christy and was standing at his doorstep. Her plump backside stuck out like a small bubble and she looked much older than her young age. She took a deep breath and exhaled quickly as she tried her best to calm herself. She knocked on the door and waited anxiously to see Guy appear.

Guy opened the door and instantly the smell of weed hit Aurora in the face like a ton of bricks, followed by the sound of trap music. Aurora looked at Guy and instantly smiled, adoring him. He was shirtless and his tattooed body was on full display. He smiled, showing her his pearly whites and his haircut was crispy and precise. Aurora couldn't help but blush while looking up at him as he hovered over her. He said nothing. He just slowly stepped to her and gently grabbed the back of her neck, causing her entire body to tense up.

"It's okay, he whispered as he sensed her nervousness.

They were now face to face and Guy leaned in and gently kissed her. He slowly slipped his tongue in her mouth and gently began to roll it around hers as he slowly massaged the back of her neck. A tingle went up Aurora's spine and a tingled happened between her legs. She had kissed boys before, but Guy's kiss was a different feel. He made her feel grown. She liked the unfamiliar feeling. As their lips unlocked, Guy stepped back, looked her up and down, and smiled.

"You're beautiful, love," he complimented. Aurora let out a nervous chuckle and dropped her head blushing. She as beaming and smiling from ear to ear.

"Thanks, Guy," she said.

"Come on…step in," he said smiling. He stepped to the side to give her a clear path into his home. As Aurora walked through the door, Guy's eyes studied her body and landed on her plump backside.

As Aurora walked in, butterflies fluttered in the pit of her stomach and she was in unfamiliar territory. She saw two guys sitting on the couch while playing a video game. They were smoking a blunt, as a thick smoke cloud dancing in the air. Aurora was surprised because she thought they would be alone. She felt Guy creep up behind her and placed his hands on her hips, steering her towards the couch. Guy quickly gave his friends a head movement and they immediately turned off the game and disappeared into the back room.

"Sorry, they're leaving soon. They were just kicking it here until you showed up," Guy said, sensing her edginess. He gripped her closely from the back and took a deep smell of her hair. She then felt his lips touch the back of her neck.

"Come on, Guy. I thought we were supposed to watch a movie," Aurora said uncomfortably.

"Oh yeah. My bad, ma. Seeing you in that dress got a nigga excited, that's all," Guy said as he walked around her and sat on the couch. Aurora followed his lead and sat on the couch right next to him. She was tense and it was showing through her stiff body language.

"Thanks for coming through. I been thinking about you all day," Guy said smoothly as he leaned back and begin to play in her hair.

"Seriously?" Aurora asked while smiling and blushing at the same time.

"Of course. Never met a girl like you. You're so mature for your age. I feel a real connection with you, feel me?" Guy said as he began to stroke her hair, sweeping it behind her ear so he could get a clear view of her face. Aurora looked over at him and for the first time, she noticed how bloodshot red his eyes were. Guy licked his lips and reached back for the rolled blunt that was in the ashtray on the coffee table. He raised it and was about to light it.

"Want to smoke one with me?" he asked as he placed the blunt in between his lips.

"I can't. I don't want to smell like weed when I go home," Aurora said, thinking about her mom catching wind of what she really had been doing.

"Oh shit. My bad," Guy said as he placed a hand on his chest as if he felt bad. " I got one better," he added as he smiled, placed the blunt back in the ashtray, and stood up. " Hold on. I'll be right back."

"Okay," Aurora responded just before she saw him stand up and disappear into the back room.

Aurora looked around the living room and was impressed. His condo was plush and comfortable. Guy was a grown man and was giving Aurora s different feeling. She looked around and admired the laid-back setting. His big screen television and fish tank was built into the wall, giving it an upscale appearance. Aurora felt comfortable as her nerves began to ease. After a few moments, Guy emerged from the back. He sat back down on the couch and had a smile on his face.

"I need you to relax with me. Let's roll," he said as he held out his hand and opened it, revealing two pills in his palm.

"Roll? What's that?" Aurora asked as she stared at the pills and frowned in confusion.

"Its ecstasy. It'll loosen you up. Your mom would never know the difference."

"I don't know about that," Aurora said as she repositioned her body, showing her uneasiness.

"Come on love, you say you not a little girl, right?" Guy asked and he released a charming grin and licked his lips.

"Far from a little girl," Aurora replied as she got turned on by his tongue.

"I already know," Guy said as he handed her a pill and then grab a bottle of water that sat on the coffee table. Aurora's heart began to rapidly beat as the nervousness and tension grew because of Guy's proposition. She had heard about the drug, but never in a hundred years would she think that she would use it.

"What does it do?" Aurora said as she looked down at the pill. Consequently, she saw Guy's penis print right below it. It was apparent that he was getting aroused and Aurora quickly looked away feeling uncomfortable.

"What does what do? This?" he asked as he grabbed his junk through his joggers and traced the outline of his pole. "Touch it," he added.

"I don't know…" Aurora said as her eyes drifted back to his large package, which was very intimidating to her.

"It's cool. Here… I'll help you," Guy said as he gently reached her hand and placed it on his crotch.

Aurora could feel it pulsating and growing as her hand went back and forth across it. Guy leaned in and slowly began to tongue kiss her as her hand remained on his growing tool. Her eyes closed and she began to feel her clitoris thumb more than she had ever experienced. She began to feel the wetness form inside of her vagina and slowly ooze onto the lips of it. She squirmed in pleasure and that's when Guy knew he had her right where he wanted her. He pulled back and placed the ecstasy pill into his mouth and swallowed it. He downed it without taking a sip of the water. He then looked deeply into Aurora's eyes.

"Open your mouth," he whispered as he held the other pill eye level.

She did as she was told, slowly opening her mouth. Guy slowly placed the pill onto her tongue and reached back to get the water bottle. He handed it to Aurora, and she proceeded to swallow the magic pill, not fully knowing what she was getting herself into.

"Yo, we have to take this shit back!" Carter demanded as he picked up a brick of cocaine off of the table.

"You have to relax, my nigga. I'll have these bitches gone in a week," Mo assured his cousin as he placed a hand on his shoulder. Carter quickly shrugged his hand off and stepped away from him, not agreeing with the forced plan.

"Nah, fuck that! You got them mu'fuckas on my arm...not yours! You think this is a game. Them mu'fuckas will cut yo fuckin' head off if that money ain't paid back. Why in the fuck would you do that?"

"What else am I supposed to do. Be your water boy while you get your brains knocked loose every few months? I'm no fuckin' water boy, my nigga," Mo said as he rubbed his hands together and stared Carter directly in the eyes, without an ounce of regret. He had a target and he was going to get there by any means necessary.

"Yo, I'm taking this shit back!" Carter said as he reached on the floor and snatched up the two empty duffle bags. He placed it on top of the table and began to placed the bricks inside while shaking his head from side to side in disbelief.

"Stop being a pussy. Let's flood this bitch and get to the money. Not sure why you're running from fate. It's in your blood negro. You can't even box anymore. What are you going to do? Huh? Riddle me that!" Mo questioned.

"You heard what the fuck I said. These going back!" Carter said as he continued to stuff the bag, not even giving Mo the courtesy of looking at him.

Joey moved his hand near his wrist where his gun was always at as he stood off and watched the two cousins argue. Mo noticed, and did a subtle head shake, signaling Joey not to do anything. It was like second nature for Joey to kill and that was the main reason Mo kept him so close. However, Mo couldn't let it play out like that. He and Carter had history and had the same blood running through their veins. He quickly deaded the situation before it could even form. He watched as his dreams began to slip away and Carter put the bricks into the bag. He decided not to put up a fuss and take another approach. He would slowly try to convince Carter to not return the joints. He knew he at least had a day because

213

Carter didn't know where Harry's spot was.

"Alright, suit yourself. Take em' back," Mo conceded.

"Trust me. I am," Carter snapped back. As he loaded the last brick, he threw the duffle over his shoulder and held the other one with his free hand. "Where is the plug?" Carter asked. Mo said nothing. He just stood there and smirked. Carter caught on to his sudden stance of silence and quickly decided to take matters into his own hands.

"Okay, fuck it. I'll ask Auntie," Carter said, thinking two steps ahead. Mo clenched his teeth in anger, knowing that Carter had found a way around him. Carter headed to the exit and gave Joey and menacing stare on his way out. He wanted it to be known that he had zero fear in his heart and he wasn't to be played with.

"Auntie wants us to be at the graveyard in the morning," Carter added sarcastically as he left the house.

"I'll be there mu'fucka," Mo said, smirking and shaking his head at his cousin's reluctancy. Carter left with the drugs, leaving Mo back at square one and without any coke.

"What's wrong with that nigga?" Joey said as the door closed.

"He's just green, bro. The real him is going to come out. I just have to find a way to click him on. He'll come around. He think telling my aunt about what happened is going to change something. But Auntie gamed up. She came from the cocaine culture. Ain't no going back once you turn on the plug switch," Mo said, smiling confidently. His time was coming, and it was coming quick.

"Don't use your teeth, bitch," Guy said as he held the cucumber to Aurora's mouth. She sucked the cucumber as if it was a penis and gagged as the vegetable hit her back tonsils. Aurora's slob was everywhere and her face was glazed with it. Guy had a smoking blunt in his mouth and lustful eyes as he watched his new victim bust it open for him. He looked over and saw his young homie fingering her. The ecstasy had kicked in and Aurora turned into another type of animal. She was out of her mind and wasn't turning down anything. She didn't even realize that she had been persuaded to participate in a full out orgy. A third guy walked over and began to play with Aurora's breasts as she worked on the cucumber.

Guy was getting twisted pleasure out of seeing Aurora obey his every command. She did whatever he said to do without any reservation. She was "rolling" and he could see it all in her eyes. Her naked body sweated profusely as she rolled her body and moved her midsection, humping against the boys finger. The drug gave her a confidence that she never had. She was liberated...or at least she thought that was the feeling she was experiencing. No sweetheart.... It's manipulation. That's what Guy should have said, but instead he just coached her to go further and further into the devil's abyss.

"Yeah bitch, suck that dick for daddy," Guy said as he guided the cucumber in and out of her mouth, disrespectfully slapping in on her lips and face. One of the boys pulled out his phone and began recording Aurora as she cut loose.

"My lil bitch a pit bull on the dick," Guy said as he controlled the cucumber and looked down at her as she behaved like a sex maniac. He was high himself and had seen enough. He was ready for the main show. He wanted to experience what Aurora's inside felt like. He waved his arm, to signal his friend to stop taping. As soon as the boy put the camera away, Guy whipped out his extra-large, uncircumcised penis and replaced the cucumber. Aurora gladly accepted Guy and slurped him up while letting the other two boys have their way with her. She was inexperienced and tight, but the drug masked the pain and she allowed them to have their way with her. Everything that one could imagine happened that night and they violated her for hours.

In the early morning, groggy and no recollection, Aurora walked up the driveway of the Diamond Estate. An Uber had just dropped her off and the sun was just coming up. Her mind felt foggy and in between her thighs were tender and sore. She tried her best to make sense of what happened and she couldn't wrap her head around what exactly had happened. Flashes of the prior night emerged, but nothing concrete. It was as if she was trying to piece a complicated abstract puzzle together. Scattered memories of Guy's uncircumcised penis and a spinning room crossed her mind. She was disappointed in herself and by the decisions she made. Her desire to make Guy like her, pushed her into situations that she now regretted. She felt a tear form in her eyes, and it was a tear of shame and remorse. Just as quickly as the tear dropped, she wiped it away. She made her way to the front door and a thought crossed her mind. That's when it hit her, that she hadn't spoken with her mother all night and the worry of a scolding overcame her.

"Fuck!" she said under her breath as she looked down at herself, realizing she had on the tube dress, which wasn't what she left home in. She pulled out her cellphone to check to see if she had any missed calls from her mom and oddly enough...there were none. Aurora got nervous because it wasn't like her mom not to be down her back when she was away from home.

Aurora reached the front door and took a deep breath, ready to take the tongue -lashing. She straightened up her dress and ran her fingers through her hair to straighten up her appearance as much as possible. She put the key in the door and tried to remain as quiet as possible while entering her home. She crept in and gently closed the door behind herself. She turned around and tip-toed into the house and to her surprise, her mom was sleep on the couch with multiple empty wine bottles around her. Aurora frowned, realizing that her mom had passed out from a long night of drinking. This was not in Breeze's character and Aurora was confused, but at that same time grateful. Just as she crept away to go to shower, she heard Breeze's voice.

"Hey baby. You look nice," she said in a dry groggy voice. As she woke from her drunken slumber. Breeze's vice startled Aurora and she turned around nervously.

"He…hey ma," Aurora said nervously. She looked down at her dress and ran her hands down her sides. In her mind, Breeze could see the sex on her.

"I wanted to look special for Papa's birthday," she said, thinking quickly on her feet.

"As you should. He deserves nothing but the best. You look beautiful. Let me get up and get dressed. What time is it?" Breeze asked as she sat up and held her head.

"It's almost seven," Aurora answered as she glanced down at her phone.

"I must have fell asleep while listening to music. What time did you get in?" Breeze asked as she stood to her feet.

"Just before curfew," Aurora lied.

"Ok good," Breeze answered as she walked to her and kissed her on the forehead. She then made her way to the kitchen in search of aspirin.

"We are supposed to meet at the cemetery at nine. Go change clothes. I don't think that little black dress is something your grandfather would have approved of," Breeze said jokingly as she opened the aspirin bottle. Aurora let out an anxious chuckle and hurried upstairs to attempt to wash the shame off her body.

Breeze grabbed her phone and sent out a group text to Mo and Carter, reminding them to meet her at the gravesite. It was going to be a difficult day for her, but it was something she knew she had to do. She rubbed her temples and prayed that her headache would subside. On that day a legend was born and he single-handedly started a movement that never would be duplicated or topped in the history of the streets of Miami.

Breeze and Aurora stood before the gravesite of Carter Diamond. The tombstone read "Diamonds are Forever. Long Live Carter Diamond." Breeze fought back tears as she thought about the good times he provided for her. Her oversized vintage shades covered half of her face and a black headwrap covered her skull. Her head was banging from the night of wine drinking, but she managed to drag herself to celebrate her father's born day. She kneeled in front of his tombstone and placed a bouquet of flowers against up. She gently rubbed her hand over the engraving and whispered.

"Thank you for everything that you built. You are the true definition of a leader and I hope one day I can find someone that's half of the man you were. I love you, daddy," Breeze said as he stood up and stepped back, giving Aurora room to put down her flowers as well. Aurora's body was still sore and her head was cloudy from the wild night before. On a regular day, Breeze would have noticed that something wasn't right, but on that particular day, Breeze had a couple of things to battle; grief and a hangover.

"Rest in peace, papa," Aurora said as she placed her roses right next to Breeze's. Aurora's legs were wobbly. Her private area was tender and swollen, making her grimace as he knelt down. It was a new pain for her and she never knew that pain sex could intel. Every time she took a step, it was an uncomfortable reminder of her being violated. Aurora's memory had slowly but surely been returning and she was ashamed of what had occurred. She tried her best to forget what had happened. However, with every thought, her mind drifted back to the vague flashes of Guy and his friends doing her wrong. Just as Aurora's stood up from placing flowers, Mo came walking up with a few flowers in hand. He first kissed Breeze on the cheek and placed his hand on her shoulder to comfort her.

"Hey Mo. Thanks for coming," Breeze said as she leaned in and smooched him on the cheek during their embrace.

"Hey auntie," he said as he smirked. Mo then focused his attention on Aurora and walked over to hug her. Mo's chains jingled loudly and swung back and forth as he made his way over. He wore an open Versace shirt, displaying his lean chiseled body and the rim of his matching Versace boxer drawers. His hair wildly pulled to the top of his head and his Dominican bloodline showed through his soft bay hair edges. It completely contrasted with his thug appearance and tattooed body, but that's what made Mo unique. He had soft features, but he was anything but that. He was a rebel and it shined through everything he did. As he reached Aurora, he could tell something was off by the look in her eyes.

"My nigga. You good?" he asked as he playfully punched her on the shoulder. Aurora looked at her cousin and instantly got nervous.

"Hi, Mo. Yes, everything is fine," she answered quickly as she dropped her head, trying to avoid eye contact. It was something about Mo's eyes that sought her truth. It seemed as if he knew that she wasn't being truthful. he could see right through her. Mo paused and never broke his stare at Aurora. He could sense something was off, but it chalked it up to grief from being at a cemetery. He made a mental note to have a talk with her at a later time.

Mo kissed Aurora on the top of her head and then proceeded to walk over to his grandfather's tombstone. He kneeled down and read the wording and felt a sense of pride. He loved being a Diamond. The respect is held in the streets was more valuable than gold and he couldn't wait his turn to prove himself. He was itching to add to the legacy of his last name and it was almost an obsession at this point. He was thirsty….thirsty for power.

"Long live the Cartel," he whispered under his breath. He slyly dug in his back pocket and pulled out a small bottle of Hennessy. He took a quick swig and then poured a small drop onto his grandfather's grave. He only wished that he could have soaked up life lessons and game from him. Unfortunately, he was murdered in broad daylight, years before Mo was born. Mo only heard old stories and urban legends about him and it was like Carter Diamond was a mystical figure. People like that only came around once every lifetime and he was proud to have that same bloodline running through his veins. He neatly placed the roses at the site. He looked to the right and added a single rose to his grandmother's grave as well, Taryn

Diamond. He kissed his two pointer fingers and touched her stone, paying homage to her as well. Just as he was standing up, Carter approached with a sweatsuit on and a stern, irritated look on his face. Carter couldn't hide the irritation for Mo. This only made his smile grow wider. In classic asshole fashion, he winked at Carter as he saw him hug and kiss Breeze.

"Hey Auntie Breeze. Sorry I'm late had to make a stop before coming here," he explained as he stared a menacing hole through a smirking Mo. He then walked over to Aurora and hugged her.

"Hey Aurora. You good?" Carter asked with his charming smile.

"I'm great," Aurora replied as she put a fake smile on, trying to mask the hurt. Carter didn't notice the mask, so he stepped towards Mo, almost immediately changing his facial expression. He clenched his teeth and spoke to Mo under his breath as his eyebrows furrowed.

"We gotta talk asap, nigga," Carter said as he forcefully brushed passed Mo, bumping his shoulder against his.

"I love you too, cuz," Mo said playfully as she smiled and rubbed his shoulder. In Mo's mind, all of this aggression was the process of Carter clicking on. In his twisted game of chess, this was all a part of the journey. Carter then kneeled at the gravesite and paid his respects as the others stood and watched him. He was mumbling something, but not loud enough so they could hear what was being said. Soon after, Carter stood up and walked over to Breeze.

"Auntie, I know this isn't a good time, but we have to talk,"

Carter said as he looked over at Mo and shook his head in disgust.

"Sure. What's going on?" Breeze said as she took off her shades and looked at her nephew who seemed to have something serious on his mind.

"This nigga is out of control. He used my name to get some work and now they won't take it back," Carter explained, speaking loud enough so Mo could hear him as well.

"Okay, baby. Calm down," Breeze said as she held her hand up to stop him from speaking any further. She then looked over at Aurora and smiled. "Go wait in the car for me. I'll be there in a sec," Breeze instructed. She waited patiently as Aurora said her goodbyes to her cousins.

When Aurora was out of earshot, she focused back on Carter. Mo approached them so they formed a circle just in front of Carter and Taryn's tombstones.

"Now, come again? Tell me what's going on?" Breeze asked as she slid her sunglasses to sit on the top of her head, trying to fully understand what was going on.

"So, this stupid mu'fucka went to the connect and used my name to get hit with work," Carter said angrily.

"Watch ya mouth," Mo said playfully, not letting the words get to him. He was just going through the motions and not taking anything serious at that point. Carter continued.

"So, this nigga took a hundred bricks and left me with the tab. I tried to give it back and he stepped all over them mu'fuckas. They said they couldn't take it back," Carter yelled. Carter had just visited Harry after calling back to the D.R. to get the info of where he was located. When he went

223

LONG LIVE THE CARTEL

to return the bricks they looked at him like he was crazy. Mo had forced his hand into something that he wanted no parts of.

"Stop being a little bitch," Mo said, finally hearing enough of Carter's bickering. "What the fuck you going to do? Huh? Tell me that. You tapped out and can't box no more. You a mu'fuckin Diamond. That means you a king. You can't be a king without money and power. You better get with the fucking program and hop off that high horse you riding. Do you know who the fuck your father was? Do you know who the fuck your mother is? You don't choose the game...the game chooses you!" Mo said with an aggressive scowl and conviction.

"Wait. I need everyone to calm down," Breeze said, taking all of the new information in. Breeze crossed her arms in front of her chest. She took a deep breath and briefly closed her eyes to gather the information that was just presented to her. She continued.

"Let me get this right. Mo used your name to get drugs and now y'all stuck with them?" Breeze asked as she frowned trying to better understand.

"Yes, that's exactly what happened. Can we get to the money now?" Mo said impatiently.

"Get it through your brain. I'm not fucking with that shit. Why don't you understand this?" Carter screamed as he stepped to Mo with aggression. Mo didn't flinch a bit. He just stood there face to face with Carter without a care in the world.

"You're a Diamond. No matter how uppity you act, you

can't change that," Mo explained while staring directly into Carter's eyes with his eyes slightly bucked. He had a crazed look on his face and he was determined to cross Carter over.

"He's right," Breeze admitted. Her response shocked Carter, which made him break the stare down with Mo and look back at her.

"Huh?" he said confused, wondering how she could side with wrong.

"I said he is right. Hate to admit it, but it's no turning back at this point. A cocaine connect isn't something you turn on and off like a water faucet. Once you start flowing only death breaks the contract. This isn't a game. No matter how it was done, it's here now. They going to want their money and when they get it back, it'll be another shipment waiting for you at your door. It's how things are. It's the way our family handled business, so we can't change the rules now because we're on the opposite end," Breeze admitted. Carter was totally taken off guard and frown while Mo began to smile from ear to ear.

"I knew you was a gangster, auntie," Mo said, feeling a sense of family pride.

"I been through things that you could never imagine. I might not say much, but I know too much," Breeze said as that gangster lineage began to show its ugly head.

"Yall have to get those off. So whatever you two have to do to end this little riff, I'ma need y'all to do that. Family is all we have. By yourself, you will go fast, but together you will go far," Breeze said, repeating words of wisdom her father used to tell her and her brothers when they were just children.

At that moment Carter knew that he was between a rock and a hard place. There was no dodging this punch. He had to take it on like a man. Mo extended his hand to shake Carter's and at first Carter was hesitant and just looked down at it. However, after a small nudge and smile from his aunt, he slapped hands with his cousin, and they embraced. Now that Carter was finally on board, he could focus his attention on Ma' Dear.

Happy Birthday, Carter Diamond.

CHAPTER 13

"I never let my right hand know what my left is doing,"
-Ma'Dear

Aurora's hands trembled as she wiped blood from between her legs. Her inner thighs felt like they had been pulled apart like chicken wings and her vagina burned so badly she could barely wipe after she peed. Every time she pulled the toilet tissue away, spots of blood dampened it. She was humiliated and her feelings were hurt so badly that it was taking everything in her to stifle her tears. Guy had been rough with her. He had let others be rough with her. She had no idea how to feel. Yes, she had agreed to it, but she hadn't really been in a position to say no, or at least that's how it had felt.

She was sick to her stomach. She felt bamboozled. No way could Guy love her the way he claimed to and if this is what love was...if this was what she had to endure to keep it, she didn't want it. The more she thought about it the angrier she became. She exited the bathroom and found her family gathered in the backyard.

"Ma, I could really use a break from all this," she said. "It's so much sadness. Can I just go hang with my friends for the rest of the day?"

Breeze nodded. "I'm sorry. I know this is heavy for you. Probably weird considering you never met your grandfather. I'm okay with you escaping all this. I wish I could. As long as Christy's mom is home you can go. Curfew still stands and call me when you get to your friend's. Somebody should smile today," Breeze said, standing to fix Aurora's hair. "Are you okay? You seem different today."

And different she was. Aurora's naïve heart was in pieces as she reflected on the ways Guy had taken advantage of her, it was getting harder to fake like she was okay. He hadn't returned one call. Her texts were unanswered. Aurora felt like an idiot. She just wanted to confront him face to face. Even Christy was ignoring her calls. Aurora just wanted to know why or more so, how...how could Guy love her one minute and then treat her like a random the next?

She was in the Uber before common sense could convince her otherwise. She had never been intimidated by the age difference before, but today, as she took this excursion to the hood, her heart clenched. Today, she didn't trust him. She overthought the entire situation during the half an hour car ride and then hopped out of the Uber as it dropped her right in front of Guy's home. She was determined to talk to him and try to get a better understanding of what went on. No matter how hard she tried to remember, only vague flashes appeared in her mind.

She tried to call Guy, one more time before she knocked on the door. But again, no answer. She saw that his car was parked on the curb right out front, so she knew that he was inside. She stood outside of his place for a second and thought long and hard before she went ahead with confronting him. After a few minutes and constantly checking her phone to see if he had communicated with her in any way, there was nothing. He just continued to ignore her. She could see that he had read her messages via the read receipts but still opted to not respond. Aurora's heart was breaking into little pieces with every unanswered call or text. She took a deep breath and mustered up enough courage to finally approach the door. She knocked. She could hear music and chatter coming from inside of the home, this only crushed her more. She heard laughing and music. How can he be happy after last night? That's what she thought as she crossed her arms in front of her chest and waited for someone to answer the door. She knocked again, but this time louder and with more urgency. Moments later, Guy snatched the door open in frustration. Aurora's heart dropped when she saw his face. She didn't know what to say. She just wanted him to make her feel better about what had transpired.

"I need to talk to you," Aurora said as tears began to form in her eyes.

"Why is you popping up at my shit like this? Huh? Banging on my motherfucking door like you the police or something."

Aurora looked at Guy in confusion. She had never heard that tone of voice from him. The care and gentleness that he used to use with her was now gone. It was nothing but irritation coming from Guy and Aurora was at a loss for words. Even the way he was looking at her was different.

"I just need to talk to you," Aurora pleaded as she sniffed and wiped the tears from her face.

"Look, now is not a good time," Guy said as he looked back into his house where the sounds of women and men resonated from.

"I have been texting and calling you. You were really rough with me. I'm bleeding and..." Aurora said, trying to make Guy aware of what she was going through. He looked at her like scum on the bottom of his shoe.

"Bitch, that's too much information. You need to go handle that and get off my doorstep," he said without an ounce of remorse. Aurora couldn't believe how Guy was treating her. It was like he was a completely different person. That's when a woman came to join them at the door. She put her arm around Guy's waist as a blunt hung from her mouth. She was much older than Aurora and her body was thick in all the right places. She was a caramel beauty queen and seemed comfortable with Guy as she leaned against him falling under his right arm.

"Who is this, baby?" the caramel beauty asked as she looked Aurora up and down.

"Nobody babe. Just a friend of Christy's. She came to pick up something," he lied as he leaned down and kissed Caramel's forehead. "Go back inside and let me finish this business up."

"Okay, baby. Don't make me wait too long," she said seductively as she smiled and looked up at him. She turned around and went back into the house as Guy's eyes followed her ass. He then focused back on Aurora who was so angry she was shaking.

"Christy's friend?" Aurora asked in total disbelief. "You hurt me! You violated me and now I'm just a nobody to you?" Aurora yelled in anger. Guy stepped out of the apartment and closed the door behind himself. He clenched his teeth in rage. Veins began to form in his temples, and he pointed his finger in Aurora's face.

"Lower your motherfuckin' voice," he said as he loomed over Aurora. He reached into his pocket and pulled out his cell phone. He pushed a few buttons and held the phone to Aurora's face so she could see the video he had just started. She saw herself on camera sucking a cucumber while having her legs spread open for one of Guy's friends. She didn't even recognize herself. Her eyes were empty as if they had no soul in them. Aurora covered her mouth in shock and tears began to fall down her face.

"This doesn't look like I forced you to do anything. Seems like you were enjoying yourself to me. Look at you," Guy said antagonizing her. Aurora couldn't stand to hear or see herself on the camera any longer, so she reached for his phone, but instead knocked it out of his hand. The phone crashed onto the ground. Guy quickly picked it up, only to find that the screen had been shattered. He instantly became enraged and smacked Aurora across the face, making her fall on the ground. He then, with his good foot, kicked her in the stomach, causing her to curl up in a fetal position. She cried out in agony. Between the cracked phone and the embarrassment that he had suffered from what Mo had done to him, he built up resentment toward Aurora. It all came out at that moment. He could no longer hide it. He stood over her and watched as she grimaced in pain and clutched her stomach tightly.

"Now run tell yo' cousin that and get the fuck on," he sneered. He turned to go inside the house and left her out there alone. Aurora heard the door slam and not only was Guy gone, but her innocence was too.

Ma'Dear stood over the stove, cooking a pot of greens and other soul food dishes. She reached into the oven and pulled out baked jerk chicken. She then walked it out to her dining area where a few young thugs were all sitting. As they did every Sunday, they gathered and Ma'Dear collected her money from the drugs she had given them on consignment. They then would all sit together and have dinner.

"Okay. Eat up, boys. Greens up next and some homemade mac and cheese," she said proudly as she disappeared back into the kitchen. She filled up the table with some of her famous soul food and sat back and watched as the gentlemen feasted. She leaned against her wall and smiled as they tore into the food buffet style.

"Y'all like it?" she asked, already knowing the answer.

"Yes ma'am," a few of them said in unison, while some nodded their heads, not being able to talk because they were so busy pigging out. She pulled off her apron and reached for her pack of cigarettes. She placed a smoke between her middle and pointer finger and lit up. She took a deep pull and quickly sucked the nicotine into her lungs. She twisted her lips to the side and blew the smoke out away from the direction of her boys.

"Listen, I'm headed out this weekend. Taking a small trip for a day or two," she said as she leaned against the wall.

"Where you sneaking out to, Ma'Dear?" one of the young thugs asked as he shoved a fork full of macaroni and cheese into his mouth.

"Aht!" she said pointing her finger at the group of men. "You know better than that. I'm ol' school. I never let my right hand know what the left is doing," Ma'Dear said half-jokingly. Ma'Dear kept what she did on the low, especially what she was doing on that particular trip. She was going away to visit her son who was a freshman in college at Bethune Cookman. It was about four hours north of Miami. Ma'Dear always kept her son away from what she did in the streets. She always kept him sheltered and managed to keep him in sleep-away private schools throughout his entire life. She would take vacations with him when he was out of school, so they could spend time together away from the place where she did her dirt. This was by design. Ma'Dear had seen so many people make that brutal mistake of putting their family in harm's way by having them around. Ma'Dear made the decision long ago that she would never have her son in direct contact with anything that could potentially hurt him.

"I need y'all to not kick up any dusk while I'm away. All dues are still owed. Drop it off to Guy and y'all can re-up with him. I'll be back tomorrow evening."

"Where you going, bitch?" Mo mumbled as he followed Ma'Dear up the interstate. A part of him just wanted to air shit out. Light up the truck she drove and eliminate his problem altogether. She was old enough to be his mother. She shouldn't even be in the game. The jungle of Miami was a young man's sport and Ma'Dear was out of her league, or so Mo thought. He had no idea she was the one who created the rules, at least the only one to do so after the era of The Cartel had faded. Everything about Ma'Dear got under Mo's skin. This wasn't her city. It belonged to the Diamonds and Mo was determined to restore the respect of his family's legacy. He made sure to keep a few car lengths between himself and Ma'Dear's vehicle, but he never lost her. If she got off the highway, he wasn't far behind. He had no idea where she was going. He suspected perhaps that she may be leading him to her connect.

Is she going to re-up? he thought.

He didn't realize how wrong he was until he pulled up to the college campus. Bethune Cookman was a historically black school and Mo frowned as he watched her get out, carrying a satchel and balancing toiletries. She appeared harmless.

"Fuck she coming to see up here?" he mumbled as he peered at her from across the parking lot.

He never exited his car, but he hawked her intensely. When he saw the young man come out of one of the buildings to assist her, Mo knew he had followed her to her weakness.

"Bitch got a kid," Mo said, as he adjusted in his seat,

peering over the steering wheel. He pulled out his phone and zoomed in on the pair as Ma'Dear kissed the young man in the school hoodie on the cheek. "Ain't this a bitch? Her ass got a motherfucking weakness."

He couldn't deny that Ma'Dear was smart. Her son was so far removed that Mo hadn't even thought of children, but now that he had discovered it, there was no unknowing it. He would use it to his advantage. He wasn't cut from the era of no women, no children. Those rules didn't apply to the young. Mo, Joey, and his little niggas were ruthless. Ma'Dear was going to learn that one way or another.

He laid in wait for six hours. That's how long her visit was. He never grew tired of preying on her. As powerful as Ma'Dear was, it wasn't often that she encountered a predator. Mo got off on the fact that he was one of few people who knew this secret. In this circumstance, she was just a mother. When she pulled away from campus that night, Mo stayed put. Her tail lights disappeared as she made the right out of the parking lot and Mo exited the car, carrying his snake in the huge duffel at his side.

He pulled his hat low over his face, avoiding cameras as he held his head down. He walked up to the dorm room that Ma'Dear had spent all those hours in and he knocked.

He hadn't seen another soul come in or out all day so he knew there couldn't have been a roommate. When the boy opened the door, Mo smiled.

"Hey man! I'm locked out of my dorm and my phone is dead. Do you happen to have an iPhone charger I can use to get some juice real quick, bro? I just need to call my roommate and have him come let me in," Mo said. His voice had never been so chipper. He had gone from goon to a good ole' college boy in the blink of an eye.

"Yeah man, of course. Shit happens, come on in," the boy said.

Mo walked in and closed the door as Ma'Dear's son went to his desk to grab the charger.

Mo set his bag on the ground before taking it. "Thanks, man. I'm Daryl," Mo introduced.

"Jackson," the kid answered. "I haven't seen you around."

"I'm lowkey man. Mostly stay at my girl's apartment off campus," Mo answered. Mo took the charger. The python in the bag began to move and Jackson jumped back.

"Aye man, your bag is moving," Jackson said.

"That's just my python bro. Can't have pets on campus so I sneak her in," Mo said.

"Wow, can I take a look?" Jackson asked.

Mo plugged up his phone and sat it face down before standing. "Yeah, man let me pull him out," Mo said. He bent down and unzipped the bag, removing the snake. "You got to wear this one." He put the snake around Jackson's neck like a rope.

"Whoa," Jackson said. "How do you hide this big ass thing from the RA?"

"I pay him to keep quiet," Mo said, chuckling.

"It's heavy," Jackson said.

"Yeah," Mo said.

"You name it?" Jackson asked.

"Yeah, Diamond," Mo said.

Mo knew that as soon as the snake heard its name it would begin to constrict. It wrapped around Jackson's body so quickly that he couldn't react.

"Aye man it's getting kind of tight," Jackson said, stumbling slightly and chuckling nervously.

"Oh, she's just playing with you," Mo said. He took a seat on Jackson's bed and his expression went cold.

"Man, get this thing off me now. It's getting too tight," Jackson said.

"Diamond," Mo repeated. The snake cloaked Jackson's neck. Before he could even let off a scream his air was cut off. Mo looked at him as he stumbled, falling against the wall as he pulled at the body of the snake.

Veins looked like they were ready to burst in his forehead as he struggled, and his eyes bulged. Blood vessels bursting turned the whites of his eyes red as he kicked. He was fighting a losing battle. The snake wouldn't let go until its prey was dead. It took two minutes for Jackson to lose consciousness and another three for his heart to stop beating. When the snake felt the last bit of life was gone, it uncoiled from around the body.

Mo picked it up, kissing the top of its head. "Good fucking girl. You a good girl for daddy," Mo said. He stuffed him back in the duffel bag, grabbed his phone off the charger, wiped everything he had touched and then pulled his hat even lower before walking out.

"Bitch better quit fucking playing with me," he mumbled. He had just shown Ma'Dear that he wasn't to be fucked with. The next life he would take would be hers.

Mo smoothly coasted down the highway listening to Nipsey Hussle without a care in the world. He drove a simple Buick that he wouldn't be caught in under any other circumstances, however, he had to move accordingly. He had just did Ma'Dear's son dirty and didn't think twice about it. He wanted to send a clear message and let her know that if you messed with the Diamonds there were consequences, deadly ones. He also wanted to establish his presence as the number one guy in the city and set an example. If your pack didn't have his signature snake on it, your days were numbered. Point blank. Some would call Mo a sociopath, but in his mind, he was merely doing what he had to do to achieve a goal. He was eerily similar to his uncle Mecca if he knew it or not. He had heard stories of him, but the similarities were undeniable. It was an urban legend that he was really Mecca's son rather than his father Monroe's, but he paid it no mind. He just knew one thing for certain and that was his last name was Diamond. And for that, he would do whatever it took to honor his family's legacy. This was the first step.

As he pulled onto the block, he saw a few of his workers on a stoop and then some were scattered down the block. The new work that they had put on the block had the whole neighborhood clicking. The sells seemed to be jumping overnight and that was just one of the blocks. He took a deep breath and smiled, knowing that all the money that was being made was coming off of his pack. He pulled the car into the driveway of the trap house and was greeted by his team like he was royalty. Everyone was extremely happy and grateful when they saw who had pulled up, greeting him with praise and head nods. This was because the money was flowing and the snake stamps were moving like hotcakes. Mo could feel the shift. He could feel the power. He could see the way they were looking at him and that's what he was chasing. It was called power.

Mo put the car in park and then reached for his cell phone that he had turned off for the trip. He didn't want anyone pinging him and placing him anywhere near the college he had just left. Mo was two steps ahead of the game and although he seemed like a hothead asshole, he was actually very calculated and this was a prime example of it. He stepped out of the car and Joey was the first to approach him.

"My nigga. We good," Joey asked as he slapped hands with Mo and briefly embraced him.

"Yessir. Need this bitch scorched," Mo said nonchalantly as he put a blunt in his mouth and pulled up his slightly sagging pants.

"I'm on it," Joey said as he whistled and looked towards the porch. Almost instantly a youngster hopped off of it and went towards the car. He quickly hopped in and pulled off, heading somewhere to set it on fire. Mo was strategically erasing any paper trail or connection back to himself. He walked over to where his car was parked and instantly felt more comfortable in the luxury of his own Porsche. As he started up the car, he checked his phone and saw that he had a string of texts from Aurora. His heart instantly dropped, thinking something had to be wrong. She was begging him to meet her at a diner, not too far away from where he was at. He instantly texted her that he was on the way and burned rubber, heading off of the block.

Aurora sat in the diner crying and waiting for Mo to pull up. Her eye had begun to swell and a bruise was forming. She didn't know what to do, so her only thought was to call her big cousin. She didn't want to go home and have to explain to her mom that she had lied to sneak out, so therefore, she was scared to face her. She had been there for hours replaying what Guy had done to her. She saw the flashing lights of a car's headlights in the diner's window. She glanced over and saw the luxury car and she instantly knew that it was Mo. He pulled in and flickered his light to signal her. She placed money on the table and walked out, joining her cousin in the car.

"Hey what's going on. I shot over here as soon as I read the text," Mo said with concern as he faced his cousin trying to understand what was going on. Aurora had told him everything about the pill, sex, etc. She left out names on the text, but he knew exactly who she was referring to. Aurora's head was down, so he didn't see her bruise but when she looked at him, he saw the damage. He paused and stared at her as he gathered his thoughts.

"Guy did that?" Mo said as he placed his finger under her chin and slightly raised her head so he could get a better look at his bruised eye. Aurora nodded her head, confirming what Mo already knew.

"Auntie don't know about this do she?" Mo asked as he was piecing the story together.

"No. I was scared to tell her. I told her I was going with a friend…."

"But you went to see him," Mo said, finishing her sentence while nodding his head calmly.

"Listen. I'm going to take care of this. But I need you to do something for me," Mo said as he mentally prepared for what he was about to do.

"Okay," she said hesitantly.

"I need you to tell your mom exactly what happened," Mo said as he rubbed his hands together and looked her directly ahead, not necessarily looking at anything in particular. He continued. "Your mom is more gamed up than you know. She has been through more than she let on. I think she can relate to you more than you think, you hear me?"

"I can't. She will kill me," Aurora said as she shook her head in fear of what would happen if she told her mom everything that's been going down behind her back.

"Trust me. Your mom is a gangster. You just don't know. You'll learn in due time. She been through some shit that you could never imagine. She looks better than what she's been through," Mo said thinking about the stories he heard about Breeze and the things she went through as a young girl while their family was in a war with the Haitians.

241

" I just don't want her to look at me differently. I never should of messed with Guy," Aurora said as she shook her head in shame and her eyes began to water again. Mo saw that she was about to breakdown and reached over and hugged her and kissed the top of her head as he rubbed her back.

"It's okay, lil' cuz. Mu'fuckas make mistakes all the time. It just makes you human," he said.

"He treated me like I was nothing," she said as she broke down crying.

"Don't worry about that. I'm going to take care of this for you. I'm going to get you home. Do you know where Guy lives?"

Needless to say, Guy got a small unexpected visit later that night. Mo made him pay back what he cost Aurora; her innocence. The next morning, Guy was found with a gunshot wound to his genital area and another two to the back of his head. One thing about those tables…they always turn.

CHAPTER 14

"Handle her with care," -Ma'Dear

Ma'Dear's soul was on fire. It was a searing of her body, from her skin to her fingernails, to the lining of her stomach, to the depth of her heart. It was the beginning of her end. The thing that would cause pain so great that she would never recover. A mother shouldn't have to bury her child. Nothing about it felt right. The sky was beneath her feet and dirt seemed to be falling on her head. Everything was upside down. Even the air was hard to swallow down like it was fleeting like she was in the coffin next to her son. She was dying slowly. With nothing left to live for, she was sure her days were now numbered. If not hers, somebody's. Ma'Dear tried to age gracefully. She drank her water. She minded her business. She tended to her garden, drank a little wine, even smoked her squares sometimes. It all kept her mood settled, it all contributed to her peace.

For many years she had run the projects fairly and quietly, getting money on the low without kicking up much dust. She respected the projects, so the projects respected her back. Then those motherfucking Diamonds came alive again. A regime that hadn't reigned in over ten years had suddenly come back more ruthless than ever. Everyone knew the rules. Her son was off limits. Even as a youngster the neighborhood boys knew that her son wasn't one of them. He was gentle. The kindest kid anyone had ever met. The hood would have eaten him alive had it not been for the love of Ma'Dear. She had done her all to make sure it didn't taint him. She didn't even know how she had ended up here. A grieving mother was something she should have never become.

"Those Diamonds are too comfortable. They think this is 2008. Too many years have passed since Big Carter ran these streets. Those kids of his ran his name into the ground. His empire crumbled under their rule. War after war. FBI. DEA. The Haitians. Everybody had a target on their backs. Watching that family lose control was like watching the Roman Empire fall. It was the end of an era in Miami. Everybody felt a little relief. Until now. Now, they're back but this isn't their city anymore. It's mine," Ma 'Dear said as she looked in the mirror, applying her earrings. There were goons all over her unit. Protection. Danger had touched her and her boys, the ones she had raised, the ones she had given condoms over the years, the ones she had fed, the ones she had washed clothes for, and babysat their kids...her boys, her hitters were overly protective now.

"They're going to pay for that. We not letting it slide, Ma'Dear."

The man over her shoulder was 25 years young and a killer through and through, but he wouldn't be going to war. No one would. Ma' Dear was a smart ruler. She believed in fair exchange. There was no need to turn up the temperature on the entire city. Just one family. Just one person. An eye for an eye.

"Dade County schools went back today?" she asked.

"Yeah," the man said.

"Hmm."

She stood and appreciated her own beauty before walking past every question she encountered on her way out the door.

Aurora walked out of the school and blew out a sharp breath. It had been a rough first day. She was the new kid and it was obvious. She couldn't break free of campus fast enough. She headed toward parent pick-up. She pulled out her phone as she looked around for her mom, but before she could dial one number the honk of a car horn pulled her attention.

"Hey, gorgeous girl. You need a ride?"

Aurora looked up, squinting as she ducked down to peer inside the car in front of her.

"It's me. Ma'Dear. I met you and your mom at the coffee shop awhile back," Ma'Dear said. "Your mom sent me to get you. She's running late."

Aurora frowned and looked down at her phone. "I'm going to just give her a quick call."

"Sounds like a plan," Ma'Dear said.

Aurora dialed her mom and it went directly to voicemail. Ma'Dear knew it would. She had put one of her boys on

Breeze. A quick pick pocket and a knife to her tires had thrown Breeze's day off kilter. She wouldn't be answering Aurora's call.

Ma'Dear needed some time with Aurora. She was too green to know the game. Ma'Dear knew that all she had to do was get Aurora in the car to get her talking.

Aurora looked around unsurely as her mom's voicemail played in her ear.

"Did you reach her?" Ma'Dear shouted out the passenger window.

"No," Aurora said, biting her bottom lip.

"Well come on. I'll take you home, sweetheart."

Aurora glanced around once more before reaching for the door handle. She slid inside and Ma'Dear patted her hand.

"It's been a long time since someone rode shotgun," Ma'Dear said.

Aurora smiled, laughing lightly as Ma'Dear pulled off. "We're going to pass my favorite ice cream shop. You mind if I stop in and grab a cone?"

Aurora sent a text to her mom.

On my way. Ma'Dear picked me up. Stopping for ice cream first.

"Yeah, that's fine," she said.

They pulled into the parking lot and Ma'Dear and Aurora climbed from the car.

"I used to come here every day after school when I was a young girl," Ma'Dear said.

"You went to school at Bal High?" she asked as they pushed into the ice cream shop.

246

"Long time ago," Ma'Dear chuckled. "I'll take a butter pecan," she called out to the boy behind the counter. "You want anything? It's on me."

"I guess I'll take a scoop of strawberry," Aurora said.

"Regular or waffle cone?" the boy asked.

"Definitely waffle cone," Ma'Dear answered for her.

Aurora smiled as they waited for their ice cream. They took their cones and Ma'Dear took a seat.

"Sit down a minute. I'll get this all over my car," Ma'Dear chuckled. "So you and your mom are new to town. How are you liking it?"

"It's different. It's okay, I guess," Aurora answered.

"Do you have a lot of family here?"

It was a way for Ma'Dear to measure the army that the Diamonds had amassed.

"Not really, just my two cousins Carter and Mo," she answered.

"Pretty girl like you must be making friends," Ma'Dear said.

"A few," she answered.

"And boyfriends," Ma'Dear said, nodding as if she knew the scoop already.

Aurora's eyes misted instantly as she thought of Guy.

"Just one. I mean there was one. I thought I knew him, but he turned out to be different than I thought he was," she whispered. Her shame was a guest at the table.

"Yeah well, that's his loss. You don't be afraid to let these men go. You be careful with these men down here honey. Demand something out of them. Don't move to fast. You set the pace. These Florida boys are something, I tell you," Ma' Dear replied.

Aurora blushed. Her thoughts instantly filled with Guy.

"See that look right there. That's what they do to you!" Ma'Dear said, laughing. "Well if any of those boys get out of line you just let me know. Most of them know me around here. I changed some of their diapers. I'll get them right in line if they ever try to take advantage. So if you ever need someone to talk to…"

"Do you know Guy?" Aurora asked, interrupting.

"I know Guy well!" Ma'Dear said. "But my beautiful girl, Guy is much too old for you. Men like Guy choose girls like you because women his age see straight through his bullshit. You be aware when you're with that one too. You're the prize, not these men. Men come a dime a dozen, but a good woman, in your case, a lovely girl, is the catch."

Aurora nodded. She wished she could just talk to her mom the way she was talking to Ma'Dear. If only she could trust her mother to listen and not react. Sometimes Breeze refused to acknowledge that Aurora was growing, and it drove a wedge between them. Rebellion was the answer to every overprotected child and Aurora was just spreading her wings.

"Thank you," Aurora said. "For not talking to me like a child."

Ma'Dear reached across the table. "Oh, you're not a child. You're a young woman and I protect young women. Sometimes all it takes is for us to listen to avoid making life changing mistakes. That's why I always run my mouth cuz I figure somebody gonna want to soak in this wisdom. I ain't got these grays for nothing."

Ma'Dear and Aurora sat in the ice cream parlor for an hour before they decided to head out. It only took 60 minutes for Aurora to fall in love with Ma'Dear. She told her everything. From Estes' inheritance to Carter's dismissal from the ring. By the time they were done eating, the bond was secured. Aurora was open for the affection and attention Ma'Dear gave. Not because Breeze didn't supply the same, but because a teenaged girl needed mentorship from someone they owed nothing to. Fear of disappointing Breeze kept Aurora from telling all. Fear of restrictions being placed on her time and how she spent it made Aurora keep secrets because she didn't want to lose freedom. The listening ear Ma'Dear gave her was needed. She could talk to her and talk she did. By the time they lifted out of their seats, Ma'Dear had information on every member of Aurora's family.

"I should probably get home. I can't reach my mom and I know she's wondering where I am," Aurora said. "Thank you for this though. It feels really good to let that stuff out."

Ma'Dear gave Aurora a smile that warmed her. She was so motherly, nurturing even, but somehow, she still felt like a good friend. "Anytime. I need to make a quick stop and then we can head to your house. It's along the way. It'll only take ten minutes. Your mom knows you're safe with me, baby."

Ma'Dear pulled out a pack of cigarettes, patting it against her palm as they walked to the car. "Lord knows I should give these up, but we all got our vices, you know? Some women are weak for men, some weak for the bottle, some weak for drugs, some of them big women weak for food..." she pulled one from the pack and lit it as she leaned against her car balancing the smoke between two fingers and tilting her head back to take a pull. She blew out the smoke and took a deep sigh. "Me, I'm gonna check a man. I make a man be a man. I ain't drowning in no bottle, I ain't never liked how it feels to be high, I'ma grow and eat my vegetables and treat my body right, but this here cigarette calms my nerves. This is my vice. Especially when my nerves are bad."

"Your nerves are bad now?" Aurora asked, truly concerned. "I haven't felt this comfortable since moving to Miami. You just seem like you really do care. I mean I know you don't cuz how could you possibly because you don't even know me, but it feels like you do and sometimes the feeling is enough."

"Ma'Dear cares, baby. I care too much," she said. "That's why my nerves are bad."

"I don't understand," Aurora said.

"You're not supposed to," Ma'Dear said. "You shouldn't get in the car with strangers, baby."

Aurora frowned. She was baffled, completely lost. "But I thought..."

Ma'Dear reached into her handbag and pulled the gun so swiftly that Aurora never saw it coming. She hit her beneath the chin in the soft skin that moved when you swallowed because she knew it would be instant.

BANG!

The second car pulled up and her goons hopped out before Aurora's body even hit the ground.

"Deliver that gift to the Diamond Estate. An eye for an eye.

I won't be the only mother crying over a fresh grave. It can end here, or we can go to war. The choice is hers," Ma'Dear said. "Handle her with care. She's somebody's baby."

Ma'Dear nodded to the ice cream boy. She owned the shop and the boy in the funny looking hat was another hitter. No cameras. No witnesses. Just revenge. Ma'Dear got into her car and pulled away. The Diamonds had another thing coming if they thought they were about to come back and terrorize the city without push back. Ma'Dear had raised every shooter in the city. There would be no army greater than hers. She hoped it didn't come to that but if it did, she had just proven that she wouldn't do anything halfway. She would go all the way. It was best to call it even and leave Ma'Dear to her garden because as soon as she stepped out the dirt and onto the concrete, lives would be lost. A lot of mothers would mourn.

"This has to be the worst day of my life," Breeze mumbled as she rode in the passenger seat of Carter's car. "Thank you for coming to get me, nephew."

"Anytime," he said. "Body shop will replace the tires by tomorrow morning and drop the car off to you. Aurora hasn't hit me back but when she does, I'll grab her and bring her home too. She's probably just out with friends or something."

"Well, she better enjoy it because it'll be the last time she leaves this house for the rest of her life. She knows how I feel about this city. She's trying to take it by storm and I just need her to slow down," Breeze said. "Miami is dangerous."

"She's just spreading her wings a little, auntie," Carter said.

He pulled up to the opulent mansion and his headlights shined on the gate.

"Fuck is this?" he asked.

A large moving box sat in front of the gate.

"I don't know," Breeze said. "Maybe one of the boxes came late or something from the move." Breeze popped open her door.

"I'll help you out," Carter said. Breeze and Carter approached the box and breeze opened the flapping lid.

"Noooooooooo!"

A mother's cry echoed over the city. Breeze knew it. She had felt it when they first stepped foot back in Miami. Her family was cursed and the city she both loved and hated had just claimed another Diamond. Aurora had been sacrificed.

Breeze stood in the walkway of the beautiful home, but her feet wouldn't carry her any further. Her entire past was behind the door in front of her. She didn't know how she was going to deliver this news. The daughter that she had concealed from Zyir had been murdered. She hadn't spoken in two days. All she could do was cry, but somehow, she had chartered a flight to come see Zyir Rich. So much time had passed. So many lonely days. So many recanting of memories. Breeze felt butterflies on top of the sickness of grief. She knew he had moved on. She knew that a woman, probably the same woman, dwelled here with him. Still, she had come. He was the only person in the world who could lift some of this hurt. She knew he wouldn't remember her. The self-imposed bullet to the head would prevent a true connection, but she just needed to see him. She needed to see the parts of him that had lived in Aurora.

"Auntie B, we got to either knock or leave. This the type of neighborhood where you linger too long, they call the police," Carter said.

"He's in there," Breeze whispered. "I can barely even breathe. Maybe just hold my hand," Breeze whispered.

Carter wrapped his hand around hers and Breeze could have sworn she was holding onto her brother and not her nephew. He guided her to the door. It was like walking down the aisle to her daddy's funeral all those years ago. She felt the same. Utter loss.

The ring of the doorbell made jealousy bloom inside her. That was supposed to be her doorbell. This porch was supposed to be her porch. This peace of mind was supposed to be her peace of mind. The man inside was supposed to be her man. When the door swung open, and Nurse Kai answered, Breeze knew...it wasn't hers. She had given it up. For the first time since making the decision to walk away, she regretted it.

"What are you doing here?" Kai's voice shook. Breeze understood why. She posed a threat. She was the woman. Every man had a woman in his life who would always occupy a space no matter, time or distance. Breeze was that bitch.

"It's time for you to give him back for a little while. I need him," Breeze said.

"You can't just come here…"

"My daughter was murdered. His daughter…" Breeze's voice broke and she stopped speaking as her chin quivered. "I need him."

Kai's conflict was palpable. "I'll fight for my man. I love him. I've been here every day."

"So have I. In the back of his mind whether you want to admit it or not, I live there," Breeze said.

"I'm only letting you into this house because there is a dead child involved," Kai said.

"That's the only reason I'm here," Breeze assured.

Kai reluctantly stepped aside and let Breeze into her house.

"I'ma wait on the porch," Carter said. Breeze nodded and followed Kai inside.

She knew everything about Zyir Rich. His scent lingered inside these walls and the closer she got to him, the harder her heart pounded.

"My nigga, we already been talking about it too long. You could have been putting shit in motion by now. I'm not with the extra words and shit. Action my nigga. Put the shit into play."

His voice. Breeze's chest hollowed. Hearing his voice ached so good.

"Baby, there's someone here to see you."

Zyir turned from the window he was staring out of and instinctively his eyes bypassed Kai's and met Breeze's.

He forgot he was on the phone. He was holding it to his ear but not speaking as a silent conversation filled the room.

"Do you remember me?" Breeze asked, her voice shaking.

He didn't say one word. He just looked at her. He hung up the phone and tossed it on his desk, but those eyes didn't leave hers.

"You remember, don't you?" she asked.

"I'm going to give you two a moment," Kai said.

She left, but didn't close the door.

Zyir was still silent. Yeah, he remembered alright. She could feel the resentment and anger in the air.

"You can hate me," she said. "I know you do."

Nothing.

"You're beautiful, Breeze," he finally said.

Relief flooded her and she rushed across the room, meeting him halfway as he wrapped his arms around her. He picked her up and Breeze bawled on his shoulder as he pushed her head into his body.

"I know you're mad at me," she cried.

"I am, B, but you're here," he said, biting his lip and holding her so tight she couldn't breathe.

"I tried to stay away. I would have stayed away, but they took her. My daughter. Our daughter, Zyir. She's dead," Breeze cried.

Zyir lost strength in his legs. The little girl he had dreamed of all those years was gone. The one who helped bring his memory back. The one who held his hand while he was asleep, leading him through a field of daisies until he discovered Breeze standing in the distance. She was gone.

He came to his knees still holding Breeze as she cried.

The only thing that tore them apart was the knock of Kai as she stood in the doorway watching them.

Breeze pulled back, wiping her eyes.

"I'm sorry," she said.

"Zyir?" Kai called.

"I'm sorry, Kai," Zyir said. "I'm incredibly sorry, ma."

"What does that mean?" Kai asked, voice rising in alarm.

"I'm not here to cause confusion," Breeze said. "I just thought you should know. I come with respect."

"After years of him not knowing, you want to come with respect? You should have buried your kid on your own!" Kai snapped.

"Be careful," Zyir said, eyes burning into Kai's like a natural instinct to protect Breeze flared. "Kai, baby…" he softened his voice. "I have to go to Miami to say goodbye to my child."

"You can come," Breeze offered. "I know you are important to Zyir. You should be there."

Kai calmed a bit. Breeze truly wasn't trying to cause problems. Zyir's arms around her were the only thing keeping her standing.

"It isn't safe," Zyir said. "For anybody, but especially for you," Zyir said looking at Kai.

"But Zyir…"

"It's decided," he said. "Give me a minute, baby."

Kai looked at Breeze and Breeze lowered her head trying to let Zyir handle it.

"If you leave here, Zyir, it'll tell me a lot," Kai said, before walking out of the room.

"I didn't mean to interrupt your life," Breeze said.

"I've been waiting years for you to interrupt my life, Breeze," Zyir said. "I just didn't think it would happen like this. You're just like I remember."

"How do you remember?" Breeze asked. She couldn't stop her eyes from prickling.

"I didn't for a long time. I would have these dreams though. You were in them. A little girl too. Took me years to connect those dots and by the time I did, it all came flooding back. The feds, the snitching, the fight, and…"

"The gunshot," Breeze finished.

"I remember it all," Zyir confirmed.

"Why didn't you come for us?" Breeze asked.

"I couldn't redeem that. Not just the deal I made with the Feds. I can stand on that. I would do that again to save you, but the moment I pulled that trigger…I couldn't redeem myself for that. The look of disgust in your eyes. Wasn't no erasing that. So I focused on starting over."

"With another woman," Breeze said, sadly.

"You walked out on me, B," he said. "You can't tell me that ain't nobody been in your life…"

"Nobody," she answered. "Nobody Zyir. I haven't loved anyone since you. Not even myself," Breeze said.

A silence filled the room.

"Look Zy," she said. "Let's just bury our daughter and put everything else between us in the coffin with her. Too much has happened. This is closure. I just thought you should know."

Another knock.

"Kai I told you…"

Zyir couldn't handle another interruption, but when he turned toward the door it wasn't Kai who stood there. It was Carter.

Zyir scoffed and looked at Breeze in disbelief.

"Carter's son?"

Breeze nodded.

"It's been a long time, Unc," Carter said.

Zyir pulled him in for a hug. "You're your father's son, boy. You're a man now."

The two embraced and Zyir held onto him extra tight. "Where's your daddy?" Zyir asked. "If you here I know he not too far behind."

"He died, Zy," Breeze whispered. "He's been gone awhile now."

Zyir pulled back, stunned to silence as emotion filled his eyes. He had been too ashamed to reach out and he wondered why Carter had never found him to finish the job that Zyir hadn't been able to. Now he knew why. Carter was no longer amongst them.

"I'm sorry, man," Zyir said, pulling his nephew in again, this time tighter. This time squeezing harder. "I'm sorry."

"We'll be at the Hyatt Regency downtown. We're headed back to Miami tomorrow on a private jet. Once you say goodbye, we can end this for good."

"You're different, Breeze," Zyir said.

"The world changed. My heart changed with it. I'm not the girl you loved anymore," Breeze admitted.

"You'll always be that," Zyir said. "I'll see you tomorrow."

Carter walked out and Breeze followed him, but before she cleared the threshold of his office, Zyir stopped her. "Breeze."

She turned to him. "I'm sorry," he said.

"For what?" she asked.

"For everything you wanted that I couldn't deliver. For the life we planned but never lived. Mostly for not being there when my daughter needed me most," he said. Breeze's melancholy was immeasurable. She couldn't find words, so she opted for nothing as she walked out.

Breeze sat on the clear port staring out of the window as the plane idled.

"Auntie, he know his way to Miami. We got to take off," Carter said.

"He's coming," she said calmly as she flipped through Vogue magazine. She wasn't even reading the pages. She just needed to do something with her hands to hold onto something to stop them from shaking. She hadn't stopped shaking since finding her daughter in that box.

"I'm going to kill her, you know that right?" Breeze asked.

Before he could answer a black executive Escalade pulled up.

Zyir emerged. She wondered how he looked so good after the nasty recovery he had endured. He had some war wounds, some scars, but it only added to his mystique. He was handsome. He was like the roughnecks who grew up in the streets who had hella scars on their arms and legs from meeting the concrete one too many times. The game had left its mark on him. Somehow, it only made him better.

He wheeled a Louis Vuitton suitcase behind him as he hiked up his pants and headed toward the jet.

"How did you know he'd show up?" Carter asked.

"I know him," Breeze said without looking up.

Zyir stepped onto the plane and looked at Breeze.

She stood and Zyir finessed her chin, forcing her to look at him.

"I'ma burn Miami to the ground," he said. "Polo's on the way too. It's time to put The Cartel back together." He removed the tear that slid down her face, wiping it with his thumb before moving to the last seat on the jet.

As the plane took flight, Breeze couldn't help but breathe a bit easier. She was assembling her army, one soldier at a time. She would need every single one to win the war ahead. She had never imagined in a million years that she would become the queen.

When the plane touched down, Breeze emerged, descending the steps. She thought her eyes were playing tricks on her when she saw her dear old friend. Aries stood in the distance, awaiting her return. There was a time when she had hated this woman, this killer, but the years and the losses had made them sisters.

"I'm so sorry, Breeze," Aries said.

Breeze hugged her so tightly crying, bawling because Aries presence signified that things were bad. Aries didn't just show up for anyone. She rarely ever came out of the cut at all, but for Aurora's funeral, her presence was necessary. She felt obliged to pay her respects.

"I didn't protect her sis," Breeze bawled. "I should have never come here."

"Shhhh," Aries soothed. "Chu' know we are going to make dis' right."

She opened up the back door to Breeze's chauffeured car and ushered her inside. She turned to Carter. "And look at chu," Aries said. "I love you. Real long, chu hear me?" she asked.

Carter kissed her cheek.

"You don't belong in de middle of no war, though. That's not what Miamor wanted for her boy," Aries said.

"I don't give a fuck what she wants, and I haven't been a boy in a long time," Carter said. "You take care of her. I've got somewhere I've got to be."

Aries turned to Zyir. "I can't stay," she said. "But when it's time to make someone pay for dis, I'll find my way back. You take care of her, Zyir. You're the only one who can."

"I plan to, Aries," Zyir said. Aries smiled.

"You look good old friend. Not a scrawny kid busting guns over his big homie anymore. You've come into your own. I've heard your name ringing," Aries said.

Zyir scoffed, but didn't acknowledge or confirm.

Aries reached for his forearm and gave a gentle squeeze before walking toward her car.

"Aye, Murder Mama!" Breeze called after her, climbing out of the car.

Aries turned around.

"I'm the queen. I need a right hand. When it's time to go to war. I need you," Breeze said.

"I never ran from a gunfight," Aries said. "And I ain't never left a bitch I love behind."

Breeze walked to Aries and hugged her tightly one more time.

"I'm not far. Just low. I'm there. Chu bury your daughter first and then we give them hell," Aries said.

Breeze watched Aries backpedal and drive away before rejoining Zyir's side.

They didn't say anything as they entered the car and pulled away. They were finally reunited, under the worst of circumstances. They were parents grieving. Everybody would feel their pain, but first, they had to say goodbye to the product of their love.

CHAPTER 15

"As long as my name on it, this gone go my way."
-Carter Jones II

Breeze felt like she was sipping air through a straw. Somehow, she was standing. She was graceful, greeting her family as they came to pay respects, giving small smiles, extending hugs, and thanking them for their support. Somehow her legs still worked. She didn't know how because her heart was now in the ground. This God forsaken city had taken everything from her. It had stripped her down to the studs. Breeze was numb to the loss. She had felt this grief before. First with her father, then mother, then every living sibling. Breeze felt like Miami was a cursed land. Aurora was the only thing she had left. She had coveted her so tightly because she was a symbol of the greatest love Breeze had ever felt. Aurora had been love in human form. Breeze watched her family. They were what was left over of what had once been an entire village. War had dwindled them down to this. Distant relatives and awkward interactions. Nephews she loved but barely knew because so much time had passed, and an uncle she hadn't seen in years. Then there was Zyir Rich. She didn't even know how he still captured her soul.

She had been such a young girl when they had fallen in love. It didn't even seem like it had once been her life. Breeze had fought the ghost of that love affair for many years and now that it was staring her in the face, she had nowhere to hide.

She had cried so many tears within these walls that they could drown her. She poured a glass of wine and then walked into the formal dining room. She took a fork from the table and tapped it against the side of the glass.

"Have a seat," she said.

Her voice barely worked.

"Breeze you don't have to host us. We know it's hard."

"I've buried my entire fucking family. I'm not feeding anyone. Just sit-down, Uncle Polo."

Any innocence that Breeze had once possessed was gone.

Zyir sat across from her. She wished he hadn't. Staring in his eyes was like putting her in a magic portal and teleporting her back in time.

She felt his eyes on her. She tried her hardest to divert his stare, but she couldn't. She never had been able to.

"My daughter…"

"Our daughter," Zyir corrected.

Breeze paused, clearing her throat and then looking around the table. Zyir, Mo, Polo, and Carter sat around her. As big as this round table used to be, with just the five of them, she felt empty. So many seats were left unfilled. There were ghosts at the table. These same ghosts gave her nightmares at night because they walked the halls of the Diamond Estate.

"Our daughter was killed," Breeze corrected. "Somebody has to pay for that. Everybody has to pay for that."

"Breeze this is emotional," Polo said.

"This is sequential," Breeze said, voice cold. "The natural order of things. Someone takes one Diamond, and a Diamond takes all of theirs. My name. My call. I want Ma'Dear's body hanging from a balcony. Closed casket."

"This is just going to go back and forth. A war is bad for business," Carter said.

"Don't want to get your hands dirty, cuzzo?" Mo asked.

"The Five Families don't do loud. They stopped doing loud when we blew this city apart the first time," Carter said. "If we go to war it will draw attention and they will pull out."

"It's too late for all that," Mo stated.

"We got to play it smart. Ma'Dear has a gang of sons that's going to ride about her if we do this the wrong way," Carter said.

"Just because we using your name to get to the connect don't mean you running the show," Mo said. "You focus on boxing."

"As long as my name on it, this gone go my way," Carter said. "Be clear bro. You the one in the streets cuz the king don't come down off the throne."

Mo stood and placed balled knuckles to the table.

"What? Nigga you just got here, this ain't your city. While you were being babied by Estes I been in the field. I rotted in that bitch while you were out pretending that you were me! You not blood! You never belonged with Estes!"

It was the same beef his father had faced years ago. When Carter Jones had come to Miami his brothers Mecca and

Monroe had doubted him, even resented him. Carter saw that in Mo.

"That's enough," Zyir stated.

"Nigga and yo snitch ass ain't got a say at this..."

Before Mo could finish his sentence Zyir was on his feet, lifting Mo by his neck and slamming him to the table.

"Don't confuse me, nephew. You don't give me nothing less than fucking respect. You a little ass boy out this bitch. Fuck your name. That name don't mean shit when it comes to me. Watch your fucking mouth and fall in line and you might live through this war," Zyir said. He jerked Mo hard before letting him go.

"Sit down, Mo," Breeze said.

"We all on the same team. The head is only as powerful as the team, Mo. Don't make the same mistakes that have taken this family out for years," Polo stated.

"Sit down, Mo," Breeze repeated.

"Before I sit you down, cousin," Carter said. No bravado. No flex.

"This is bullshit," Mo said stepping back from the table. "Fake ass family."

He stormed out, leaving the table in silence.

"Give him some time to cool his head," Polo stated.

"Carter your father led this Cartel. He was smart. He was fair. He was cunning, but most of all he was not to be fucked with. Mo is probably right. He knows these streets. He has a team. He's been getting it in the mud since he came out of lock up. I can't imagine what you have done and seen under Estes, but Estes operate at the level of the connect. It's time for you to tap into the streets, Carter. Tap into your father, cuz he was the biggest hustler these streets ever saw and he's in you," Polo said.

"You need a team," Zyir said.

"Mo has a team. He's the same as he was when we were kids. He won't be mad forever. By morning he'll be back rocking," Carter said.

"You need your own team. Mo's team is loyal to him first. They'll hold you down, but he'll always come first. His team can eat, but you need to assemble your own. Young, hungry, niggas that you feed first, so they'll be loyal to you," Zyir schooled. "Your daddy was my best friend. My brother. I can't see his only son be sent out into the jungle unless he's the king of the shit."

"You can't half do it though. One foot in one foot out will get you killed. You got to breathe it. I've seen the stories. I know you're trying to get back to boxing," Polo said.

Carter had a lot to think of. He had never wanted to be his father. He disdained everything the man was.

"It's been a long day. We have a lot to go over. Mo has to be a part of the fold. It won't get resolved in a night. The Cartel is back and we're going into another war. Most of us at this table won't make it out of it alive. I don't care. I want revenge for my daughter," she said. She grabbed her wine glass and pushed back from the table. "Now get out of my house so I can cry."

Breeze went into her father's old office and walked out onto the attached terrace.

Silent tears rolled down her face as she looked over her family's massive estate. It felt like a museum now that it was just her. Living in it alone would destroy her. She almost wanted to sell it, but her heart wouldn't allow it.

She heard the footsteps behind her. She knew he would stay. She hoped he wouldn't. The altercation to come wouldn't be pretty. They had gone a whole two days without addressing the elephant in the room. Apparently, it was too large to ignore any longer because the scent of him filled her bedroom.

He didn't say anything. He just stood there. He watched her. She wondered how much he actually remembered. Was it all back? Or just fragments? How much of her actions would she have to face?

"Breeze. You gonna look at me?"

Breeze didn't know if she could, but she knew she owed him too much, not to. She turned to him and her soul bled all over the room. She felt her tears building. Rising and rising as her nose burned from the emotion building in her. She had convinced herself that Zyir Rich, her Zyir, was no longer alive. That he had died when he put that bullet in his head. That he'd never remember, never be the same again, but here he was. He was in front of her and she could tell by the way he looked at her that he remembered. Breeze wasn't the same weak girl. She closed her eyes, pushing down the girl he used to love. The vulnerable girl. The one he used to read books to. The one he used to rock to sleep. "You're my baby," Zyir used to say. She could still hear him. Still feel his breath on her ear. Still smell the scent of his cologne.

Breeze pulled in a deep breath and when she lifted her eyes the tears were gone.

"I'm sorry," Zyir said.

"Sorry for what," Breeze said.

"For it all," he answered.

Her heart clenched, but she said nothing.

"When I found out I was pregnant, I never imagined this. I couldn't have foreseen this in a million years. I looked at her every day and pulled power from her. I pulled you from her because I knew you were somewhere inside her. She was made of you and you always built me up. Always kept me safe, so I felt strong when I looked at her. Felt you."

"You walked out on me, Breeze," he said. "I gave up everything to protect you and you turned your back on me."

There it was. The bomb was dropped.

"I thought I was right back then. To stand up for something. For family. You snitched on my family…"

"To save you, B," Zyir said calmly. "I would have sacrificed anybody to save you."

"We had an empire, Zyir. An entire kingdom to take care of. My father's kingdom. Sometimes you sacrifice one to save the kingdom."

"What would you have me do?" Zyir asked.

"Sacrifice me! Maybe Carter would be alive. Maybe Miamor wouldn't be in jail. Maybe Carter and Mo would have never been put in the system and our daughter would be alive if the family was still standing!" Breeze shouted.

"And I would have lost you!" Zyir's voice boomed. He

wasn't a yeller, but he raised his voice so passionately that Breeze's stomach dropped in doom.

"You lost me anyway, Zy," she whispered, pain in her tone. "Look at us? I haven't seen you in years. We're strangers."

"Nah, I'ma always know you, Breeze," Zyir said. "It took me awhile to remember. Took me some time to figure out why it hurt so bad when you walked out of that hospital room. I felt every step you took when you left."

"Stop," Breeze whispered.

"I knew I loved you. I knew it in my gut. I knew I loved that little girl."

"Stop it, Zyir!" Breeze yelled.

He deadpanned on her. "At the end of the day, I loved you. I gave up my brother for you and you left me to die. My wife left me to die."

"Maybe I didn't know that love was supposed to come before all, come before them," she whispered as her eyes prickled.

"The love we lost…" Zyir paused and cleared his throat before flicking his nose and turning toward the door. "I loved you, Breeze Diamond."

"I never required love Zy. All I needed was loyalty," she answered.

Zyir's gaze was filled with disdain and disappointment, but behind all of that, she still saw affection. He was too real to hate her. Too good to unfeel all the good they had once experienced with one another.

"When I first came down to Miami with Carter, I thought you were the prettiest girl I'd ever seen. You were surrounded by your daddy's Cartel. A princess. Killers all in your space, but you were nothing like them. You were innocent. Special. The streets hadn't tainted you at all and I was stuck on that every time I looked at you. I just wanted to fuck with you the long way. Prove to Carter and your brothers that I could hold it down when it came to you. That I wouldn't do no shit to corrupt you cuz you were so damn good man. It was in your eyes. The way you looked at me. You made a nigga heart feel like it was in a cage. Like you had the key, B. Now, when I look at you, you look just like them. You look like a Diamond."

"I am a Diamond. I'm going to always be a Diamond. I'm the queen of Diamonds, Zyir. It's why I could never be a Rich."

Zyir nodded and knocked on the wall.

"I'll stay in town long enough to teach Carter the game. He's Carter's son. I won't feed him to the wolves. You and me though. We buried everything we had today," Zyir said. He turned, put his hand in the pockets of his designer slacks and walked away.

CHAPTER 16

"People die in war," -Breeze

Breeze heard the storm outside her window, and she squeezed her pillow tighter as she allowed her levees to break. She was right. She was the queen, but the throne was lonely. She had never known how heavy the crown was because she had never been the one wearing it. Now that it was her turn the weight of it felt like it would crush her neck.

Her bedroom was spinning or maybe that was her head. The bottle of expensive wine had drowned her, the rain that pounded her windowpane was finishing the job. She wondered if her baby was cold. Aurora out there in all that rain on her first night made Breeze's stomach turn. She was so hurt it felt like she wouldn't make it. She remembered this feeling of loss. She had just never expected to feel it again. She had thought her days of experiencing grief were over, but they were just beginning. The burden of burying a child was unlike anything she had ever felt. It was worse than every other death combined.

The sound of breaking glass pulled her from her bed. She could barely hold herself up she was so devastated. It felt like her energy had been buried today. Like Aurora had taken all her strength to the grave with her. Breeze heard the howl of the wind as it infiltrated her home. Storms weren't uncommon to Miami. This one seemed fitting. No way could the sun shine after what had happened. It never deserved to shine again.

She took the house by heart. She knew every corner, but when she entered the living room the silhouette of the man sitting on the couch shook her to her core. She screamed and then flicked the light, illuminating the room.

Zyir didn't move. Didn't speak. He just rubbed his hands together as he sat leaned over onto his knees. His eyes were on the floor. She didn't even know he had stayed. Had he been sitting there, listening to her cry the entire time?

"I didn't mean to scare you, B," he said.

"What are you doing here?" she asked, voice trembling. The howling wind pulled her eyes to the broken kitchen window.

"It's just a tree branch from the storm," he said as he stood. "You got some wood?"

"I think there is some storm stuff in the garage," she said, voice faint. He nodded and then bypassed her. Breeze was stuck. She didn't know what to do or say. He appeared in minutes and went to work covering the broken window.

"Zy, why are you here?" she asked.

"I don't know, man. Leaving. It felt permanent."

"We've been apart for more than ten years," she said.

"Half of those years I couldn't remember shit, Breeze. I kept seeing your face in my head. From the hospital. Every time I closed my eyes, I saw those eyes. I just didn't know who they belonged to. I couldn't place you. Couldn't even remember your name," Zyir admitted.

"But then you did. You started to remember, and you didn't come after me. I saw you with that girl. I saw the way she took care of you. The way you touched her, looked at her. You were already gone, Zyir. You might have been breathing but you weren't mine anymore."

"Kai's a good woman," Zyir admitted. "She's honest and beautiful. She's loyal."

"I can't do this. I don't need to hear this. You should leave," Breeze said. "You should go back to her, back to your life. Carter will be fine. Go home Zyir."

"I'm trying," he said. He took a step toward her, taking one hand to trace her jawline. Breeze's chin quivered. "But I can't, B."

"Why?" she said.

"Because walking away gone kill me," Zyir said. "I still love you, Breeze. I lay up at night with Kai and I don't sleep, all night I'm up, with my fingers in her hair and she's laying on my chest, but my mind is a million miles away. My mind is on you. From the day I started to remember who I was until this moment; I've thought about you."

"Then why didn't you come find me? Why didn't you come find your daughter?" Breeze asked.

"I ain't know how to make you not hate me," he answered honestly.

Breeze felt the tears fall down her face. He cleared them. "I'm so sorry," she said, crying, struggling not to fall apart, but it was inevitably happening.

"Stop crying, B," he whispered, kissing her lips softly. She wanted to stop him, wanted to not be the woman to sleep with another woman's man, but he had been hers first. She had loved him first. That had to count for something.

Passion and grief fueled them as he lifted her off her feet, holding her under her ass while taking wide steps toward the couch. Breeze cupped his face, inhaling him, tasting his tongue, as he laid her on the couch.

He hovered over her and Breeze reached up, touching the scar on his temple.

They stared at one another as their entire history played in their minds. She had a split second to change her mind, but just as fast as the moment came it went as Zyir lifted the short silk gown. He pulled the thin straps down exposing her breast and took it between his mouth, biting gently with his lips folded over his teeth. Breeze reached for his belt, fumbling hands undoing it, then the button, the zipper slid south, and she felt him. She held her breath. Zyir was a king, always had been, always would be and in bed he conquered her. He was inside her and Breeze was in heaven. Hell was put on pause as he moved in, then out, stroke so smooth and official that she felt a little lightheaded from the pleasure.

There was years of emotions between them. Years of pent up anger, resentment, love, yearning. They had time to make up for and Breeze felt him, carving out days he had missed, fucking his need for her away.

276

Breeze was a beautiful woman with a hideous past and tremendous pain. Her sad eyes revealed all as they stared at one another, transfixed.

Body to body, Zyir held her face, nose to nose...so close that not even the absence that had filled them fucked up the moment. So many voids existed when they were apart. His flesh inside her flesh was completion. Breeze's legs shook.

"Zyir, I'm..."

He pulled out, stroking himself as he came, going down to capture her clit and suck the orgasm out of her soul because he needed to remember the way she tasted, just in case he never tasted it again.

"Zyir," she moaned as her stomach collapsed, convulsing as she reached between her legs to grip his head as he cleaned her up.

"Mmm," he groaned, tongue still mopping. He sucked on her until she stopped shaking and began shaking all over again until she couldn't take anymore because her clit was so sensitive that even when he blew on it, she started cumming back to back.

He came up her body and hovered over her, gripping her face as Breeze cried.

He squeezed on the side of her, taking up most of the space on the oversized couch and then pulled her on top of him. His baby. She always had been. Even in his dreams. Even when they were apart. Even when the sight of her face was the only thing that pulled him out of bed on those long, painful days of recovery. He hadn't known why her face was ingrained in his mind, but she never went away. The crushing moment when he remembered it all had pulled him out of a nightmare one night, a cold sweat covering his body as it all came flooding back to him. Animosity and fear of her hatred had kept him away. A reluctance to hurt Kai, the woman who had been by his side through every moment of his recovery, convinced him to leave the past where it was at. Being here, however, seeing Breeze, made it impossible.

"I don't expect you to blow up your life. I don't even like the idea of putting this kind of hurt on someone who took care of you all these years. She did my job Zyir. She made sure you were okay. I can't hate her for that," she whispered. "But if you can just stay tonight. Just the night of our daughter's funeral, you can leave again in the morning."

Zyir had some decisions to make.

"I'm not leaving you down here, B. You're heading into a war. Kids have died. One on their side, one on ours. You were smart to put Carter in place. Mo's actions escalated a petty beef and turned it into something that only death will settle. This is far from over. Shit gonna get cold in Miami. Blood is going to flow. We both know what the last war did to your family. Everybody not going to survive. Let's get through this war and then we'll figure out what's next for us. I ain't leaving you down here to handle the gunplay alone though. I might have forgotten a whole lot, but I ain't never forget how to put my murder game down. I'ma cover you."

Breeze didn't know she would feel so much relief. His choice was clear. If there was ever a priority in his life, she was it, even after all this time. Even after the way she had abandoned him. His disdain for her in those moments were equal to his love for someone else. The way he had loved her simply couldn't be replicated. She didn't know what would happen between them once this war was over, but she had him until then. She would enjoy whatever time he allowed them to share.

"People die in war," Breeze whispered.

"We've been up against worst," Zyir said. "The Cartel will live long, B. Close your eyes."

I'm going to make this entire city bleed for my daughter, Breeze thought. She had no idea that Zyir was thinking the same.

Carter found himself at Ashton's door. A hundred-dollar tip to the doorman allowed him entrance to the building. She wasn't answering his calls and he didn't want to put his weight on her, but he couldn't deny that for the first time since losing his father he had felt peace. Between her thighs, Carter felt at ease and as the ghosts of his father chased him down, he was seeking refuge with her. He knew it was a lot to ask. They had just started fucking around. She didn't owe him anything, but when she pulled open her door, the look on her face told him that she was going to give him all she had. He left her no time to say anything. He backed her up into her condo and her weighted breaths labored as she wrapped her arms around his neck.

"Carter, you can't just show up like…"

Her words were swallowed and replaced by moans as he kissed her. His hands slipped up her thighs and he ripped the panties she wore. She reached for the buttons on his shirt and she slid her hand over his hard abs. He was so solid, a machine of a man but she could see him malfunctioning. There was uncertainty and pain in his eyes that hadn't been there before. She undid his belt, then the button and Carter didn't even pull his pants all the way down. They hung off his hip as he pulled out, diving into her as he braced her back against the wall. No time to take pause. Neither thought twice about protection. He just wanted to get it out. Whatever this was. This resentment. This fear. This expectation of legacy. He wanted to fuck it away and if her wetness was any indication of her intentions, she wanted to let him. Pussy this wet had to be a hazard. She needed a sign or something, warning niggas that things got slippery in the trenches when she got in the mood. She took his mind away from the turmoil he was in because he only felt one thing. His dick throbbed as he hit it. Pussy gripping. Tight and warm. He groaned as each stroke hoisted her up the wall a little. The first time he had been gentle. This time he was rough. A do both ass type of nigga and Ashton loved it...loved it so much she hated that she had an agenda. Carter was making her heart go against her brain. She told herself she wouldn't get attached. That she would honor Miamor's wishes, keep him safe, watch his back, until she made it home, but this man was like food. She wanted him in her mouth, all the time, even when she wasn't hungry because the nigga tasted so damn good.

Carter had dick that didn't end. Dick that felt like it reached parts of her that dick wasn't supposed to be acquainted with. She held on extra tight as he went still inside her. Heavy breathing filled the inches between their faces.

"I break all my rules when it come to you, girl," he panted.

She rubbed his head. "We've only been on one date, Carter. It shouldn't feel like this," she whispered. Her eyes burned into him. She was right. He knew it. Didn't stop him from seeking her today though. The newness of this thing they were doing didn't make him take pause at all. He had buried family today and been seated at the head of The Cartel, a position he never wanted, but one he had inherited. This fuck was more than a fuck. He had pulled up for therapy. The pussy was talking to him. Healing as fuck.

His stroke was perfect, and Ashton fucked him back with a passion, squeezing all the juice out her peach.

"Carter, yes!" she shouted as she came.

His stroke grew more desperate, he hit it harder.

"Carter let it out. Pour it all into me," she moaned.

He growled the pussy was so good. Every stroke sent her further up the wall. The feeling of him pulsing inside her made her feel powerful. She felt life, a heartbeat in his dick, inside her.

"If you don't pull out, you're going to make a baby," she whispered.

"Damn," he groaned. "Fuckkkk." He planted his seed inside her and then pulled her off the wall, dick still in her, as he carried her through her condo, all the way to her bedroom.

"Carter this scares me," she admitted as he laid her down.

"Let me have my way anyway," he instructed. Round two made Ashton submissive. She gave in completely, letting him touch her without limits, letting him fuck until he couldn't anymore, until he was exhausted.

As they laid in bed on twisted white sheets, Ashton's eyes closed slowly.

"You can't come to me like this, like you need me because it's going to make me fall in love with you," she said, lazily.

His arm around her shoulder as she rested in the crease of his arm. His fingers in her hair.

"I ain't never wanted nothing like what you give me," he said.

She turned toward him and caressed his face.

"You want to tell me what happened today?" she asked. "Cuz while it was amazing, I don't know if you even knew I was in the room. Your eyes changed since I last saw you. It's like they're empty."

Carter took her hand and lifted it in front of his face, focusing on her dainty fingertips, playing with them as his mind raced.

"Boxing is over," he said. "My career is done. My family has tapped me to take over the family business."

"Is that a bad thing?" Ashton asked.

"They run Miami, Ashton. My family is The Cartel. I am The Cartel," he said.

Ashton deserved an award for the way she feigned ignorance. Like she hadn't known. Like she was still a bit confused.

"The Cartel?" she asked.

"Biggest drug organization the state of Florida has ever seen," he mumbled. "And its mine. I've run from that my whole life. Didn't want to be anything like my father, but I'm tired of running. I will never outrun my family name so I might as well say fuck it and be the best fucking drug dealer these blocks have seen since my father was running em'."

Ashton came up on one elbow and stared at him. She couldn't help but think of Miamor. Would she want this for him? He was stepping into a game his father had left behind with unknown enemies lurking. The Cartel had a lot of love in Miami, but they had a lot of hate too. Carter was inheriting a problem.

"Carter, you're not a killer. You're not a drug dealer. What about your career?" she asked.

"I've seen things you wouldn't even be able to imagine. Been so close to death that I saw the other side. I grew up around Estes. He taught me everything I needed to know to run a drug cartel, then made sure I didn't have to use it, but just in case, I knew how. Niggas in Miami don't scare me. I scare me. Once I get into some gangster shit, I know I won't get out. I'll be too good at it and I like to be good at shit," he said.

"You want to be king of Miami," she said, a little breathless because she believed everything he said. She liked clean cut Carter, but this was a side of him she loved. It was a side she was surprised existed. This was the ghost of Carter Jones. No way was he dead. He was living and breathing through his son. Ashton had never been so wet. This was what Miamor had told her about. The allure. The confidence. The fucking royalty that flowed through his veins was the sexiest thing Ashton had ever seen in a man and she wanted parts.

"You can't run the city without soldiers," she said.

"So they tell me," Carter said.

"I know soldiers," she said, climbing on top of him.

She reached down and lifted a little until he slid inside.

"Does that make me the queen? If I gather your army, can I be your queen, baby?"

She rode his dick and then laid flat against him, her breasts against his chest as Carter pumped her hard, massaging her ass cheeks in circles as he beat it up. Didn't matter that she was on top, he still put in the work.

"Carter!" she moaned, raining on him as he filled her.

He pulled her hair and then kissed her lips.

"Who you got in mind?" Carter asked.

"Ris. Ris and his niggas are loyal and they're strong out here. From New York all the way to Florida, they're respected," Ashton informed.

She climbed off of Carter and reached for her nightstand where her phone sat.

She sent a text to Ris.

"What you doing man?" he asked, taking her phone and tossing it aside. "I ain't done with you yet."

Ashton giggled as he pulled her back to him. "We can lay here and fuck or we can get up, shower, and go meet Ris at his club. He's expecting us. After that, I'll suck your dick til' morning."

"Can't say this don't surprise a nigga," Ris said as he greeted Ashton with a kiss on the cheek.

"Stop it," she said, blushing.

"I ain't think lil' baby had a heart, dawg. But here she is, pulling rank for you," Ris said, pouring two drinks before taking a seat. Carter took a seat and shook his head, declining the drink. Discipline. It wasn't just a habit in the ring. It was a habit that would keep him alive and one step ahead in the streets. He had been trained by the best so he would be the best.

"She said you need hitters. I got hitters, but why would I work for you?"

"Because it beats robbing niggas after a night at the club," Carter said.

Ris leaned back in his seat.

"You think I don't know? Niggas might not see how you move, but I'm aware of every move I make before I make it. The parties are the bait. These rappers and industry niggas that show are up the fish. You eat after every party. That's beneath you, bruh. I'm offering you the opportunity of a lifetime. I'm talking weight in the tons, not no corner bullshit, not a few expensive chains snatched off the necks of mumble rappers either," Carter said.

"Ain't nobody got access to work like that," Ris said. "Not for a long time down here since..."

"My father, Carter Jones. Not since The Cartel ran shit. The Cartel has returned. I need loyalty. Shooters," Carter said. "Shooters that are loyal to me above anybody and everybody. I've had bread before though. I ain't asking you to do it off the arm. I cut advances. I'll give you a million upfront."

Ris scoffed as he bit his lip.

"That should show good faith," Carter said.

"You drop a milli in my lap my nigga and you can consider us in business, bruh," Ris said. "Who you need taken care of?"

"First thing I want to know is who killed Estes? That's personal. I want his head. After that, we'll flood the streets and get Ma'Dear out the way."

Ashton's body went cold when Carter gave the order. It almost knocked the air from her lungs. She had to grit her teeth to stop her eyes from watering. Her nose burned and she held her breath. The feeling of his hand on the back of her neck made her jump, startled.

Carter stood and Ashton did too, but she was shaking; she could barely keep her cards tucked, she was showing her hand. Her feelings were involved and now she was his enemy. Estes had meant something to him, and she had taken him away.

"You good?" Carter asked, leaning into her ear, nipping it a bit with his teeth and then lingering there. He didn't care that Ris was watching and Ashton loved it. Aggressive with everyone but her, and unafraid to show that she was the weakness because he knew nobody had the power to exploit it.

She nodded.

Carter stood. "She'll drop the bag off to you in cash in the morning," he said. "Then you bring me the nigga who hit Estes. I want him zipped up."

"No doubt," Ris said. They shook hands and Carter walked out of the club with Ashton clinging to his arm.

Ashton was silent as they drove back to his place.

"I don't have clothes," she whispered as she looked out of the window. Her heart was anxious. Her soul unsettled.

"I'll buy you clothes," he stated, smirking. "I'll buy you whatever. Give you whatever. All I ask is that you be loyal. That you make love to a nigga like you did earlier and you stay down. You do that and I'ma make sure we come up."

"Are you sure you want to do this?" Ashton asked.

"It's all I got left," Carter stated.

Ashton found herself floating through the rest of the night. She could never quite clear the tears from her eyes. He wanted to love her. He trusted her. When all along it was her. She was the one he was after. She had done the act he wanted to avenge. Her heart hurt because she knew she would have to leave him, but the ways he had her folded in his bed, the way he stroked her all night, the way his tongue lapped at the most tender parts of her flesh made her want to stay.

Ashton came back to back for hours. Overindulging in a man that she knew she couldn't keep. The sun came up and Ashton felt him, kissing her forehead, moving her wild hair out of her face.

She turned to him and held his face as she looked him in the eyes. "Carter I don't want to see you hurt," she said.

"And you won't," he answered. "I got to get up, meet Mo and my family at the Diamond Estate. I need you to make that run for me. Take the money to Ris. Can I trust you?"

No, no you can't, she thought. Her lips said. "Of course, you can. This feels a lot like love," she said.

Carter smiled lazily and climbed out of the bed, slipping into expensive boxers and gripping his dick before leaning down over her. He stole kisses. She was a willing victim.

"Glad it feels good. It's only gone get better," he said. "I got to shower then break out. I got some shit to fix with Mo. Get some sleep. I'ma leave a bag for you in the living room. Deliver it to Ris and text me when you're done. I'll meet you back here tonight."

"Here?" she asked.

"You no longer sleep at your place. You're mine," he said.

Ashton couldn't hold the lone tear that fell. He cleared it. Another kiss. Then he swaggered out of the room, headed to shower. Ashton listened to every drop of water hit the tiled floor. She inhaled the smell of his body scent and the steam, memorizing it. The cologne he used. Then she closed her eyes and squeezed her pillow tightly as she listened to him walk out of the villa. She knew it would be the last time she saw him. She loved him and now she had to leave him because if he found out she was behind Estes' murder, he would kill her. It was the price to pay for fucking with The Cartel.

Ashton laid in his bed, basking in the leftover sex on the sheets before she climbed out of bed. She showered and removed one of his button-down shirts from the drawer, tying it around her waist so that it would fit better. It smelled like him and she tucked her nose inside the collar and closed her eyes. Miamor had been right. She had fallen for him fast and effortlessly.

"You can't stay here," she said aloud. She grabbed her things, went to the living room and halted when she saw the two large duffel bags on the living room floor. She unzipped one and blew out a deep breath. Neat stacks of hundred-dollar bills filled it. Her lips quivered as she called an Uber. She had five minutes to change her mind, but she knew she wouldn't. She couldn't.

Ashton waited curbside with two large duffels and when the Uber pulled up, she hopped inside. She needed to get to her condo, pack her things, and get in her car. She needed to get as far away from Miami as possible before any loose ends involving Estes' murder led back to her. It was time to go home, back to her sisters, where she would be safe from The Cartel's reach. She couldn't be Miamor's eyes and ears into Carter's world anymore. She had to think about herself. All she had to do was keep running and she would get to keep her life…a million dollars would go a long way. All she had to do was make it to her sisters. Her heart couldn't help but feel weighted, however.

Don't think about him, just run. Run far away from The Cartel and don't ever look back.

TO BE CONTINUED IN MONEY DEVILS

Available on August 18th
Everywhere Books Are Sold

Head over to the Ashley and JaQuavis Reading Club on
Facebook to discuss this surprise release.
Follow the authors
@realjaquavis
@ashleyantoinette

Head over to www.thebooklovers.co for information about a
new mobile app for readers and bookfans.

Book Lovers: Coming Soon